**A BOOKS
BY THE BAY
MYSTERY**

Killer
Characters

Ellery Adams

BERKLEY PRIME CRIME
New York

BERKLEY PRIME CRIME
Published by Berkley
An imprint of Penguin Random House LLC
375 Hudson Street, New York, New York 10014

Copyright © 2017 by Ellery Adams
Excerpt from *A Killer Plot* copyright © 2010 by Ellery Adams
Penguin Random House supports copyright. Copyright fuels creativity, encourages
diverse voices, promotes free speech, and creates a vibrant culture. Thank you for buying
an authorized edition of this book and for complying with copyright laws by not
reproducing, scanning, or distributing any part of it in any form without permission.
You are supporting writers and allowing Penguin Random House to continue to
publish books for every reader.

BERKLEY is a registered trademark and BERKLEY PRIME CRIME and the B colophon
are trademarks of Penguin Random House LLC.

ISBN 9780451488442

First Edition: May 2017

Printed in the United States of America
5   7   9   10   8   6   4

Cover art by Kimberly Schamber
Cover design by Rita Frangie
Book design by Tiffany Estreicher

To You, Dear Reader,

Despite having thirty novels under my belt, this book,
Killer Characters, *was incredibly difficult to write. But
whenever my fingers flagged, one of you—a reader-
friend—would magically pop up with a message of encouragement or a funny anecdote, and I'd suddenly
discover the words that had been evading me.*

*With the completion of this novel, it would seem that
we've traveled with Olivia and the Bayside Book Writers
to the edge of the water, and it's time to board a boat to
another shore. See how the lighthouse beacon illumi-
nates the ocean before us? Let's follow that path and
see where it takes us. If we're lucky, the journey will
make a great story. And I know this much, my friends:
I couldn't ask for better company along the way.*

~~~~~~

*End? No, the journey doesn't end here. . . . The grey rain-
curtain of this world rolls back, and all turns to silver
glass, and then you see it.*

—J. R. R. TOLKIEN

Friends should be like books, few, but hand-selected.

—C. J. LANGENHOVEN

"You have been my friend," replied Charlotte. "That in itself is a tremendous thing."

—E. B. WHITE, *CHARLOTTE'S WEB*

Chapter 1

*The flesh would shrink and go, the blood
would dry, but no one believes in his
mind of minds or heart of hearts that
the pictures do stop.*

—SAUL BELLOW

"All I think about is death," said Laurel Hobbs to her friend and fellow Bayside Book Writer Olivia Limoges. After uttering this morose remark, Laurel pushed her empty mug closer to the edge of the table and glanced around Grumpy's Diner in search of Dixie. "I know I sound selfish and whiny, but death has become the theme of my life. Death and dying. It hangs in each room of our house like a light fixture or a pair of curtains. Steve and I whisper about the inevitable moment before we go to sleep at night. When will it happen? Will we be forewarned? Or will it be sudden? Will there be a phone call in those dead hours between midnight and dawn?" She reached behind her head and tightened her ponytail of honey blond hair. "Even the twins are depressed. They can see their grandmother withering day by day."

Olivia nodded in sympathy. "It sounds really hard. How's Steve doing?"

"He puts on a brave face," Laurel said. "But I worry about him burying his feelings. This is his mother, and she's dying. Yet he barely talks about how her loss will affect him." Seeing Dixie emerge from the kitchen carrying a glass coffee carafe, Laurel raised her arm and waved.

Dixie responded by holding up an index finger. She then skated over to the *Evita* booth to drop off a check. As she worked her way toward the front of the Andrew Lloyd Webber–themed diner, she paused at the *Cats* and *Starlight Express* booths to top off her customers' mugs with fresh coffee.

"There won't be anything left by the time she gets here," Laurel complained. "And I don't have time to sit around while she brews another pot."

This grumbling wasn't like Laurel. Olivia studied her friend in concern. Laurel's face was puffy from lack of sleep and she hadn't bothered to put on makeup or earrings. In all the years Olivia and Laurel had been friends, critique partners, and amateur crime solvers, Olivia couldn't remember seeing Laurel venture out in public looking this frayed at the seams. Laurel also couldn't keep still. Her fingers moved from her empty coffee cup to her napkin to her wedding band, conveying a sense of anxiety that worried Olivia. Laurel was always full of energy, but it had been a controlled and positive energy—not this neurotic restlessness.

Seeing Dixie stop again to refill a mug at the *Tell Me on a Sunday* booth, Olivia tried to distract Laurel before she leaped up and grabbed the carafe right out of Dixie's hands. "You said that you and Steve talked about things before you went to sleep. Doesn't that count as him discussing his feelings?"

Laurel shrugged. "It's all details. Wills, funeral arrangements, what will happen to his dad—Steve hasn't once said that he's sad or scared. I feel like he's a million miles away these days. I'm trying to be patient and understanding, but I'm taking care of the boys, my work, the house, the yard, the bills. I also visit his mom when I can, and that's not much fun. You know she doesn't like me."

Olivia covered Laurel's hand with her own. "Men don't communicate the way women do. I'm sure Steve is grateful for your support, but you need to take care of yourself too, Laurel. You're running yourself ragged."

Laurel barked out a humorless laugh. "I have no other choice. A woman comes in once a week to help with the cleaning, and a landscape service is handling the lawn, but I have to keep up with everything else. Between Steve's work and his parents, he doesn't seem to have anything left to give to me or the boys."

"Here I am!" Dixie exclaimed. She skidded to a halt in front of their table and performed an elaborate series of one-hundred-and-eighty-degree turns by balancing on the toe of her left skate. "Service with flair! You can't get *that* at the Boot Top Bistro, eh?" she teased, referring to Olivia's five-star restaurant.

"It really is shameful that we don't have a single tutu-wearing dwarf in our employ," Olivia admitted with exaggerated embarrassment as Dixie refilled their mugs. "Do you know of a skilled dwarf who'd be interested in working for a demanding female proprietor and a moody French chef? My waitstaff says the tips are great, but they have to deal with extremely persnickety customers. Being adept at smoothing ruffled feathers is a must-have of any potential employee."

Dixie snorted. "Grumpy's feathers have been ruffled for the last three days over this fishin' trip he wanted to go on and couldn't because of family stuff. Instead of smoothing his feathers, I told him *exactly* where he could shove them! Sometimes that man takes me, and his whole beautiful life, for granted. When that happens, I need to remind him how much the two of us need each other for things to work. Not just around here, but at home too." She stopped and furrowed her brow. "Laurel, honey, what's wrong?"

Olivia looked across the table and saw that Laurel was crying. "Sorry, Dixie. I'm just tired and stressed. We have a meeting with Rachel's palliative care team today and I'm dreading it."

"Rachel? Is that Steve's mama?" Dixie asked, resting the coffee carafe on the edge of the table.

"Yes," Laurel said. She wiped off her tears with her napkin. "Steve and his dad, Milton, argue about Rachel's care at every meeting. It's just awful. The meetings are scheduled every two weeks, and the closer we get to . . . the end, the more Steve and his dad argue about her care. They've always gotten along so well, but lately the friction between them comes out during these meetings."

Dixie made a sympathetic noise. "It's hard to let go of the folks we love. But what about Rachel? Doesn't she get a vote on how she lives out the rest of her life?"

"Of course," Laurel said, bristling. "She's stated more than once that her main objective is to avoid pain. She isn't interested in adding weeks or days to her life if it means suffering, but Steve isn't really listening to her, and Milton seems to be shell-shocked by what's happened to his wife. I've never gotten along with Rachel, but I've been trying to make sure her wishes are being heard. Luckily, the palliative care doc and both of the hospice nurses are very focused on her goals."

Dixie put a hand on Laurel's shoulder. "I can almost feel

the weight on you, sweetie. How much time do they think she has?"

"Six weeks." Laurel took a sip of her coffee and then glanced out the window. She watched the passersby for a moment before adding, "I think she'll go sooner. She's been trying to hang on until Christmas for Steve's sake, but whenever I visit, she talks about how tired she is." Laurel sighed. "If Steve and his dad don't make peace with each other *before* she passes, things are going to be even worse once she's gone."

Dixie gave Laurel's shoulder another squeeze and then swept her gaze around the diner. A customer was signaling her for the check, so she turned back to Laurel and said, "I'm gonna pack up some treats for you to take home. I know how much those darlin' boys like Grumpy's apple pie. You hang in there, honey. We're here if you need us."

When Laurel nodded absently, Olivia felt a pang of guilt. Other than taking Laurel out for the occasional lunch or coffee, she hadn't been a very supportive friend. She knew that Laurel was stressed, and even though she and the other Bayside Book Writers had bemoaned her absence during their last two meetings, they'd all assumed that she'd bounce back and make it to the next meeting. Laurel always bounced back.

"Have you been able to write at all?" Olivia asked softly. "Outside of pieces for the newspaper, I mean."

Laurel was still staring out the window, but her eyes had a glassy, unfocused look. "No," she whispered.

"That settles it. I'm coming with you to this meeting," Olivia said. "Even if I sit outside in the hall, you'll know I'm close by. You need a friend, whether you realize it or not. And while I'm terrible at all the touchy-feely stuff, I *can* be present." She pulled some bills from her wallet and placed them on the table. "Haviland will be at the groomer's for another hour. He's getting the works today—shampoo, trim, massage—so I'm all yours."

"Maybe I should trade places with Haviland," Laurel said as she shouldered her purse. "I'd love a day of pampering."

Dixie reemerged from the kitchen and skated to the front of the diner, blatantly ignoring the customer in the *Phantom of the Opera* booth who was waving what Olivia assumed was an empty syrup jug in the air in an attempt to flag down his diminutive waitress. However, Dixie wasn't going to miss her chance to show Laurel some love by thrusting a loaded take-out bag into her arms.

"I don't want to hear any thanks from you either," Dixie warned when Laurel opened her mouth. "You've always been there for me and mine. It's our turn to repay the favor. Kiss those boys for me, ya hear?"

And then she skated off, her pink taffeta tutu billowing like the bell of a gelatinous sea creature.

Olivia held open the diner door and gestured for Laurel to precede her outside. "That poodle is shamefully spoiled. It's better not to compare our existence to his. It'll only make you feel glum. Besides, why shouldn't you have a spa day? If you need a fresh crop of helpers, I could ask Kim for the names of reliable babysitters and you, I, and Millay could spend a few hours in New Bern being treated like royalty."

Not only was Kim Olivia's sister-in-law, but she also managed Olivia's second restaurant, the Bayside Crab House, and had two young children. If anyone could help Laurel with child care, it was Kim Salter.

Laurel turned toward her minivan, which looked as if it hadn't been washed in months, and sighed. "What if something happened while I was off getting a facial? I couldn't live with the guilt."

Would you feel guilty or would your husband make *you feel guilty?* Olivia wondered, and then tried to erase the uncharitable thought. She wasn't a fan of Laurel's husband. None of the Bayside Book Writers were. They were friendly to Steve for Laurel's sake, though it seemed clear to all of Laurel's friends that her husband didn't put as much effort into the marriage as she did. Even after the couple had undergone a year's worth of marital counseling, Olivia continued to doubt Steve's sincerity. It wasn't fair, she knew, to judge a man she didn't really know, but her gut told her not to trust him. With her history of being abandoned or betrayed by men, Olivia believed it was foolish to ignore her baser instincts.

He's Laurel's husband. Not yours, Olivia reminded herself.

Laurel, who'd been rooting around in her purse, proffered a business card. "Here's the address. The meeting starts in thirty minutes. I doubt Steve and Milton will be thrilled to see you, but if you're sure . . . well, I'd love to have you there."

"I'm sure." Olivia smiled. "See you in a few."

The offices for Tidewater Hospice were located halfway between Oyster Bay and New Bern and they looked relatively new. Laurel was greeted warmly by a receptionist and told to proceed to the conference room.

"Everyone's in-house. We're just waiting on your husband," the woman called after them. "He said he was running late, but that he'd get here as soon as he could."

Though Laurel's shoulders tensed, she smiled and thanked the woman as though Steve's tardiness were no big deal.

Steve's father was far more overt in expressing his annoyance.

"He's *late*?" Milton demanded angrily after Laurel repeated the receptionist's message to the group of people gathered in the small conference room. Laurel's father-in-law was bent over the watercooler in the corner. Now he stood erect and glared at Laurel. "Are his patients more important than his dying mother? And who's this?" He gestured at Olivia with his paper cup, causing water to slosh over the rim and onto his shirt. "Goddamn it. Now look at me."

A woman in her late twenties with large breasts, wide hips, and dark brown hair pulled into a loose bun eased the cup from Milton's hand. "Why don't you sit down while I refill that for you?" She spoke in a soothing, almost maternal voice and gave Milton a winsome smile. "I'm sure your son will be here real soon. Dr. Zemmel had to grab some paperwork from his office, so the timing might turn out just fine. Come on, sit down by me."

Judging by the woman's purple scrubs, Olivia guessed that she was one of Rachel's nurses. The second nurse was taller, thinner, and older. She was in her mid-thirties and had luminescent mocha-colored skin and hazel eyes. Beside her sat a clergyman, and next to him was a dour-faced matron in a wool cardigan. The chair at the head of the table remained empty, but a young woman with an athletic build occupied the chair directly next to it. She wore a white scrub top with pink piping and pink pants and was drawing leaping dolphins and bubbly hearts on a legal pad.

Is she a college student? Olivia wondered. *High school? Maybe she's an intern or a volunteer.*

"Dad, this is Olivia Limoges," Laurel said. "She's here for me. She won't say a word. I just needed a friend today. I hope that's okay."

Milton was clearly taken aback. "*You* needed a friend? What does *any* of this have to do with you?"

Laurel's face reddened. "You and Rachel are my husband's parents, and I care about you both, so this *does* concern me. Rachel's illness also affects my family. My sons. My husband. And me. I want to do everything I can to help, and I don't appreciate being made to feel as if I don't matter."

"Well, I don't see how—"

Milton's rudeness was interrupted by the arrival of the palliative care doctor.

"Good morning, everyone," he said in a tone of affable authority. He strode into the room with an air of urgency common to most physicians. However, once he'd settled into his chair, he took a long moment to simply sit and be quiet. A calm came over him and the room. He glanced at each person at the table, greeting him or her with his eyes. Olivia liked him for taking the time to do this.

When his gaze fell on Olivia, Laurel spoke up. "This is a good friend of mine, Olivia Limoges. I invited her to be here today," she added, and again, Olivia heard a note of defiance in her friend's voice.

"Jonathan Zemmel," he said, extending his hand. "It's a pleasure to have you with us, Olivia." He then quickly introduced the rest of the team members. The busty, dark-haired nurse who'd successfully soothed Milton was Stacy Balena and the older nurse with the beautiful skin and eyes was Wanda Watts.

Dr. Zemmel went on to explain that Haley Wilson, the baby-faced woman in pink-and-white scrubs, was a nurse's aide, before moving on to the clergyman. His name was Bob Rhodes, and he served as the associate pastor of the church Rachel and Milton attended. Dr. Zemmel finished up with Lynne Chester, the dour-faced matron who served as a volunteer for both the hospice and the church. The introductions completed, Dr. Zemmel shifted his attention back to Laurel. "Will Steve be joining us?"

"He's late!" Milton snapped before Laurel could answer. "Apparently, his practice is more important than his mother."

"Having gotten to know your son a little, I doubt that's the case," Dr. Zemmel said kindly. "Let's review how things are going. Hopefully, Steve will slip in while we're talking. Okay?"

"Okay." Laurel flashed the doctor a grateful smile.

Olivia listened as the hospice team discussed Rachel's condition. She was impressed by how they presented the facts without sounding remotely distant or cold. If anything, they all seemed to know Rachel and to genuinely care about her welfare. The team didn't focus on just the medical details either. Once those had been reviewed, Dr. Zemmel asked for feedback from everyone present, and by the time each person had spoken, an entire range of subjects had been covered. They discussed changes in Rachel's diet, her current emotional state, her spiritual needs, her favorite sources of entertainment, and anything else that might have come up since their last meeting.

The team had been sharing for twenty minutes when Steve arrived, out of breath and murmuring apologies about a tricky case.

Milton rolled his eyes and shook his head in unconcealed disgust. Steve ignored these gestures as he pulled out a vacant chair on the opposite side of the table from his father. Spotting Olivia, he paused to glare accusingly at Laurel before asking, "So, where are we?"

"The team just finished updating us on your mother's condition," Milton said tersely. "I'm sure they don't have time to repeat everything, so I'd like to talk about our next step." He quickly swiveled his chair in order to address Dr. Zemmel. "As you know, because Rachel is at home with me, I notice every little change in her health. Lately, I've noticed that Rachel is eating less and less. When will you consider putting in a feeding tube?"

"I don't think Mom needs one yet. Does she, Doctor?" Steve spread his arms wide, placing his hands flat on the table. He inhaled deeply, filling his chest with air. Olivia wondered if Laurel's husband was trying to appear physically domineering or if it was a subconscious movement.

Jonathan Zemmel weighed the pros and cons of inserting a feeding tube and patiently and attentively listened to the concerns Milton and Steve had on the subject. Olivia had never encountered a physician with such an unhurried manner. He listened with every fiber of his being—maintaining eye contact, nodding, and repeating each person's concerns to make sure he correctly understood. By doing so, he managed to defuse the tension between father and son.

Olivia was most impressed by Dr. Zemmel.

The meeting was eventually called to an end when Stacy's pager went off.

"Excuse me," she said, moving to a far corner of the room. Pulling a cell phone from the pocket of her scrubs, she dialed a number and listened. She then assured the caller that she was on her way.

"Is it Rachel?" Milton asked, his eyes fearful. "Is she okay?"

It was at that moment that Olivia saw him for what he truly was: a man who would give anything to have more time with his wife. And what of Steve? He undoubtedly wanted his mother to live as long as possible too, but he didn't want her to suffer. Was he ready to let her go if letting her go meant that she'd have a peaceful death?

Does such a thing actually exist? Olivia thought dubiously.

She wanted to believe in the possibility of people slipping away in their sleep, caught up in the arms of a sweet dream, but she'd seen too many violent deaths—too many murders—to invest much faith in the other kind. The kind where a person dies in her own bed, surrounded by loved ones. It seemed like a foreign concept to her, and yet that was precisely what Milton, Steve, Laurel, and the people of Tidewater Hospice were trying to give Rachel. A graceful exit. A departure on one's own terms.

"She's asking for me," Stacy said, looking at Milton. "I'm late for my shift and you know how changes in her routine can upset her. I'm going to head out to your place."

"Thanks, Stacy." Dr. Zemmel rose to his feet. "Okay, folks. Let's see how Rachel does over the weekend. I'll check in with the dietitian on Monday and we can revisit the topic of the feeding tube then. Feel free to call if other concerns arise. We'll keep working together to provide Rachel with the best possible care."

With the meeting adjourned, the hospice employees left. Steve informed Laurel that he wouldn't be home for supper because he wanted to spend the evening with his mother, and then he and his father also departed, arguing all the way down the hall.

Pastor Rhodes made to leave as well, but Lynne asked him to wait. "I want to tell Laurel about Rachel's request. I'm sure she'll want to do something to help."

Olivia didn't care for the woman's tone. The implication was that Laurel's efforts had been found wanting but that she was now being offered the chance to remedy her lack of daughterly devotion.

"Of course," Laurel said, playing right into Lynne's hands. "What is it?"

Lynne smoothed the material of her cardigan with a self-satisfied air. "You know Rachel's collection of Hummel figurines? One's broken and she'd really like to see it repaired as soon as possible. It's her favorite piece. She's asked both Milton and Steve to take care of it *several* times, but I guess they're both just too overwrought to get it done."

Laurel looked nonplussed. "I don't know how to fix—"

"Fred Yoder would," Olivia cut in brightly. "Give me directions to your in-laws' condo, Laurel. I'll get the Hummel and take it directly to Fred."

Laurel's relief was nearly palpable. "Really? Because that way, I could still make it to the grocery store and meet the twins when they get off the school bus."

Olivia directed her reply at Lynne. Beaming at the pug-nosed woman, she said, "Problem solved. Thank you *so much* for bringing this to Laurel's attention."

Lynne gave her cardigan another tug, muttered something about her Christian duty, and marched out of the room. A baffled Pastor Rhodes followed in her wake.

"I don't envy you," Olivia said to Laurel. "You're in the middle of a very trying ordeal. I can see why you can't work on your novel, but do some journaling so you can vent. Don't hold everything inside. Okay?"

Laurel promised to do her best. After Laurel gave Olivia directions to the condo, the two friends parted ways.

Olivia wasn't about to face a dying woman alone. She wasn't good with strangers under normal circumstances, and she had no experience with the terminally ill. Also, everything she knew of Rachel Hobbs came from what Laurel had told her over the years, and these anecdotes had not left a favorable impression. Rachel was a doting, overly involved mother. Steve was her only child, and she'd never forgiven him for getting married. She was fond of her grandsons, Dallas and Dermot, but had never shown an ounce of warmth toward Laurel. In fact, she seemed to look for excuses to criticize her son's wife. Nothing Laurel did was ever good enough, even though everyone who knew the Hobbs family believed that Laurel did a great job balancing a successful career with her homelife.

Maybe Rachel has become kindhearted now that her days are numbered, Olivia thought hopefully. She doubted this was true, however. She found that people rarely had major personality reversals. Even when death was a certainty, and in Rachel's case it was close at hand, Olivia didn't think people suddenly just stopped being who they'd always been and started being someone else. She knew fear had the power to change people. As did love. She had been molded by both emotions, but she was still Olivia Limoges.

"The captain now looks more like an admiral," the owner of A Pampered Pooch told Olivia as she led Captain Haviland into the front room.

"He *is* a handsome fellow," Olivia agreed, and leaned down to kiss her poodle on his black nose. He rewarded her with a lick on the cheek and then pranced over to the door, his caramel-colored eyes lit with an anticipatory gleam. He was ready for a ride in the car.

"You wouldn't be wagging your tail so vigorously if you knew where we were headed," Olivia said once she had Haviland safely fastened in his dog harness in the backseat of her new Range Rover Evoque. This was a novel arrangement for them both. Previously, Haviland had enjoyed sole proprietorship of the passenger seat. Now that Olivia was married, however, Police Chief Sawyer Rawlings claimed ownership of that seat, leaving Haviland the bench seat.

As Olivia drove through downtown Oyster Bay, her spirits were lifted by the sight of the tinsel candy canes fastened to the top of each streetlamp and the wreaths of fresh greens festooned with red velvet bows hanging from every shop door. Christmas hadn't meant much to her until her half brother and his children had come into her life, but now she enjoyed the holiday, reveling in her role as the doting aunt.

"We have arrived, Captain. Sandcrest Condominiums," Olivia said, reading the gilt sign attached to the wall of a small gatehouse. Unlike most of the newer planned communities in Oyster Bay, this one actually boasted a working electronic gate and a uniformed security guard. Olivia put down her window as the guard approached.

"Who are you here to see?" he asked with complete disinterest.

"Rachel Hobbs."

"One moment."

The guard returned to his miniature cottage and made a quick call. Olivia clearly passed muster, for the gate slid open and the guard gestured for Olivia to drive forward. She did, wondering for the first time how the Hobbses had acquired their wealth. She'd never thought to ask Laurel what line of work they'd been in, but she knew that their Oyster Bay condo was one of several residences Milton and Rachel owned. Because of Rachel's illness, it had become their primary residence.

The condo, which was originally a place for them to stay when they were visiting Steve and his family, was an end unit with a large patio, a lovely garden, and a two-car garage. The interior was also impressive, and when Stacy, the hospice nurse, invited Olivia to wait in the living room while she fetched the broken Hummel, Olivia took note of the expensive furnishings as well as the top-of-the-line appliances in the kitchen.

It wasn't until she moved closer to the locked bookcases that the extent of the Hobbses' wealth became more apparent. Each shelf was crammed with costly leather-bound first editions, delicate Staffordshire and Meissen figurines, and Chinese porcelain that looked, even to Olivia's inexpert eye, like very early pieces. Now thoroughly intrigued, she tiptoed into the hallway and was rewarded by the sight of a row of framed Picasso drawings.

Olivia was drawn deeper into the condo by Picasso's bold, fluid lines. As she marveled over a series of female nudes and then ogled a splendid study of a horse, she couldn't help overhearing voices at the end of the corridor. She recognized them as belonging to Stacy and Rachel.

"Laurel sent a stranger to pick up my Hummel?" Rachel Hobbs sounded tired and weak, but still managed to convey disgust. "It's too bad Steve didn't marry someone like you, my dear. You're so good to me and I bet you'd know how to take care of him too."

"I like to think so," Stacy replied with a confidence that bordered on arrogance.

Standing in the dim hallway, Olivia balled her fists. She didn't care for the possessive note in the nurse's voice. And why did she say "I like" instead of "I'd like," as though it wasn't just wishful thinking?

Olivia retreated to the living room and tried to calm down. She'd come to Rachel's place to relieve Laurel of one of her burdens, but what if she'd just stumbled on a truth that could tear her friend's world apart?

Is Steve having an affair?

This question was foremost in Olivia's mind as Stacy walked into the living room and gave her the box. It was the question that ran on an endless loop as Olivia drove back through town.

This time, she didn't notice the Christmas decorations. She didn't see the tinsel candy canes wink in the December sun or draw a comparison of the red cheeks on the plastic Santa outside the hardware store to a pair of crab apples.

Olivia was far too focused on getting to her husband, Chief Sawyer Rawlings, for any of these things to register. She needed to talk about what she'd heard—and what she'd felt—with him. She needed his good sense and his reason. She needed him to make her believe that she was blowing this way out of proportion.

Because if Rawlings didn't convince her not to, Olivia would ferret out the truth concerning Steve Hobbs. And if it turned out that he was cheating on Laurel, Olivia would hurt the man. She didn't have a plan yet, but she would do something. If Laurel suffered, then Steve would suffer.

Olivia would see to that.

Chapter 2

You want to believe that there's one relationship in life that's beyond betrayal. A relationship that's beyond that kind of hurt. And there isn't.

—CALEB CARR

Haviland was thrilled to be entering the Oyster Bay Police Department building. Not only did he revel in the attention he received from nearly every human within, but there was also a chance that he might run into Greta, the attractive K-9 officer.

As luck would have it, Greta's partner was eating lunch in the break room, so Haviland was able to approach his favorite German shepherd looking and smelling like a participant in the Westminster Kennel Club Show.

Olivia was too impatient to stand around while Haviland and Greta greeted each other with an elaborate series of sniffs, snorts, and tail wags.

"Can I leave the captain here for a few minutes?" Olivia asked Greta's handler. "I'm on my way to the chief's office, and Haviland's obviously in no rush to follow me."

The officer, who'd taken an enormous bite from his meatball sub while Olivia was speaking, gave her a thumbs-up before his gaze returned to his car magazine.

Sawyer Rawlings rarely closed his door, so Olivia wasn't surprised to find it partially open.

"Hello, you." Rawlings, who had had both hands buried inside the top drawer of his filing cabinet, sensed that someone had walked in. He looked up and, seeing Olivia, smiled. "To what do I owe this unexpected vision of beauty in the middle of my day?"

When Olivia didn't respond, but strode over to the window and crossed her arms over her chest, Rawlings immediately abandoned his filing.

"You're angry," he said. "Did I leave dirty dishes in the sink? Put my white socks in the dark-load hamper?" He grinned, expecting his banter to elicit a smile from her too. When her mouth remained a thin, tense line, Rawlings gently spun her around and searched her face.

"It isn't you," Olivia said.

Rawlings let loose an exaggerated sigh of relief. "Which poor sucker has incurred your wrath? A lazy employee? A tourist? Was someone rude to Dixie?" Rawlings watched his wife's eyes for a sign that he was getting closer to discovering the source of her discontent. "No, not Dixie. She can take care of herself. Officer Cook and I have a long-standing bet on whether or not she keeps a knife concealed in the toe of her left roller skate like Ian Fleming's Rosa Klebb. Remember *From Russia with Love*?"

"Stop," Olivia snapped. "This is serious."

Rawlings took Olivia's hand and led her to the chairs facing his desk. "I'm worried now. What is it?"

"I'm not sure." Olivia looked at the man she'd been married to for over a year and a half and saw how his concern had deepened the lines on his forehead and around his mouth. She reclaimed her hand, tenderly touched his right cheek to show her gratitude, and then said, "I'd better start from the beginning."

Rawlings nodded. "That's usually the best place."

Olivia told him about her lunch with Laurel. "She's doing everything in her power to hold her family together, but the stress is getting to her. She looked exhausted. She just drags herself from one commitment to another. There's no light on her horizon. So when I heard she had to attend the semi-monthly hospice meeting for Steve's mom, I offered to go along."

"You did?" Rawlings couldn't conceal his astonishment.

His bewilderment made Olivia smile. "I know. I could hardly believe it myself. But I had this vibe that Laurel couldn't bear another weight on her shoulders, and if my being with her at that meeting could provide her with the tiniest bit of comfort, then I had to go."

"You'd better watch it," Rawlings warned. "If this gets out, your ice queen reputation will suffer."

Thinking of Stacy's comment, Olivia felt a fresh surge of anger. "I'm sure I can do something to maintain that." She gave Rawlings a brief summary of the meeting, including details about all the participants. Next, she explained how she ended up inside Rachel Hobbs's condo.

"Do you remember Laurel ever mentioning how her in-laws made their money?" Olivia asked Rawlings.

He shook his head. "Honestly, whenever she mentioned Steve's family during our critique group meetings, she mostly talked about how Rachel criticized her or how her in-laws were spoiling the twins with lavish gifts."

"That sounds about right," Olivia agreed. "In any case, they have some impressive items in their condo. Rare books, expensive porcelain, what I believe to be original Picasso drawings. Costly antiques. I'm mentioning these because I might have been distracted when I heard what I heard. And I need to tell you about it so you can help me form a clear judgment."

Rawlings waited without speaking. His ability to be quiet was one of his finest qualities, and Olivia especially valued it now. Still, as she returned to that moment in the hall when she'd been surrounded by those wonderful Picassos, she knew that no matter what Rawlings said, she'd already decided that something was going on between Steve Hobbs and Stacy Balena. They were crossing some sort of line. Or lines.

Olivia repeated the conversation she'd overheard between Rachel and the hospice nurse, trying not to influence Rawlings in any way. She merely recalled the words and then asked, "What do you make of Stacy's reply?"

Rawlings carefully considered the question. Frowning, he asked, "Are you sure she didn't say '*I'd* like to think I could'?"

"She didn't, which is what I found strange," Olivia said, inwardly pleased that Rawlings had noticed the same discrepancy. "There's more to it than just the phrase. Stacy spoke with such arrogance. Such smugness. As though she were saying, 'Believe me, I already know how to take care of your son, Mrs. Hobbs.'"

Holding up a cautionary finger, Rawlings said, "Isn't that a great deal to infer from such a short phrase?" The rest of his fingers joined the first to create a flat palm as he staved off Olivia's protest. "You wanted my opinion. Let me give it to you." Lowering his hand, he placed it on her knee. "Were you able to see her face?"

"No," Olivia admitted. "She was in what I presume was Rachel's room, though I believe she was headed in my direction. Her voice was louder and clearer than Rachel's. I think

Stacy was definitely standing close to the doorway when she said that line. I could feel her words impact me, and they made me instantly angry on Laurel's behalf." She paused and looked at Rawlings. "I've learned not to ignore my instincts when it comes to strangers, and my instincts told me that I couldn't walk out of that condo and forget what I'd heard."

"Fair enough." Rawlings fell silent. After a long moment, he asked, "How old is she? This nurse?"

Olivia shrugged. "In her late twenties, I'd say."

"And Steve is in his early forties?"

"Yes. Why?" Olivia tried to read the chief's face, but his expression gave away nothing.

Rawlings stroked his chin. "Is she attractive?"

Olivia glared at him. "*Laurel* is attractive. She's still every inch the cheerleader she was back in high school. She's fit, pretty, smart, sweet, generous, and loyal. What's more, she's Steve's *wife* and the mother of his children. Who cares what this nurse looks like?"

Raising both hands in a conciliatory gesture, Rawlings whispered, "*I* don't. There's only one woman in this world for me, and that's you. But I'm asking you to consider if Steve might have found Ms. Balena attractive."

Forcing herself to be subjective, Olivia had to concede that men might have been drawn to the hospice nurse. "She's well-endowed. A mass of long, dark hair, which she wears in a messy knot. Fake nails. At least five piercings per ear. I don't know, Rawlings. She's the complete opposite of Laurel. She's curvier. Darker. And *so* much younger. But I suppose a certain man could find a much younger woman very sexy."

Olivia's last statement hung in the air like clouds weighed down by rain.

"So she could be appealing," Olivia said very softly,

"especially if you're a married man in your forties and you feel trapped by a life that isn't what you'd once envisioned. Suddenly, this young woman comes along and expresses an interest in you. She doesn't have to be beautiful, does she? She only has to be attractive enough to catch your eye. Her real function is to inflate your tired ego and make you feel a little less old."

Rawlings winced. "Isn't that a harsh summary? We have no idea what's going on between Laurel and Steve. Marriages are private."

"Which is why certain hospice nurses should keep out of them!" Olivia hissed.

"Agreed," Rawlings said. "The question before you is what to do next. Do you share your suspicions with Laurel?"

Olivia grimaced. She couldn't imagine a more uncomfortable conversation. "Couldn't you just put a tail on Stacy? See if she and Steve meet at some roadside motel or something?"

"No, I can't." Rawlings tapped his name plaque. "I'm not going to abuse my position to investigate your hunch. No crime has been committed. And don't get angry because I'm refusing you. I trust your instincts, Olivia. I always have. However, I see no choice but for you to tell Laurel what you heard. It'll be up to her to decide what to do with the information."

"She's already so stressed." Olivia sank back in her chair and moaned. "She might lash out at me for bringing this to her attention. This could totally turn into a 'shoot the messenger' situation."

Rawlings nodded gravely. "It's quite possible." He picked up Olivia's hand and cradled it between both of his. "What are you going to do?"

Olivia met her husband's kind, intelligent gaze. "If our

roles were reversed—and God help you if that should ever happen—I'd want to know. So I'm going to tell her."

Leaning over to kiss her forehead, Rawlings said, "You never need to worry about me, my love. I know better than to tangle with you. Not only are you a crack shot with a rifle, but Haviland would swiftly go for the jugular, should you give him the command." His lips moved down the tip of her nose before finding her mouth.

Olivia, who'd entered Rawlings's office taut with anger, felt the tension leave her shoulders. Closing her eyes, she gave in to his kiss. But only briefly. She needed to speak with Laurel now.

Pulling away, Olivia tapped the face of her watch. "I think I'll need a double come cocktail time."

"I'll be waiting." Rawlings helped her to her feet and then glanced around. Suddenly, it dawned on him that she was without her constant companion. "Where's Haviland?"

Olivia pointed at the hall. "Wooing Greta."

Rawlings grinned. "If only human romantic relationships were as simple as toothy smiles and wagging tails . . ." His grin faded. "I wouldn't dream of telling you what to do, but I want to give you one piece of advice. Don't say more than is absolutely necessary. When conveying news that has the potential to cause great pain, I've found that it's best to use as few words as possible."

Olivia knew that Rawlings, in his role as police chief, had had too much practice imparting the most devastating news. The kind of news that tore lives apart.

"Okay. I'll keep that in mind," she promised. She then issued a low whistle, waited for Haviland to join her in the hall, and left the police station.

"We can't go home just yet," she told her poodle once they were outside. Olivia folded her arms across her chest as though bracing against the cold. "I have to break Laurel's heart first."

When Olivia pulled up in front of Laurel's house, her friend was standing by the lamppost, attempting to untangle a mass of multicolored Christmas lights.

"We're so late with our decorations this year," she lamented upon seeing Olivia. "But the boys love the lights so much that I have to make an effort to hang a few." She gave the string a fierce yank as a cluster of bulbs caught on the branch of an overgrown azalea bush. Laurel kicked at the bush and swore.

"That's how I feel about putting up lights too," Olivia said with forced levity. "Come on, let's untangle the knot at this end. If we do that, it won't keep catching on that branch."

"Fa-la-la-la-la-la-bleeping-la," Laurel sang grumpily. "Why the hell am I out here anyway? This is supposed to be Steve's job. Or it *was* supposed to be his job, I should say. About three years ago, he decided that he didn't feel like doing it anymore, so I took over. I swear, Olivia, by this point in our marriage, I've taken everything on."

Though Olivia didn't like the direction the conversation was heading, it did provide a segue for her to say what she'd come to say.

"Laurel," she began, focusing her gaze on the knotted string of lights, "it sounds like this is a difficult time for you and Steve. But prior to this, you two were seeing a marriage counselor. Were things better then?"

Laurel hugged herself. Decembers in Oyster Bay were mild, but locals still wore sweaters and thin coats while outdoors. Laurel had come outside dressed in only a blouse and a knit cap. Olivia was tempted to shoo her friend back into the house, but she was afraid that Laurel might clam up in the boys' presence. And with good reason too. The twins didn't need to hear that their parents weren't getting along, though they probably already knew something was amiss. Children had an innate sense for such things.

"Things were better for a time," Laurel said. "But then Steve withdrew again. Like I said, he kind of left me to handle everything. The boys, the house, the bills. He went to work and came home. There were good days sprinkled in. But overall, I felt like he wasn't really *here*. Like we weren't really connected. I did his laundry and cooked his meals and took care of his needs. He didn't do much to take care of mine, though. I think . . ." She stopped and swallowed. "I think I've become invisible to him."

Laurel spoke these last words so quietly that Olivia barely heard them. However, they floated to her across the brisk air and she felt chilled. She saw the hollowness of her friend's cheeks. The sorrow in her eyes. The loneliness and worry etched into the fine lines on her lovely face.

And she, Olivia, was about to make things worse.

"I have to tell you something," Olivia said. "It might be absolutely meaningless, but had our roles been reversed, I would have wanted you to come to me. So here I am." And without further explanation, Olivia went on to describe her visit to Rachel's condo. When she was finished, Laurel stood very still. She didn't respond for a long time, and when she did, she sounded remarkably calm.

"I asked Steve if he was having an affair. In fact, I've asked him twice. Both times, I was looking right at him. He looked right back at me and told me that he wasn't." She released a pent-up breath. "I have to believe that."

Olivia didn't see why, but as Rawlings had said, marriages were private, so she simply nodded to show Laurel that she was listening.

"I was suspicious, you see, because he started acting weird. It happened at about the same time his mother took a turn for the worse." Laurel gave a shrill little laugh. "He'd send me texts with these naughty emojis. He's never done that before. It freaked me out because I was worried someone at work would see. Or one of the boys would grab my phone—they're always taking it to play some game—and see a dirty message from him."

"So he was trying to spice things up?" Olivia asked.

Laurel shook her head. "Only virtually. In person he was still distant. The discrepancy was what made me suspicious, and that's when I asked him the first time."

"And the second time?"

Laurel hung her head. "He brought me flowers."

"That's it?"

"You don't understand. Steve's only given me flowers once before. And it was to apologize for something he'd done," Laurel explained. "To get out of the doghouse. He'd never bought flowers for me other than that one time. Not when I landed my first job or when my first article went national. Not even when the twins were born. He just doesn't do stuff like that. He'd buy me other things, but not flowers. So when he came home with this big bouquet, an alarm bell went off. I know that paints him in a terrible light, and that's not what I mean to do, but we just haven't been close lately."

Olivia thought Laurel was being very generous in her choice of words. So generous that she wasn't sure if Laurel was being deliberately obtuse about Steve's behavior. "So, did you ask him then? Directly?"

"If he was having an affair?" Laurel's eyes turned glassy

as she tried to remember. "I commented on how men only bring flowers to their wives and start writing love notes when they're having an affair and looked right at him. He smiled and kissed me on the cheek and said something about wanting to rekindle things with me. That's what I wanted too, so I believed him." Her hand flew to her mouth. "Oh Lord! Have I been totally blind?"

"We don't know anything for certain," Olivia was quick to remind Laurel, though her gut feeling that Steve was a louse was growing stronger. As was her anger.

"First things first," Laurel said, dumping the lights on the ground. "I need to see if Steve's still at the office. Come on."

Heading into her house, Laurel marched into the kitchen and scooped up the cordless phone. She pressed a single button and waited.

"Joyce? Hey, it's Laurel. Is Steve with a patient?" She waited several heartbeats before continuing. "Oh? What time was this?"

Olivia watched the abrupt shift in Laurel's expressions. They went from curiosity to surprise to a quiet fury in a matter of seconds. Olivia didn't need Laurel to tell her that Steve wasn't at the office.

At that moment, Olivia's phone started vibrating from inside her coat pocket. Millay Hollowell was calling, and since Laurel had a notepad out and was politely questioning Joyce, Olivia decided to retreat to the foyer and briefly speak with their mutual friend and fellow Bayside Book Writer.

"This isn't a good time. I'll have to get back to you," she whispered urgently.

"What's with the husky voice?" Millay demanded good-naturedly. "Are you and the chief having an afternoon delight?"

Olivia scowled, even though her fellow Bayside Book Writer couldn't see the expression. "I'm with Laurel. She's . . ." Olivia stopped. It wasn't for her to share Laurel's suspicions.

"Who is it?" Laurel appeared in the doorway. She'd donned a coat and had a determined set to her jaw.

"Millay."

Laurel nodded as though she hadn't heard. She held up a piece of paper. "I have Stacy's address, and I'm going there right now. A neighbor is coming here to watch the boys. As soon as she shows up, I'll leave."

"What's going on?" Millay asked. "Laurel sounds funny."

Laurel gestured for the phone and Olivia passed it over.

Moving to the front door, Laurel peered outside and murmured, "I think Steve is sleeping with his mother's nurse. I'm driving to her place now to try to catch them in the act."

The expletive that Millay bellowed came through the cell phone speaker loud and clear. Laurel listened for several seconds before ending the call and handing the phone back to Olivia.

"Millay's on her way," she said. "She insists on coming with me. She says I need a posse."

Olivia pocketed her phone. "I have to agree. We have no idea how this afternoon is going to end."

"Is Haviland in your car?" Laurel asked. "Because I might want him to rip someone's throat out." She made a clumsy attempt to tie her scarf around her neck, but her hands were shaking so badly that she was unable to form a knot. Olivia took hold of the ends of the scarf and tied it for her friend.

"Yes, Haviland is with me," she said. "And I think it's best that I do the driving."

* * *

"Stacy Balena?" Millay couldn't hide her astonishment. "*No way!* I *know* her." She ran her hands through her short hair, which she'd recently dyed from its natural black to a shade of silvery violet. "She's, like, twenty-eight. And she has kids."

"*What?*" Laurel and Olivia cried in unison from the front seat of Olivia's Range Rover.

"Yeah. She's been divorced for a few years, I think. We're not exactly tight." Millay put her arm around Haviland's shoulders as Olivia swerved around a driver who'd suddenly decided to turn without indicating his intent by using his signal. "Her ex lives in New Bern, which is where the kids go to school. He's remarried and has the more stable homelife, so Stacy gets them every other weekend, or something like that."

Laurel pivoted in her seat. "How do you know all this?"

"Because Stacy and I hang out at some of the same bars and clubs. I've run into her at Bayside Ink too." Millay pointed to the hoop protruding from her left eyebrow. "That's where I buy my body jewelry."

"So she has . . . piercings?" Laurel's voice rose an octave.

Millay hesitated. "Other than the ones in her ears, I have no clue. I know she has a tattoo on her lower back. Nothing too creative. Flowers and curlicues with her name in the center. Harris calls them tramp stamps, though I've told him a million times that it's a derogatory term."

"Harris might be more accurate in his word usage than he realizes," Laurel muttered darkly, and Millay fell silent.

Olivia was relieved that their younger friend decided not to choose this moment to defend trends favored by the millennial generation. After all, Millay was Stacy's age, while Laurel was a decade older and Olivia was in her mid-forties.

"What else can you tell me about her?" Laurel asked.

Millay hesitated. "Not much. We're not friends. We're just friendly. She hangs out with a group of nurses. They're into selfie sticks and posting pics of themselves online every five seconds. That's not my thing. But I figured Stacy was into that because she hadn't gotten over her divorce and she was looking for positive reinforcement, you know? And also, she was probably following that fake-it-till-you-make-it mantra. No one smiles that much and actually means it."

"Why did her marriage end?"

"Her husband cheated on her with a woman . . ." Millay suddenly became very preoccupied with her thumbnail. She chewed on it ferociously and stared out the window.

"Go on," Laurel commanded.

Millay sighed. "He left Stacy for a woman your age. She looked a little like you too. Petite and blond."

"Jesus," Olivia breathed.

Laurel glanced down at the paper in her hands, and Olivia could see that she was gripping it so tightly that her knuckles had gone white. "Turn left at the next light."

Complying, Olivia pulled into a neighborhood with small homes dating from the seventies. Laurel read out the number and as they progressed deeper into the subdivision, the houses seemed to become more derelict.

"This is it," Laurel said, pointing at a split-level ranch painted in what Olivia could only describe as a vomit yellow hue.

Olivia parked at the curb and the women alighted from the car, leaving Haviland behind.

"That car was at the condo when I stopped by earlier. It must be Stacy's," Olivia said, indicating the gold Hyundai sedan. The rear window was covered with a hodgepodge of decals, and the side panels were dinged and scratched from bumper to bumper.

The garage door was closed, but there was a row of

rectangular windows along its upper quadrant. Though it was too high for Laurel to look through, Olivia had no problem seeing into the space. One glance at the vanity plate attached to the luxury sedan parked in the garage and she knew that Laurel's life was about to be forever altered.

"Does Steve's plate read 'smile for me'?" Olivia asked. "As in S-M-Y-L-4-M-E?"

Laurel's face went gray. "Yes." She touched the garage door. "So he's in there."

Olivia nodded. And before she or Millay could react, Laurel was off like a bullet, racing up the tiered steps for the front door.

Millay cursed and ran after her.

Olivia, who wasn't much of a runner, took longer to catch up. By the time she did, Laurel was already twisting the knob and pushing against the door. It opened without resistance.

Laurel entered the house and quietly mounted the stairs leading to the second floor. Olivia and Millay followed, but when they reached the top, Olivia grabbed Millay's elbow. She turned to her friend and shook her head, signaling that Laurel had to travel to the end of the hall by herself.

A woman's shrill laugh tripped out of the last bedroom. Olivia caught a glimpse of beige carpet and dark purple walls. A large silver cursive letter *S* affixed to a floral satin ribbon hung from the door. Laurel's shoulder brushed against it as she crossed the threshold and came to a halt. The letter swung back and forth on its nail and then a man cried, "What the— *Laurel!*"

"Surprise. It's me. Your wife," Laurel said with a chilling calm. "Put your clothes on and get out. I'll deal with you at home." She crossed her arms over her chest and waited. Seconds later, Steve came scurrying out of the bedroom. He flew down the stairs past Olivia and Millay as though they weren't even there.

Laurel didn't move. She didn't so much as cast him a backward glance. "As for you, you low-life piece of trash," she said, her voice filled with menace, "you're going to suffer for trying to destroy my family. You should be burned like a witch. I love the idea of you doused in gasoline. Yes! I could easily pour on the gas and strike a match. And the whole time you're burning, and experiencing just a smidgen of the pain you've caused me, I'd laugh. Because you'd be getting the exact punishment you deserve."

Chapter 3

Rawlings handed Olivia a drink and stood next to her on the back deck. She stared out over the winter-stark dunes to where Haviland raced along the water's edge, his paws leaving depressions in the damp sand. The poodle was untouched by the chilly air, unfazed by the pain his human companion had witnessed and was now trying to process.

"I'm so sorry," Rawlings whispered. Though his shoulder was close to Olivia's, he sensed that she wouldn't welcome his touch. "What happened after you left the nurse's house?"

"We took Laurel home," Olivia said. "Steve was waiting for her. He'd asked the neighbor who'd been watching the twins to take them back to her place so he and Laurel could talk in private." She took a large swig of her Chivas Regal and readjusted the blanket Rawlings had draped over her shoulders. "I don't imagine there'll be much talking. Screaming maybe. Some broken glass. Frankly, I hope Laurel takes a swing at Steve with his four-iron."

Rawlings sipped from his beer bottle and frowned as he gazed at the darkening water. "Too many good marriages are torn apart because of infidelity. I know two officers who recently separated after their spouses had affairs with people they met through social media. It's just too easy to pretend to be someone you're not on those sites. Too easy to avoid the hard work and commitment required by a real relationship and indulge in a fantasy instead." He leaned over the railing, his eyes tracking Haviland as the poodle jogged toward the lighthouse. "How did Steve get to know this woman so well? By chatting with her online? Or did he spend time with her while she cared for his mother?"

"I have no idea," Olivia said tersely. The sight of the Atlantic and the steady rhythm of the waves curling into the shore had never failed to calm her, but she was unable to tamp down her anger. Draining the rest of her drink, she turned to Rawlings, her sea blue eyes filled with cold fire. "Why does it matter how or where they flirted? Whether it was by voice mails or Facebook messages? Or e-mails? Or all of the above? This woman was *supposed* to be seeing to the *medical needs* of Steve's mother. And Steve was *supposed* to be focused on spending quality time with his mother before she passed. Would you define quality time as sleeping with her nurse?"

"No, I certainly wouldn't." Rawlings took Olivia's empty glass from her hand. "Do you want to go inside? The sun's setting and I have the fire going in the living room. I don't want you to catch cold."

Olivia shook her head. "I'd like to feel numb for a bit. Because after today, everything's going to be different. Our Bayside Book Writers' meetings, for example. Laurel won't come anymore. How could she?" She snorted over the absurdity of the notion. "She's hardly going to ask us to critique the next chapter of a manuscript detailing the life of a busy wife and mother struggling to find individuality in a seemingly loveless marriage."

A single tear rolled down Olivia's cheek and she wiped at it with an irritated flick of her wrist. Rawlings grabbed that same wrist and held it fast.

"I know you're boiling mad right now," he said. "But I am on your side. And I'm on Laurel's side. What can we do for her, Olivia? What can anyone do for her?" Rawlings moved closer. "She's in terrible pain. If anyone understands pain, it's you. What can you do to help her survive this trauma? What can I do? Or Millay? Or Harris?"

Once Olivia surrendered to Rawlings's touch, she was able to put aside her own emotions and consider his question. "The shock will hit her first. That will last for a little while. It's only when that wears off that the pain will truly begin. I can only guess at how world-shattering that will be. My pain was unlike hers. I was a child deserted by a parent. I didn't realize until later exactly what had been done to me." She glanced down at the simple gold band on Rawlings's ring finger. "Laurel's been betrayed by the man who slept next to her every night. By the man whose laundry she folded and whose dinners she cooked. By the man who fathered her children and stood at the sink in the bathroom, brushing his teeth, as she brushed hers. She trusted him to keep the vow they'd made to each other, but he didn't. And in breaking that vow, he has broken her heart."

Rawlings opened the sliding door and ushered Olivia into the house. He steered her over to the sofa and spread another blanket over her legs.

"I saw it, Sawyer," Olivia whispered. "When Laurel entered that tramp's bedroom, I saw her chest cave inward. It was like she'd been shot. Like she'd taken an impact. It was horrible."

Rawlings wrapped his arms around Olivia's shoulders. "Laurel is strong. She can get through this. This agony. She can do it. She'll do it for her boys. And we'll help her."

Olivia nodded. "Yes. She needs to know that she isn't alone. Betrayal is horribly isolating. And I can only imagine how this will affect Laurel's self-confidence. Steve is such a bastard. I hope she takes him for all he's worth!"

"She may still love him," Rawlings said in a soft voice. "The boys love him. Maybe, just maybe, they can find a way to stay together. To fight for their marriage. To fight for their family. It won't be easy, but wouldn't it be worth it?"

Olivia was about to lash out at Rawlings for so much as mentioning the idea when she bit back her harsh words.

Is he right? Is it better to swallow the pain and try to find a way to forgive? Is it even possible?

Haviland appeared at the closed door, pressing his nose against the glass until he made an erratic trail of half-moon smudges.

"I'll get him," Rawlings said.

Haviland darted inside the opening and trotted straight into the kitchen to examine his dinner dish.

"You're welcome!" Rawlings called after him.

"What do you expect?" Olivia asked caustically. "He's a male. He's biologically wired to satisfy his primal appetites."

Rawlings gave her a hard look. "Do you plan on punishing every man under this roof for Steve's actions? Because I'd like to pour you another drink, fix some dinner, and be grateful for what we have instead. Can we try to do that? I'd also like to comfort you if I can. You've experienced a shock too."

"I'm sorry." Olivia ran her hands through her short, moon-pale hair. "I can't stop being angry."

"Come here." Rawlings pulled her to her feet and held her tightly. "You don't have to let go of your anger. You have every right to feel what you feel. I just want you to know that I'm on your side. And I'm on Laurel's side. Okay?"

That night, before she went to sleep, Olivia sent Laurel a text to say that she was thinking of her and that she could call at any time. *"I'll check on you tomorrow,"* Olivia typed. *"You're not alone."*

As she reached over to turn off the lamp on her bedside table, she wondered if her friend would sleep at all on what was bound to be the worst night of her life.

Olivia didn't hear Rawlings leave for work the next morning. She slept so soundly that she didn't wake until after he was long gone. He left a note by the coffeepot telling her that he loved her and to call him if she wanted to talk. The note had been written on the back of a scrap of paper taken from Rawlings's recently revised manuscript and bore green pen marks from where he'd made editorial changes to a line of dialogue. Olivia thought the new line was much improved and smiled over how Rawlings had torn his discarded pages into uneven strips to be used as grocery or to-do lists. Or, in this case, a note of affection.

Olivia filled a take-out cup with coffee, put on a warm sweater, a pair of jeans, and a down vest, and took Haviland outside for a walk on the beach. Laurel hadn't replied to her text, and though this didn't surprise Olivia, she couldn't stop thinking about her friend. What had Laurel decided to do? Had she thrown Steve out of the house? Or was he sleeping in the guest room until Laurel had a chance to cool off? And where were the twins? Had they heard their parents screaming at each other? Were they scared and confused?

The winter sun set the water aglow with a gentle light, and the horizon was free of clouds. Far off in the distance, freighters chugged along the shipping lanes, and Olivia knew that the booths at Grumpy's Diner would be occupied by Oyster Bay's working-class folk. The ones with the callused hands and weathered faces. Those who rose early and went to bed late. All across Olivia's picturesque seaside town, people would be going about their routines. Everyone but Laurel Hobbs. Her life would never be routine again.

"Come on, Haviland." Olivia turned toward home before they'd even reached the Point—the long finger of sand jutting out into the ocean. "I'm going crazy. We might as well take Rachel's broken Hummel figurine to Fred. I promised to help Laurel by dealing with that errand, and I didn't get to it because of yesterday's drama."

Haviland glanced back over his shoulder at the Point as if to say, *This isn't our usual routine*, but he was such a good-natured dog that he didn't hesitate for long before falling into step with Olivia.

"We'll stop at Decadence and get Fred a chocolate croissant and a latte. It's been ages since we've dropped in for a visit." She gave her poodle a quick pat. "You must miss Duncan," she added, referring to Fred Yoder's Westie.

At the sound of his canine pal's name, Haviland released an exuberant bark and gave Olivia a toothy grin. Olivia firmly believed that her dog understood everything she said and that he was more intelligent than many of the humans she encountered.

At Decadence, Shelley Giusti, the wife of Olivia's head chef at the Boot Top Bistro, and an accomplished chef in her own right, was busy making adjustments to the window display. The desserterie offered a variety of coffee and pastries throughout the day. In the evening, the lights were dimmed, the music shifted from sprightly jazz to what Harris Williams, Olivia's ginger-haired computer genius friend and the other male member of the Bayside Book Writers, described as "sexy Cuban social club instrumental," and Shelley set out menus featuring a list of artisanal desserts and seasonal cocktails.

Olivia's gaze traveled over a veritable army of foil-wrapped chocolate Santas to the marzipan fruit and the rows of homemade fudge in the display case. She stared at the block of Candy Cane Fudge, a white chocolate fudge featuring ribbons of peppermint, and felt a wave of despair.

"What's wrong?" Shelley asked, peering down at Olivia from the second rung of a stepladder. "You look like you just found coal in your stocking."

"Sorry." Olivia produced a weak smile. "I heard some bad news yesterday, and I'm having a hard time shaking it off. I know one of your butter croissants will help. I'm also going to bring a chocolate croissant to Fred at Circa."

Shelley seemed unconvinced but was too polite to pry. She climbed down from the ladder and scooted behind the massive display case filled with a heavenly array of handmade chocolate, candy, and pastries. After telling the young woman manning the register that she'd take care of Olivia's order herself, she disappeared into the kitchen.

When she reemerged a few minutes later, she held a white paper bag and a take-out coffee cup. "You have to see my design before I put the lid on," she told Olivia. Her face was shining with pride. "I've been working on this for weeks."

Olivia approached the scrubbed pine counter where Shelley's customers collected their drinks. She looked into the steamed milk of her latte to find a Christmas tree, complete with star, captured in the froth. "Wow," she breathed, though the tree only made her think of Laurel's boys again. "It's beautiful, Shelley. Did Fred get one too?"

"I bungled his." Shelley winked at her. "Don't tell him. At least your croissants are fresh from the oven. Enjoy!"

Olivia devoured hers at the next red light, ignoring Haviland's whines and frantic lip licking. "This is my breakfast," she scolded. "You've had yours. Besides, Fred is bound to give you a chew stick and you know it."

Fred didn't open his antique store until ten, but Olivia knew that he arrived well before that time in order to drink his second cup of coffee while reading the paper at the table in the shop's small but cheerful kitchen.

"The light is better here than at home," he'd once explained to Olivia, but Olivia sensed that the truth had more to do with Fred's outgoing personality. A lifelong bachelor, he loved interacting with people and could talk to anyone who drifted into his shop. Even the most taciturn passersby soon found themselves showing Fred photos of their grandchildren or sharing a favorite story or joke.

Unfortunately, Fred had bought a house on the outskirts of town because he'd been attracted by the large attached workshop space. He quickly discovered, however, that he didn't care for the remoteness of the location.

"It's been too long since I've seen you," he reproached Olivia after opening the front door and inviting her inside. Duncan, his Westie, barked a chorus of happy hellos to Haviland. The two dogs sniffed and grunted before making their way into the kitchen.

"I brought a peace offering," Olivia said, proffering the Decadence bag and cup carrier.

Fred smiled. "You are forgiven all sins. Come on back."

"I also have an injured antique in my handbag," Olivia

added as she followed Fred into the kitchen. "I brought it in as a favor to Laurel."

After Fred put the goodies on the kitchen table, he took a pair of chew sticks out of a chipped Little Red Riding Hood cookie jar made by Hull and turned to address the two canines. "Gentlemen? Sit, please."

Both dogs obeyed and Fred distributed their treats.

Olivia removed the Hummel from her bag and gently unwrapped it.

"In general, figurines don't get my blood racing," Fred said, watching her. "I'm certainly not going to put this chocolate croissant down for a Hummel."

Olivia laughed. It felt good to laugh after feeling so angry yesterday and so glum this morning. "I can't say I'm fond of these particular figurines, but to each his own."

Fred nodded. "That's right. The world is full of unique collectors and the things that are dear to them. So let's see what happened to this poor child." He squinted at the Hummel in concern. "Messy break. The paint's all chipped where the arm came off."

"Can it be repaired?"

"Yes, but it needs to be shipped to a Hummel expert," Fred said. He popped the last bite of croissant into his mouth and wiped his hands on a paper napkin without taking his eyes off the figurine. When his fingers were suitably clean, he turned the Hummel over and peered at the base through his bifocals. Olivia knew that Fred wanted to verify that the piece was genuine by examining the maker's mark. However, he seemed unable to see it.

Reaching for the magnifying glass lying next to the newspaper, Fred muttered, "Damn it all."

Olivia glanced at her friend. "Is the mark faded?"

"My vision just isn't what it used to be and I'm having a

hard time making out the mold number. It's embossed here. Can you read it?"

Fred handed her the magnifying glass, which Olivia didn't need but used anyway. She recited the number while Fred jotted it down. He then searched for the figurine on his laptop and informed Olivia that not only was it genuine, but it was also a fairly rare one.

"There's no time to send it out," Olivia said. "We need a patch job—something to make it look good enough to comfort Laurel's mother-in-law. Isn't there anyone in the area who can help us? I'll pay whatever they ask for a rush job."

Fred cradled the Hummel in his palm and seemed to be waging an internal debate. Finally, he said, "I know a guy. I'll give him a call and see if he can work some magic for us."

"Thanks, Fred. You're the best."

"Anything for you, Olivia." Fred held up a finger. "But next time, promise that you'll drop by just for a chat." He grinned. "Though I thoroughly enjoyed the pastry bribe."

After promising to call as soon as the Hummel was repaired, Fred walked Olivia and Haviland to the door. Duncan plodded along after them but didn't make it all the way across the shop. The allure of his doggy bed, which was behind the display counter containing coins and other small items, was apparently too great to resist. He curled up, closed his eyes, and released a sigh of contentment.

"They lead a tough life, don't they?" Olivia pointed between Haviland and Duncan.

Fred shot his dog a brief but troubled glance. "He's showing signs of age. Duncan needs insulin shots now." He paused to gather himself. "At least his diabetes is treatable. We've been together so long that I can't imagine this place—or any place—without him."

Knowing exactly how Fred felt, Olivia squeezed her friend's hand. "You keep him healthy. And yourself too. This world needs more gentlemen like you, Fred Yoder." An image of Steve Hobbs popped into her head. "Trust me. These days, a real gentleman is as rare as that Hummel."

Olivia decided to call Rawlings before heading into the Boot Top Bistro, but he didn't answer his cell or office phone. This was unusual and Olivia wondered if he'd caught a new case.

"Harris will know," she said to Haviland, and dialed his number.

Once, Harris had been a full-time computer geek, writing code for a computer gaming company. However, he now only worked for that company part-time in order to pursue his other passion: serving as a consultant for the Oyster Bay Police Department. Harris had proved so gifted in being able to find people and things in cyberspace that he'd quickly become a valuable member of the chief's team.

As soon as she got Harris on the line, Olivia knew that he wasn't at the station. The buzz of background noise sounded as if he were standing on a crowded subway platform.

"What's going on?" she asked.

"It's bad," Harris whispered nervously. "The chief's a few feet away, so I can't say much."

Fear tiptoed up Olivia's spine. "Don't do that, Harris. Just tell me."

"Hold on. Let me walk around to the other side of the car." Harris continued to speak sotto voce and Olivia had a hard time hearing him over the background din.

"Harris? Where are you?" she demanded.

"In a parking lot just outside the security gates of the

condos where Laurel's in-laws live," Harris said. His voice came through clearly now and there was no mistaking the anxiety in it. "Olivia, there's been a murder."

The fear tightened its grip on Olivia. It wrapped an icy hand around her stomach and squeezed. "Who's the victim?"

"It'll be a while before her ID's confirmed. She was in her car and the whole thing was set on fire." Harris paused. "But I saw the name on the registration."

Olivia, who had yet to pull away from the curb in front of Circa, turned off the Range Rover's engine and closed her eyes. After fighting back a wave of nausea, she drew in a fortifying breath and asked, "Was it a gold Hyundai? With decals all over the rear window?"

"Yeah," Harris murmured reluctantly. "The vehicle belongs to Stacy Balena."

Keeping her eyes shut, as if blocking out images could forestall any more information from entering her brain, Olivia willed Harris's words to be false. "No, no, no," she protested. "It can't be."

Of course, she knew he was telling the truth. Harris never lied. Not only that, but he had more facts about this case. More facts than he wanted to share with her. These were facts that he was loath to share because these facts were going to wound her. They had already hurt him. She knew this by his subdued, hesitant tone.

"Harris?" She spoke his name gently. "What else do you want to tell me?"

"The chief has asked to be excused from the case," Harris explained gruffly. "Cook will take over. I can stay involved because I'm only a consultant. And that's a good thing, because I need to know what's going on. Especially since I don't think she—Laurel—did this. The chief told me about Laurel catching Steve."

Olivia opened her eyes. She stared first at her poodle, but his restless gaze refused to be held, so she glanced to the east, beyond the shops and the boats at anchor, searching for the beacon she'd always looked for when in need of comfort. The landmark of her past. From when she lived in the lighthouse keeper's cottage as a girl. Her eyes found the lighthouse lamp. Her beacon in the dark.

She found where it rose into the pale sky and focused her sights on the place where the December sun winked off the glass. "Laurel's a suspect?"

Harris didn't respond for a long time. "She's the prime suspect," he said eventually and with great reluctance. "The security guard saw her screaming at Stacy. Stacy was in her car at the time. The guard recognized both women. He said that when he tried to intervene, Laurel hurled a wine bottle at him. He threatened to call the cops on her, so she got in her minivan and left. He said she drove erratically, like she'd been drinking heavily. Stacy said she was too upset to drive and wanted to take a few minutes to calm down. She was still alive when the guards changed shifts, but Laurel was the last person seen with her."

"No, no, no," Olivia repeated.

A cloud covered the sun. There was no more glint on the lighthouse glass or on the water below. Everything seemed to turn dull and gray. Hopeless.

"What happened next? Did Stacy leave?"

Harris sighed. It was the weighted sigh of a man steeling himself for a terrible outcome. "The guard doesn't know. After seeing that she was okay, he returned to his shack or hut or whatever. A different guard called in the fire an hour later. He'd barely started his shift when he made the call."

"Where's Laurel now?"

"I guess she's still at home. Cook is on his way there now." Harris paused. "Why? What are you planning to do?"

Olivia pushed her ignition button, and the engine roared in response. "I'm going to be there for her, of course."

"I'll see you at the station," Harris said approvingly. "Take care of her."

"I will," Olivia replied. Tossing her phone on the passenger seat, she put the car in drive, told Haviland to brace himself, and pulled out onto Main Street.

She headed for Laurel's house, breaking half a dozen traffic laws as she drove. She wanted to believe that if she could beat the cops to her friend, somehow this nightmare would not be real. That it would all prove to be a mistake.

But as Olivia entered Laurel's development and saw the two cruisers parked in her driveway, she knew that no amount of speed could have spared her friend what was coming.

Steve stood out on the front lawn—his shadow forming an elongated and faceless creature with hands in its pockets—watching in stupefied horror as a female officer helped a mute and docile Laurel into the backseat of one of the police cars.

Doors slammed. Engines started. Neighbors gathered on stoops and porches to gawk.

Olivia hurriedly drove past the surreal scene, which looked like a still frame from a horror movie, and sped toward the end of the street. Here, she turned around so quickly that her tires squealed, and then she caught up to the cruiser carrying Laurel into town.

Chapter 4

Secrets, silent, stony sit in the dark
palaces of both our hearts: secrets
weary of their tyranny: tyrants willing
to be dethroned.

—JAMES JOYCE

When Olivia arrived at the station, Rawlings was waiting at the entrance.

"No one will be interviewing Laurel tonight," the chief quickly assured his wife. "She's passed out in the holding cell. Cook will talk to her in the morning. You should go home. There's nothing you can do here."

Olivia immediately dismissed this with a curt shake of the head. "I need to see her."

"I can't get you back there, honey. I'm not on the case."

Inexplicably, the endearment angered Olivia. How many times had Steve called Laurel "honey" or "sweetheart" while he was deceiving her? And after all the pain, humiliation, and heartbreak she'd already suffered, Laurel could now look forward to waking up in a cold, dim jail cell.

And Laurel wasn't some drunk sleeping off a bender. She wouldn't come around feeling momentarily scared and confused. Her situation was far worse. She'd struggle to consciousness and have to face the memory of being read her Miranda rights. And then it would all come crashing down. The arrest. Steve's affair. The end of the life she'd known.

Olivia couldn't stand the thought of her friend staring down such a frightening dawn alone.

"I'll wait in your office all night if I have to," she insisted. "But first, I want to go back to Laurel's and pack her a change of clothes. She'll want to know who's taking care of the twins too, so I'll find out what I can from her louse of a husband."

Rawlings put his hands on Olivia's shoulders. "Steve is on his way to us. He also has to account for his whereabouts and undergo questioning."

"And the boys?" Olivia's anxiety rose. "Who's watching the twins?"

"I'll have the dispatch operator put us in touch with the officer accompanying Mr., er, Steve," Rawlings said. "Come inside."

Olivia followed Rawlings into the station, wondering if her husband had almost called Steve "Mr. Hobbs" because he viewed him as a suspect. Rawlings had always addressed the victims, suspects, and persons of interest involved in his cases with the utmost respect. Whether a person had shoplifted or committed murder made no difference. Rawlings never used first names. Those were reserved for friends, family, or, in Steve's case, acquaintances.

I won't be able to take it if he starts referring to Laurel as "Mrs. Hobbs," Olivia thought. The very notion filled her with an intense rage, and her step nearly faltered.

Rawlings, interpreting Olivia's unsteady gait as a sign that she needed both physical and emotional support, put a hand under her elbow.

She twisted away. It was a subtle movement, creating just enough distance to make it awkward for Rawlings to keep his hand raised. He shot her a puzzled look before lowering his arm.

The dispatch operator had no trouble contacting the officer escorting Steve, and Steve was able to explain that arrangements had been made for the twins to spend the night at a neighbor's house.

"We wanted to be able to talk about what happened without them overhearing," Olivia heard him say as though from a very great distance. Steve said something else that began with "Oh God, what have I—!" but the rest of his words dissolved into sobs.

Olivia listened to his crying without feeling an ounce of pity for him.

"Those children are probably far more aware of what's been going on than their parents realize," she murmured, and the dispatch operator, an older woman with gray hair and a kind face, nodded in sorrowful agreement.

"Poor lambs," she whispered.

Rawlings thanked the operator and steered Olivia several feet away from her desk.

"Are you still planning on going to Laurel's?" he asked. "Because I'll have to clear it with Cook. He has a team assigned to search the house for evidence."

"Evidence," Olivia repeated numbly. "I don't think they'll find proof of murder, but they will discover plenty of motives on Laurel's part in that house. The moment Harris gets into Steve's computer—and undoubtedly his cell phone too—Laurel's humiliation will no longer be private." She could almost hear the opening lines of tomorrow's news reports. "Tell Cook that his officers can watch every move I make, but I need to pack a few necessities for Laurel. I'll wear gloves. I'll wear shoe covers. I'll wear damn coveralls, but I'm going in that house. Tonight."

Olivia expected Rawlings to argue, but he didn't. Instead, he walked mutely beside her as she strode over the frost-crisp grass to the parking lot. Neither of them spoke, but their plumed breaths intertwined over their heads like two phantom tornadoes that instantly dissipated, re-forming again several seconds later.

It was only when Olivia opened her car door that Rawlings reacted. Putting his body between the door and the car body to prevent Olivia from shutting it, he said, "I hate this too. Every bit as much as you do. Maybe more. Because I'm caught between a rock and a hard place. I can't be Laurel's friend and confidant. Neither can Harris. We'll have to entrust those most important roles to you and Millay. But neither can I be involved in this case. Cook will throw me bones, but he knows damn well that it's impossible for me to be objective. And he's right. I can't. I don't want anything that happened tonight to be true."

He pressed the tips of his fingers across the bridge of his nose, and Olivia saw that his fingers were trembling. She felt the hardness that had been growing over her heart like a layer of barnacles since she and Millay entered Stacy's house crack and soften.

"I don't want Laurel to be in that cell," Rawlings went on. "I hate that she's there, and I can't predict what morning will bring. But I know that we have to stick together. You and me. Harris and Millay. All of us. We're not on opposite sides. Laurel is *our* friend."

Olivia put a hand on his cheek. "I'm sorry. I didn't mean to take my anger out on you. I'm just so scared for her. Things look really bad." This last phrase was spoken in a low whisper. "I feel like Judas saying that, but isn't it true?"

Rawlings gave her a little smile. "You know I've read nearly every book about pirates and buried treasure, right?

Well, I've always remembered something that Robert Louis Stevenson wrote. It goes, 'Keep your fears to yourself, but share your courage with others.'" He laid his hand over Olivia's. "We have to follow that creed. Don't let your worry show. It will take an incredible amount of courage to push aside the fear, but that's what Laurel needs from us more than anything else now."

The wisdom of Rawlings's advice allowed Olivia to momentarily forget her own anxiety. She nodded, her mind already conjuring a to-do list of tasks that had to be seen to before Laurel woke.

"You have that look in your eye," Rawlings said. "You're coming up with a battle plan."

"Yes. Pack a bag for Laurel. Hire the best defense lawyer in the state. Call my sister-in-law and ask her to help me find someone to look after Laurel's children."

Rawlings cocked his head. "Steve's a cad, but he's still their father. He'll be back home in a couple of hours and should be able to take care of his own sons."

"The only needs he knows how to fulfill are his own," Olivia snapped. "That man is weak. Only a weak man would cheat on a strong woman. You watch. Steve Hobbs will shatter into a thousand pieces now that his wife has been arrested and their lives are going to be put on display. I wouldn't entrust the boys to his keeping for more than a couple of hours. Laurel would never forgive me if I did."

Rawlings threw up his hands. "Just remember that he has the law on his side. Don't make arrangements without informing him. That's all I'm suggesting."

"Recommendation noted." Olivia pulled on her seat belt and clicked it into place, signaling her readiness to leave. "I won't cross any lines. That would only make things harder for Laurel, and that's the last thing I'm looking to do."

Olivia watched Rawlings step away from the Range Rover and head back into the station. As she drove out of the parking lot, she wondered what it must feel like for the chief of police to stand off to the side while one of his subordinates took over the most important murder investigation of his career.

He must feel as helpless as a rookie, she thought.

But there would be time to comfort her husband later. Olivia pressed a button on her steering wheel and directed a command toward the microphone built into her dashboard. "Call Kim Salter. Home." A female computer voice repeated her orders and within seconds, Olivia's sister-in-law was on the line.

"Kim. I'm sorry to bother you, but I need a favor. It's urgent," Olivia said.

There wasn't the slightest hesitation before Kim replied, "I've been hoping for a phone call like this. For a chance to thank you for inviting our family to Oyster Bay and for giving us the life we'd been dreaming of. So tell me. How can I help?"

Though Olivia was touched by Kim's words, she didn't let it show. She was afraid that if she lowered her emotional defenses any more tonight—that if she allowed herself to express another deep feeling—she would fail to be the unyielding rock of a friend that Laurel so gravely needed.

After uttering a brief thanks, Olivia explained that she needed to find a kind, discreet, and reliable person to care for Dermot and Dallas.

"Why?" Kim asked. "Did something happen to Laurel?"

And here it was. The question Olivia should have been prepared for but wasn't.

Gripping the steering wheel tightly, Olivia took a moment to collect herself before answering. "Laurel is being held as a murder suspect. She didn't do it, of course," she hastily added, knowing she'd have to tack on this caveat every time she told people what had happened. "But I don't know when she'll be able to go home."

"Good Lord, those poor boys." Kim's voice went very quiet. "And Steve! He must be going out of his mind."

"Oh, he lost his mind well before tonight," Olivia said acidly. "This is all his fault, but Laurel will end up bearing the full weight of his sins."

There was silence on Kim's end. Finally, she said, "I don't—"

"You'll hear the sordid details soon enough," Olivia interrupted. "Listen, Kim. I don't mean to be abrupt, but I'm desperate. Can you find me a warm and trustworthy woman to watch the boys?"

Kim's reply was a firm "Yes. I'll start making calls right now."

Olivia relaxed her grip on the steering wheel by a fraction. "Thank you so much. I'll check in with you in the morning. The boys are with a neighbor, so we have until then."

"Tell Laurel that her sons will be okay," Kim said. "If I can't hire someone, I'll relocate them to our place until I find a solution. You tell Laurel not to worry about those boys. They're going to be okay."

After promising to relay the message, Olivia ended the call and issued more commands through her Bluetooth connection. By the time she arrived at Laurel's, she'd spoken to a paralegal at the Raleigh-based law firm Olivia believed would provide Laurel with the best defense. The paralegal, a shrewd and ambitious young man, was working late on a case and instantly recognized Olivia's name. His boss rarely took vacations, but when he did, he opted for long weekends at the beach. His preferred coastal getaway was Oyster Bay, and he never booked a rental house overlooking the ocean without also booking a table at his favorite restaurant: the Boot Top Bistro.

"It's an honor to be of service, Ms. Limoges," the paralegal gushed.

"You might not agree when you hear which service I require." Olivia put forth her request, and the paralegal began to hem and haw. He described their heavy caseload and an assortment of other obstacles that made her request impossible, but Olivia smoothly cut him off and insisted that he call his boss to deliver her message.

"At home?" the paralegal squeaked. "At this time of night?"

Olivia glanced at the facade of Laurel's house. Every light blazed, creating rectangles of illumination on the lawn. In addition to a pair of police cruisers, Harris's Chevy Volt was parked in the driveway. The search had begun.

Her anxiety spiking, Olivia's anger surged. "You could always give me the number, but I believe Rand would prefer to hear a summary from you first." Her use of the attorney's first name was deliberate. "Here's my cell phone number." She rattled off the number. "Please tell Rand that I'll be expecting him in the morning."

"Yes, ma'am," the paralegal said.

Olivia's final call was to Millay. She needed fresh air for this conversation, so she grabbed her smartphone, brought up Millay's contact card, and listened to the line ring several times.

Growing impatient, Olivia began walking up the flagstone path to Laurel's front door. Just as she reached the lamppost—the same lamppost Laurel had decorated with Christmas lights in an attempt to bring a little cheer to her

family in the face of her mother-in-law's impending death—
Millay picked up.

"Are you at work?" Olivia asked, hearing the telltale din
of a bar crowd in the background.

"That I am, Miss Marple. I'm popping the caps off bottles of Bud as fast as Harris gets in line to buy the latest
iPhone." Someone shouted a raucous greeting at Millay.
Olivia was on the verge of losing her temper when Millay
sensed that something was wrong. "Hey. You don't usually
call me here. Is everything okay?"

Olivia told her.

After releasing a torrent of expletives, Millay asked,
"Where are you?"

"Parked in front of Laurel's house. I'm going inside to
pack a change of clothes for her. I plan to be there when she
wakes up tomorrow. Even if Cook won't let me see her, I'm
going to be there."

"I'll be right over," Millay said. "It's the women against
the men now, you know. The chief and Harris have to view
Laurel as a suspect. They don't have any other choice. That
leaves it to us to exonerate her. This totally sucks!" she suddenly yelled. "All because Steve had a midlife crisis, which
resulted in his not being able to keep it in his pants, the Bayside Book Writers are now officially divided. It's going to be
a civil war. Painful and bloody and nobody really wins."

Millay hung up and Olivia remained frozen in place,
weighing her friend's words. Absently, she pinched one of
the Christmas lightbulbs between her thumb and forefinger.
The light, which turned her skin a sickly orange hue, gave
off almost no heat. Olivia released it and continued her
march to the front door.

She knocked forcefully and drew herself to her full
height. The cops hadn't been in the house for long and

wouldn't have had enough time to handle and shift all the objects that represented the life of the Hobbs family, but the idea that they would soon be doing so vexed Olivia more than she cared to admit. She wanted to get in and out without bearing witness to the assault on her friend's cupboards, cabinets, closets, and drawers.

A very pale-faced Harris opened the door. He wore a funny expression and Olivia realized that he was on the verge of being sick to his stomach. She immediately put a hand under his elbow and pulled him outside.

"Breathe in through your mouth," she said calmly. "That's it. You're going to be fine."

Harris inhaled great gulps of fresh air, and some of the color returned to his cheeks. Studying him, Olivia guessed that Harris must have gained access to Steve's computer and found something that caused him serious distress.

Because it makes things worse for Laurel? Olivia worried.

Without considering the consequences, she stepped into the warm, bright entry hall and turned toward Steve's office, Harris reluctantly trailing behind her.

The office, which was located on the opposite end of the house from the master bedroom, was a cavelike room. The walls were painted a shade of deep merlot, and other than a single window covered by dark plantation shutters and a group of framed diplomas, the space was bare of decoration. There were no family photos or mementos. No souvenirs or trophies. Just paperwork, file folders, golf magazines, and bookcases filled with dental journals and reference books.

Steve's desk was covered by a mass of random papers, sticky notes, and newspaper articles—most of which were stained with splatters or rings of red wine. After pulling a tissue from a tooth-shaped box perched on the corner of the desk, Olivia gave the computer mouse a nudge to bring the black screen to life. Suddenly, she found herself staring at half a dozen images of a naked woman.

Olivia jumped back, startled.

She recognized the woman, of course. It was Stacy Balena. She had arranged herself in several provocative poses and wore a sly smile in every shot. The last image, however, looked different, and Olivia realized that it was a video file.

"Christ," she murmured.

"Don't watch that," Harris warned from behind her. "It's pretty lewd."

Color had returned to Harris's cheeks. In fact, as he glanced from Olivia to the computer, he flushed from neck to forehead.

"I wouldn't think a man of your age—a man who's grown up in the digital world—would be shocked by what appears to be amateur porn."

Harris scuttled between Olivia and the computer, obscuring her view of the screen. "It's not the video itself. It's all the messages the two of them exchanged. When I started reading them, I couldn't help imagining—"

"How Laurel must have felt when she read them," Olivia guessed. "And it doesn't seem like Steve made much effort to hide them. But why would he? Laurel trusted him."

Harris nodded miserably.

"Are you sure that she read them?" Olivia asked.

"Unless Steve shoved a chair under the door to keep anyone from entering this room—you can see the marks under the knob—and printed about a hundred pages of documents capturing every picture, e-mail, and Facebook message, and a record of Steve's cell phone charges for the past two months, then I'd say that yes, Laurel read everything."

Olivia glanced around. "How do you know she printed a hundred pages?"

"I checked the printer history," Harris said. "She must have stashed the printouts somewhere. Maybe she was gathering evidence because she planned to sue for divorce on grounds of adultery. Seems like it would have been an open-and-shut case." He chewed his lip. "But seeing all this stuff. Reading their messages. Him calling her 'my princess,' and crap like that. It must have hurt Laurel so badly."

"*Princess?* Are you serious?" a voice asked caustically. "I think I might lose my dinner."

Olivia turned to find Millay standing in the doorway. With her moon pale face, black hair, heavy black eye makeup, and black leather jacket and boots, she looked like a vengeful angel. Anger radiated off her body and shone from her pupils like twin sparks.

With Millay's arrival, Harris seemed to suddenly remember his duty. "You two shouldn't be in here. Cook said you were just coming for some clothes for Laurel. And it was supposed to be just you, Olivia."

Millay glared at Harris. "Chill out, Columbo. I won't touch anything. But I'm here because this is about *Laurel*. Remember her? She's our *friend*?"

Harris was about to reply when he stopped and put a finger to his lips. "Another officer is coming. You two had better hustle back to the other end of the house. We could all get in trouble, and I'm lucky I'm even being allowed to work this case. The other cops know I'm Laurel's friend, but since I'm only a consultant, no one sees me as possibly compromising the investigation."

Olivia followed Harris's advice and quickly returned to the foyer. She and Millay introduced themselves to a junior officer who escorted them to the master bedroom and watched as they selected clothes and toiletries for Laurel. At the last second, Olivia scooped up a framed photograph of the twins and added that to the pile she'd assembled on Laurel's bed.

"I found this duffel bag in her closet." Millay held out a pink-and-teal number, complete with Laurel's monogram.

"That'll do," Olivia said, and then looked to the cop for permission. After being given a brief nod of acquiescence, she took the bag from Millay and dropped it on the bed. When she pushed a pair of jeans inside, her fingers brushed against the hard edge of a file folder.

Sensing she'd found the printouts Laurel had made from Steve's computer, Olivia was now eager to leave the house. She and Millay needed to read them. At least, they needed to read some of them. They needed to see if any of the material could have caused Laurel to become so enraged that—

No! Olivia ceased the rest of the thought from forming. *Laurel did not kill that woman.*

Outside, Olivia and Millay faced each other. They said nothing. The initial shock of Laurel's arrest had worn off. What remained was the horror and misery of Laurel's situation. She was being held as the prime suspect in a murder case. Her house was being searched. She had a compelling motive for killing the victim.

"This is utter bullshit," Millay muttered, her breath pluming in the winter air. "You and I know Laurel didn't do this." She jerked her thumb at Harris's car. "No offense to Harris and the chief, but they'll have no choice but to play by the book and treat our girl like any other suspect pulled in off the street. That means it's on us, Olivia. We're all Laurel's got. Watch how fast the rest of her friends desert her." She made a derisive gesture at the surrounding homes before pointing at Laurel's bag. "So, what was in there? Something flashed across your face when you put your hand inside."

"Remind me never to play poker with you," Olivia said. "You're far too adept at reading people." After setting the bag in her backseat, she turned to Millay. "I think we're in possession of Laurel's adultery file. She's a journalist, remember, and she knows her way around a computer. She has years of experience gathering documents and data in order to piece together a story."

Millay's gaze slid to the bag. "And when she finished assembling that story, then what? She started to pack an overnight bag, stopped, and decided to confront the other woman instead?"

Olivia arched her eyebrows. "That's a tame term, coming from you."

"I'm still absorbing the craziness of our new reality, okay?" Millay raked her hands through her hair. "Stacy's *my* age. She hangs out in clubs. She has piercings and hooks up with men who sport lots of ink. What the hell was she doing with Steve? A middle-aged dentist with a beer gut. A suburbanite with a wife and kids. What was she thinking?"

"Steve owns his practice. He makes a very good living." Olivia slammed her car door shut. "You said that Stacy had kids. Maybe she thought Steve would help her financially. Maybe he already has. We'd have to go through Laurel's files to see how serious this affair was."

A look of unease entered Millay's eyes. "Crap. That means reading all their gross seduction messages."

Olivia shared her friend's displeasure at the thought. "We'll skim them. But we need to know everything if we're going to help Laurel."

"And how will the chief feel about your taking evidence from the suspect's house?"

Olivia shrugged. "Everything we have in that bag is also on Steve's computer. Harris will make the same discoveries and put everything together the same way Laurel did. It'll just take him longer. We need this head start."

Millay reached for the passenger-door handle and then paused. She glanced at Laurel's house and then looked at Olivia. Her face was etched with fear. "What she found must have wounded her so badly. A total knife in the back. What if—"

"Don't even say it." Olivia pulled her keys from her pocket and walked around to the driver's side. Eager to get away from Laurel's house, she yanked her seat belt across her chest, started the car, and switched on the headlamps.

Because she'd parked at the curb, the lights fell directly on Laurel's mailbox, illuminating the brass letters spelling out THE HOBBS FAMILY.

Olivia and Millay both stared at the letters for several seconds before Olivia performed such a violent U-turn that her tires left black scars on the road.

Chapter 5

The fact is that being seductive is an
addiction that can never be satisfied.

—GABRIEL GARCÍA MÁRQUEZ

"Where are we going to read this?" Millay asked, jerking her thumb toward the bag in the backseat. "We can't take it to your place. The chief might come home and catch us with it. We can go to my apartment, but I don't stock your fancy booze. In fact, my liquor supply is pretty low. Things haven't been going well with my writing and . . ." Leaving the thought incomplete, she gave a curt shake of her head. "None of that matters right now. I just wanted to warn you about my Mother Hubbard situation."

Olivia deliberated over whether she could wade through the verbal—and potentially pictorial—history of Steve's affair without alcohol. Deciding that she needed a dose of liquid courage, she made a quick stop at the ABC store, where she bought a bottle of twenty-five-year-old Chivas Regal for herself and a six-pack of Devils Backbone lager for Millay.

While Olivia was making these purchases, Millay darted into the convenience store next door to buy snacks.

"I have no appetite whatsoever," Olivia said ten minutes later as Millay unceremoniously dumped a bag of pretzels in the center of her kitchen table.

Millay dropped two ice cubes in a glass and plunked it down in front of Olivia. "Of course not. I don't either, but we should put something in our stomachs. It's going to be a long, hard night and we don't want to end up sloshed. The booze is to keep us from losing our minds while we read through this crap, but if we drink too much, we'll lose our perspective."

Olivia poured two fingers' worth of Scotch into her glass. "Do you think that's what happened to Laurel? She drank too much and lost her perspective?"

Pulling a church key from her back pocket, Millay expertly uncapped her beer. The cap skittered across the table, spinning on its axis like a serrated coin until Millay's hand shot out, flattening the cap with her palm.

"I think Laurel sat in her husband's chair and drank and read." Millay touched the edge of the cap to the folder sitting in the middle of the table. Neither woman had yet to open it. "I think she drank and read and visualized everything that happened between Steve and Stacy. I think she heard their words in her head. She heard them whispering to each other. Laughing together. And sharing fantasies. Parts of her broke then. The softer parts. The parts of her that once trusted her husband and believed in her marriage. And I guess the rest of her went into rage mode."

Olivia took a fortifying sip of Scotch. "Fueled by wine and fury, she set off to confront Stacy. To what end?"

"We won't know until we start reading." Millay sighed

and reached for the folder. "It's going to be miserable, but here we go."

"Maybe we'll find something to indicate another suspect," Olivia said, accepting the first printout. "Stacy complaining about an abusive ex-boyfriend or a stalker. Anyone to take the heat off Laurel."

Millay was already frowning. "It looks like this is the first contact. Stacy initiated it through Facebook. See?"

Olivia scooted her chair closer and read the message.

Hi, Steve. I hope it's okay for me to call you that and to message you. I wanted to tell you how much I like spending time with your mom!! She's told me so much about you that I feel like I already know you!! We might not be the same age, but we like a lot of the same music. She said that you rock vinyl in your office. Me too!!! Only I keep my player in my bedroom. I like to play my records before I go to bed. Tonight I'm listening to Cheap Trick. What are you spinning right now? Stac☺

Millay said, "It's going to be a long night if we have to read crap writing like this. What's with the tween girl use of exclamation marks or the smiley face emoji replacing the *e* of 'Stace'? Is she twelve or twenty-eight?" Millay mimed sticking a finger down her throat. "Still, she's a good manipulator. Gets the married guy to picture her bedroom right away and then ends with a question. Steve didn't have to answer, but it would seem rude not to. After all, she's his mother's nurse."

Olivia had already moved on to the next conversation. "She inflates his ego immediately too. Says how impressed she is that he has his own practice and that she understands what it's like to work long hours because you love your job and because you want your kids to have everything. She tells him about having to pick up her kids here." Olivia turned to Millay. "I thought you said that they lived with their father."

"That's what Stacy told me." Millay chewed her lip. "Maybe she wanted Steve to feel sorry for her—to think of her toiling away without the support of a husband. A good husband like him."

Olivia nodded. "She might have been manipulating him. But why? What did she hope to get out of this? Maybe her motive will become clearer as the affair gets more serious."

The messages continued for the next few nights as Stacy and Steve's relationship developed from a seemingly innocuous exchange of personal details to casual flirting. The flirting quickly escalated, and within a week's time, it was clear that Steve had crossed a line—verbally, at least.

Stacy, encouraged by Steve's receptiveness, changed the tone of her messages altogether. No further mention was made of music or of her record collection. She focused all her attention on seduction. Her messages alternated between attaching stock photos of attractive couples in sexually charged positions, to which she added steamy captions, and asking Steve questions about his life.

"She must have made him feel like he was the most interesting man in the world," Millay scoffed.

"And he never stopped to wonder what a woman her age would want with a man his age," Olivia said. "He was too busy having his ego fed."

Millay pointed at one of the images Stacy had sent toward the beginning of the affair. "I'm sure those pics didn't hurt either. They got him thinking about what it would be like to get physical with Stacy. And eventually, I guess he wanted to turn their fantasy into the real thing."

Olivia, who was doing her best to skim over several days' worth of salacious language, signaled for a writing implement. "This is the day Stacy tells Steve to call her. She gives him her number and he says he'll try on his way to work. It looks like Laurel has printouts of Steve's cell phone bills from the last two months and has highlighted every call and text to and from Stacy."

Spreading the bills out on the table, Millay whistled. "Damn, it's a miracle the guy had time to clean anyone's teeth, let alone catch a few hours' sleep or visit his dying mom." She shook her head. "The man was more addicted than a teenager with a smartphone."

How did he hide this from Laurel? Olivia wondered. The calls and texts occurred throughout the day. Even during mealtimes. Surely, Laurel must have heard Steve's phone ringing or pinging or noticed how he never had it far from his person. And many of the calls started after eleven at night and lasted for anywhere from sixty to ninety minutes. Obviously, Steve spoke to Stacy while the rest of his family slept.

He probably locked himself in his office and whispered so he wouldn't wake the twins, Olivia thought, feeling a resurgence of anger as she imagined how innocent Laurel's sons must look in sleep. She could picture plaid pajamas and sports-themed bedding and perhaps a plush toy tucked protectively under one arm.

"Hey, I think I found something," Millay said, forcing Olivia back to the moment. "They must have started hanging out by this point. Sounds like they met for coffee, because he makes an obscene reference about the Starbucks between here and New Bern. Anyway, see what she says here."

Olivia read the message next to Millay's index finger, grimacing over the plethora of exclamation marks.

It was great!!! I can't wait to do it again!!! Sorry if I acted weird at first, but I was freaking out because my ex contacted me right before we met and threatened me. He was really mean to me when we were together. He's a BAD person who does BAD things. I know now that he was abusive, but I was young and I thought I loved him. He wasn't nice to me like you are. You're a real gentleman. I can tell!! You're the kind of man who knows how to treat women like they deserve!!!

A jolt of excitement ran up Olivia's spine. "This is what I was hoping for. Could Stacy be referring to her ex-husband? Was he violent? Is he still a threat? Had she recently done something to provoke him?"

Millay shrugged. She'd already begun reading ahead. "Steve doesn't seem very interested in hearing about Stacy's past. Whenever she raises the subject of her ex or her kids, he wastes no time bringing the topic back around to himself. She always takes the hint and follows along. Man, I never saw her as the submissive type."

"She hasn't hooked him yet, that's why." Olivia flipped to the next page. "Right now he's just paying for coffee. In Steve's mind, he probably doesn't even think he's cheated. Once he goes to Stacy's house, we should see a change in the tone of these messages. We should be able to get an idea of what she wanted from him. Maybe it was protection from her ex."

Millay looked unconvinced. "She didn't strike me as the

type to be afraid of any guy. She acted like she could control them—not the other way around."

"But you're talking about the men in the clubs, right? Men close to your age?"

"Yeah." Millay drew her eyebrows together. "Late twenties to early thirties, pierced, tatted up. So wouldn't you assume these guys would pose more of a threat than another middle-aged dude with a potential beer belly?"

Olivia felt that zing again. That quickening in her blood that told her she was onto something though she wasn't quite sure what. "Her ex is older too? Like Steve?"

The coincidence struck Millay too. "That's weird, isn't it? Her going for a second guy *that* much older—especially after she told anyone who'd listen how much she hated her ex. She always mocked his suburban lifestyle and his new wife's minivan and all that."

"Let's take a break from this nauseating exchange of messages and research Stacy's ex-husband," Olivia suggested, reaching for her glass.

"I'll drink to that." Millay poured Olivia another finger's worth of Chivas Regal and opened a bag of snack nuts. After pouring the contents into a bowl, she pushed the bowl toward Olivia. "You need to eat. Chow on those, Philip Marlowe."

Olivia picked out a handful of cashews from the mix and glanced around for Millay's laptop. "In the past, we would have just called Harris and asked him to handle this step for us, but we're on our own. I guess we could pay for one of those online background checks."

Millay left the kitchen and reappeared a minute later with her laptop in hand. "I got this."

Having no immediate task to complete and no desire to read more of the sickening messages, Olivia stood, stretched, and checked her phone for messages. Rawlings had sent a single text informing her that Laurel was still asleep and that Cook had finished questioning Steve.

He'll be home for the boys, which is good, Rawlings wrote, referring to Dallas and Dermot.

At the moment, it was impossible for Olivia to view Steve as anything but a terrible father. He'd put his desires ahead of the needs of his family and because of that, she felt the twins were better off staying with the neighbor. But as she stopped to consider this, she realized that the boys would need the familiarity and comfort of their house more than ever in the coming days. They were going to need as much comfort and reassurance as possible, and it pained Olivia to know that no matter what happened, Laurel's sons were unlikely to emerge from this experience unscathed.

"I have no idea who Stacy's ex is, so I'll run a background check on her first." Millay tapped on her keyboard, her gaze fixed on her screen. "We should be able to learn his name that way."

"Do you need a credit card?" Olivia asked, already digging in her bag for her wallet.

"I prefer PayPal," Millay said. She hit the enter key three times and then gave a satisfied grunt. "Here we are."

Olivia returned to her seat and scooted her chair closer to Millay's to read Stacy Balena's background report. "She's from Detroit? How on earth did she end up in Oyster Bay?"

"Looks like her family moved down when she was in high school," Millay said. "That's when she got the first of—let's see—seven speeding tickets." She whistled. "And I thought I had a lead foot."

"According to this, she's on every social networking site known to man. Is that a millennial thing?"

Millay shrugged. "Not for all of us. I'm only on Facebook

to interact with readers, and to be honest, it can wear me out. I'm no Kardashian. You don't see me posting selfies every five seconds and sharing the intimate details of my relationships. I keep the private stuff private."

"You're smarter than most of your peers," Olivia said.

"It's not about being smart. It's a cultural thing," Millay argued. "We all grew up with technology. It's normal for us to communicate via text. The problem is that some of us don't communicate well in person because we're so used to doing it through an instant message. It's kind of messed up. I got lucky because being a writer gave me a reason to study how people connect. Plus, I had the Bayside Book Writers. You guys forced me to talk and taught me how to listen."

Olivia made a noise to show that she'd heard her friend, but she was busy scanning Stacy's rather unremarkable biographical details.

"Aside from Stacy graduating from high school, getting married ridiculously young, and completing nursing school, this report doesn't tell us much," Olivia grumbled.

"At least it provides her ex-husband's name." Millay pointed at a section entitled Known Relatives. "Gordon Bruce. This must be him. See? She's listed as Stacy Bruce under 'other aliases.'"

Millay launched a new search on Bruce. When the results loaded, the first thing Olivia noticed was Bruce's birth date. "He's Steve's age, all right. Almost to the month. Looks like he got remarried almost immediately following his divorce from Stacy and now lives in New Bern. If Stacy lives here, she can't be spending much time with her children."

"She didn't talk about them," Millay said. "But then again, not many guys our age want to hook up with a divorcée who has two kids. Kids don't really fit with the club scene."

"No," Olivia mused aloud. She watched Millay scroll down the page and then cried, "Stop! Click the button that can show us Bruce's arrest history."

Millay plucked an almond from the bowl of mixed nuts and popped it into her mouth. "It's probably just more traffic violations. The guy's a chiropractor. How . . ." Her words died as the first arrest record appeared on-screen.

"An arrest for assault," Olivia read. "He and Stacy were married then. He was found guilty too."

"And there's a second assault charge," Millay said. "About a year earlier in a different county. He received a not-guilty ruling that time."

Olivia experienced a stirring of hope—the faintest flutter, like the brush of an insect wing against one's cheek—that they'd stumbled on a lead. Perhaps they could convince Cook that someone else had killed Stacy.

Olivia paused to consider if it was wrong to want Gordon Bruce to be guilty instead of Laurel. He was a husband and a father with a single arrest tarnishing his name. That arrest didn't exactly paint him as a hardened criminal. And yet Olivia would gladly have thrown him to the wolves in exchange for Laurel's freedom. "Stacy's ex could be a factor. Cook should at least find out where he was last night."

"We should check to see if Stacy mentions him to Steve again," Millay suggested. "If her ex was really an issue, she'd tell Steve because she'd want him to feel protective of her." She focused on the printouts. "I had no idea she was such a conniving manipulator. I thought she was just a normal chick who liked alternative music, piercings, tats, and blowing off a little steam every now and then. Talk about hiding a dark side behind a smile. Damn."

The women returned to their reading. It wasn't long before they discovered messages containing evidence not only that Stacy had an antagonistic relationship with her ex-husband, but that he also went out of his way to insult her education, sophistication, appearance, and class. He never tired of criticizing her parenting and was constantly comparing her to his second wife, a high school principal who was fifteen years older than Stacy and held a PhD to boot.

"Look at this." Millay directed Olivia's attention to several lines of text written beneath a graphic of a curled fist. It said: If anyone tries to hurt you. Your ex. Someone from work. A stranger on the street. You call me. I'll leave work in a heartbeat. I'd even leave the house. Night or day. You don't have to feel like you're alone. You're not alone anymore. You have me.

"Steve to the rescue. He'd race right over in his luxury sedan and go after his tramp's assailant with a periodontal probe and mint-flavored floss," Olivia muttered acerbically.

Millay didn't respond. She was gazing off into the distance and Olivia quietly waited for her friend to return to the present.

"What if *Laurel* was the assailant?" Millay asked in a very soft voice.

Olivia couldn't believe what she was hearing. "You don't honestly think—"

"No. I don't think she burned a woman alive. But what if she *did* lose it? What if she turned that minivan around and drove back to where Stacy was still parked? What if she screamed or even punched the woman who'd been screwing her husband?" Millay persisted. "After seeing all this crap? Who wouldn't want to? I'd beat her black-and-blue." She suddenly shoved her chair back and leaped to her feet. It was such an abrupt movement that the chair struck the wood floor with a loud clatter.

"Me too," Olivia said, watching Millay closely. There was something about this situation that had touched a nerve in her young friend. It was more than Laurel's dire situation. Olivia could sense that, but she wasn't sure exactly where Millay's anger was coming from. Millay's mother and father were still together, and though she rarely spoke about her parents, as they weren't close, she'd never mentioned being affected by marital conflict or infidelity during her childhood. What was it, then? Had a lover cheated on her? Was this anger personal?

Millay gave the chair a careless kick, sending it skittering toward the refrigerator. "The best of us would be tempted to punish the invader. That's what Stacy was. An invader. She started this whole thing by coming on to Steve, and Laurel knows it. After catching them in the act and then reading this stuff while drinking a bottle of wine, even sweet Laurel might have wanted revenge." Olivia was about to speak when Millay held up her hand to stop her. "Hear me out. What if the ex had been following Stacy? What if he was hanging around during this confrontation outside Rachel's condo?" Millay kicked the chair again. "What if he saw an opportunity to get rid of this albatross once and for all? No more child support payments. No more shared custody. No more headaches."

Olivia nodded. Other than theorize, there was nothing more they could do to establish Gordon Bruce's guilt. It would be up to the police to determine whether Stacy's ex-husband should be questioned and, if so, if he had a solid alibi for the night of her murder.

Trying to distract herself from images of Laurel confronting Stacy, Olivia flipped to the last page of the printouts. She wanted to know what the relationship between Steve and Stacy looked like leading up to the night of the murder.

However, it was becoming difficult to concentrate on the seemingly endless exchange of messages. Also, it was very late. Olivia's body felt heavy. It was as though a rock had been tied to her ankle and she was slowly sinking through cold, dark water. Her mind was growing sluggish too. She kept cycling through the same thoughts in an effort to keep a single thought at bay.

But when she read the final string of text messages from Steve's phone, her heartbeat accelerated and she blinked away the grit from her eyes. "There was trouble in Lovers' Paradise right before Stacy died. She and Steve had a fight. Must have been a big one too. Look at all these exclamation marks!"

"I can't tell exactly what it's about, but Stacy starts off playing it very, very cool." Millay had come to stand behind Olivia and was now reading over her shoulder. "By the end of the conversation, however, she's obviously pissed off. If I had to guess, I'd say she's tired of waiting for Steve to make a decision. She wants him to give her a clear sign that he's going to leave Laurel. She wants proof."

"I agree," Olivia said. "Which is why she blows up at him when he writes 'My situation is complicated.'"

Millay put her hands on her hips. "Smart girl to not let him come over for their prearranged date. An exciting sexual relationship is what Steve wants most, and Stacy denies him that. Now he's back to being miserable with his life, even though he has a much younger girlfriend."

"Miserable, yes. And possibly desperate too. What if this fight escalated?" Olivia tapped on the printouts. "What if Stacy made demands that Steve wasn't willing to meet? What if she threatened to contact Laurel? If Steve had wanted to leave Laurel to be with Stacy, he would have left. I don't think he was prepared to make that move and he wouldn't have welcomed Stacy forcing his hand."

Millay understood the implication. "If his affair became

public, he'd lose his family and his reputation. Maybe more. Some of his clients might leave too. Doesn't he advertise his practice as 'Dentistry for the Family' or something like that?"

"But why would Steve try to track down Stacy last night?" Olivia attempted to visualize the scene. "Laurel already knew they were having an affair by then, so there was no need for Steve to stop Stacy from talking to his wife. Unless Stacy knew other secrets that Steve would kill to keep."

Releasing a frustrated sigh, Millay scooped up the folder and said, "At least we can throw some doubt on the cops' case against Laurel. No matter what they have on her, we can still press them to consider multiple suspects."

"Cook won't take shortcuts," Olivia said. "Neither will Rawlings. You know that."

Millay hugged herself. "Sorry. I'm not thinking straight anymore. It's not the time of night—this is normal for me. It's just the way we're all split up. I hate it. I hate the thought that things might not turn out okay."

Olivia couldn't reply to that. She was afraid that if she spoke, she might confess that the same fear had been running like an icy current through her blood since she heard of Laurel's arrest. The fear that things would never be okay again. That, in the end, Cook, Rawlings, Harris, and the rest of the Oyster Bay police force would uncover enough evidence to convict Laurel of Stacy's murder. And this would only happen in one terrible and unfathomable set of circumstances.

That Laurel had actually committed the crime.

Chapter 6

After checking in with Rawlings by phone, Olivia drove home to catch a few hours of sleep.

Despite her determination to be with Laurel the moment she woke from her alcohol-induced stupor to face the worst dawn of her life, Olivia knew that there was little sense in her sitting in one of the rigid lobby chairs until someone from the holding area allowed her in to see her friend. Olivia would best help Laurel by seizing what rest she could and recharging her taxed brain.

Haviland must have recognized the sound of her car, because he didn't bother meeting her at the kitchen door. He issued a groggy bark from upstairs and Olivia smiled as she ascended to the second floor and entered the master bedroom.

The winter moon cast a feeble light on the bed, but it was enough for Olivia to discern the black shadow stretched out across the length of Rawlings's side.

"And here I thought you'd adjusted to him by now," she whispered to her poodle as she collapsed onto the bed without bothering to undress. Worming her way under the covers, she moved up against Haviland and stroked his hair. His familiar scent and the rhythmic rise and fall of his chest comforted her.

She didn't remember drifting off. It felt as though she'd just closed her eyes when she heard Rawlings whisper something. His hand was on her shoulder and he gently shook her. "Olivia. It's early, but I knew you'd want me to wake you."

Olivia wanted to linger in the half-life between sleep and full consciousness. This silent place was nothing but warmth and softness. It was the under-the-covers feeling as opposed to the covers-ripped-away feeling.

"Is Laurel up?" she croaked.

Rawlings set a mug of coffee on the nightstand. He was already dressed and, judging from the dampness of his hair, fresh from the shower. "I just got a call from the station. She's showing signs of coming around."

Olivia swung her feet to the floor and blinked several times, trying to bring Rawlings into focus. When she could see well enough to notice that he hadn't bothered to shave and was holding a travel cup in his left hand, last night's sense of urgency swiftly returned.

"Can you stay long enough to talk to me while I do a quick rinse?" she asked, heading for the bathroom. "I feel disgusting."

"I can give you five minutes and pour your coffee into a take-out cup on my way out the door," Rawlings said. "That's the best I can do."

Olivia turned the shower to the hottest setting and stripped off her clothes. "What did you learn from Steve's interview?"

"Not a whole lot." Rawlings had to raise his voice over the sound of the water. "He was in shock. He kept saying that he couldn't believe what he'd done—that he'd gotten lost. That he'd gone down a dark path. He begged Cook to help Laurel so that he, Steve, could make things right with her and fix their marriage. Cook had to keep redirecting him to the question at hand. His mind was all over the place."

"I think it's a bit late for him to make things right!" Olivia shouted from inside the fogged-up shower stall. "Where was he during the time of the murder?"

"Home," Rawlings replied. "After the twins went to the neighbor's house, he and Laurel talked. And yelled. And said very hurtful things to each other. Finally, Laurel stormed out of their bedroom and barricaded herself in Steve's office. Steve claims that he was too worn-out from the shock of being discovered with Stacy followed by an emotionally charged two-hour-long talking, yelling, and crying session with Laurel to try to coax her out, so he went to bed."

Olivia shut off the water and Rawlings handed her a towel. "Can you verify his claim that he stayed at home while Laurel was out?"

"Not as of this point. We'll have to interview the neighbors to see if anyone saw either of their cars leaving or re-entering the neighborhood."

Though Olivia dried herself as quickly as possible, her skin was covered with gooseflesh and she hated to step off the bath mat onto the cold tile floor. "Are you viewing Steve as a suspect?"

"Let's just say that we're not discounting the possibility," Rawlings said.

To Olivia, this sounded deliberately vague. Rawlings was being cagey, which wasn't like him. In the past, rules and procedure had prevented him from sharing certain details of an investigation with her, but he'd never been cagey. And this was the most important investigation of his career.

Olivia, who'd been on the verge of suggesting that Cook and Rawlings should pay a visit to Gordon Bruce, suddenly realized that if she told Rawlings about the printouts, he'd know that she'd taken evidence from Laurel's house. Not only did Olivia hope to hide that fact from her husband, but she also wanted to keep the documents for further review. If Rawlings learned of their existence, he would undoubtedly take them.

So now I'm keeping secrets from him, Olivia thought with a twinge of guilt. *But it's for Laurel's sake. I can make it up to Rawlings later. When this is all straightened out and our friend is no longer a murder suspect.*

"I should go now," Rawlings said, moving back into the bedroom.

Olivia followed him. "What about Stacy's ex?" She tossed the question casually over her shoulder as she stepped into her walk-in closet in search of a warm sweater and clean jeans. "Is he on your list?"

"We'll get to him, but we have to question Laurel first. You know that. We'll be very gentle with her. I'll make sure that she gets a chance to change her clothes and brush her teeth. She'll get food and coffee. I'm even bringing a bottle of aspirin for the headache she's bound to have." Rawlings darkened the doorway of the closet. "You might have to wait a bit to see her. As hard as this is, Cook has to interview her."

"I know," Olivia said. "But she might not say a word until you can reassure her that the twins are okay. Tell her how they spent the night at the neighbor's and how, starting today, a friend of Kim's will be going over to the house to look after them. Tell her that Millay, Kim, and I will check on them too."

Rawlings nodded. "That's good. That'll give her something to cling to—the thought of the boys being at home and of a group of women fussing over them and filling them with too much food."

He'd clearly offered Olivia the lighthearted comment in hopes of being rewarded with a small smile, but she merely said, "I'll see you soon," and turned away to finish dressing.

By the time she reached the station, two news vans were already parked in the lot. A pair of indiscernible blondes in light wool coats was checking their hair and makeup in preparation to film sound bites next to the Oyster Bay Police Department sign while their cameramen chatted. Seeing them made Laurel's nightmare all too real and propelled Olivia toward the rear entrance at a rapid clip. Haviland trotted by her ankle, his tail wagging in anticipation of a rendezvous with Greta.

As expected, the door was locked. Olivia pounded on it a few times and a bleary-eyed officer opened it a crack and, after a moment's hesitation, admitted her and Haviland.

"The chief's in the interview room, ma'am," the officer informed her.

Assuming he was with Laurel, Olivia asked, "I'm looking for Harris. Is he at his desk?"

The officer nodded before veering off into the break room.

Olivia deposited Haviland in the chief's office. After telling him he was free to go back to sleep, she walked down the hall to the largest room in the building. The space, which held a dozen desks, was filled with the constant cacophony of ringing phones, chatter, printers and fax machines spitting out documents, and the click of fingers striking keyboards.

This morning, it seemed as though half of the department had been called in and was already hard at work. Other than an occasional chin dip, no one paid attention to Olivia as she made her way to the back of the room where Harris had been given a desk in a somewhat dim corner.

As the only man in the room not dressed in a uniform, he might have been expected to appear out of place in wrinkled khakis and a T-shirt reading PROGRAMMER OUT OF WORK, WILLING TO DO WINDOWS, but he looked very much at home in his little nook. In true Harris style, his desk featured an assortment of action figures from *Star Trek*, *Star Wars*, *Doctor Who*, *Terminator*, and *Battlestar Galactica*. There was also an alien stress ball and a mouse pad covered in binary code.

"Hey," he said, briefly glancing away from his screen. After closing several windows, he turned to Olivia. "Is that coffee for me?"

Olivia looked down at her travel cup. "It's half gone, but you're welcome to the rest." She proffered the cup and Harris took it without hesitating. "Did you get any sleep?"

Harris shrugged. "About three hours, give or take. Probably the same as the chief. What about you?"

"Closer to four. I feel like I haven't had any." Olivia gestured at the paperwork on Harris's desk. "What's your role in this investigation?"

"The usual. Deep background checks. Criminal history. Financial status. Known relatives. Cell phone records. Examining recent history on social media . . ." Harris trailed off, seemingly too focused on guzzling Olivia's tepid coffee to continue.

"Whose profile did you start with, Stacy's or Laurel's?" Olivia asked.

Harris's neck turned red. "I worked them at the same time. Except the social media stuff. Laurel's only active on two places, Facebook and Pinterest. And she didn't post to Facebook that often. Mostly around holidays. Pics of the twins doing cute stuff—that kind of thing. And she hasn't visited Pinterest in months."

"Probably because she's been too busy juggling her career and acting as both mother and father to Dermot and Dallas," Olivia muttered, unable to keep the hostility out of her tone.

"I'm sure that's true," Harris agreed. "Stacy, in contrast, is on nearly every social media site known to man. She doesn't keep up with all of them, but it took me all of five minutes to see that she had one goal on each and every site."

Olivia's curiosity was instantly piqued. "Which was?"

"To put it in complimentary terms, she tried to make herself look irresistible to men. Some of her posted images were as close to porn as the Web site rules would allow." Harris took another swig of coffee. "I'm waiting for the all-clear before I can start digging around on her desktop. I figure I should focus on getting a complete picture of the victim. I can't really do much else, seeing as how Steve refused to share his social media or e-mail passwords with us. If Cook wants to see Steve's side, we'll have to get a warrant. As for Laurel, I tried to get into her phone to see her most recent calls and texts, but I don't know her password."

"What if she doesn't share her password?" Olivia asked.

Harris set the travel cup down and splayed his hands. "I could get locked out by guessing an incorrect password, and then we'd never know what was on her phone."

Olivia gaped at him. "Are you listening to yourself? If Laurel doesn't answer all of Cook's questions, it's because she's in shock. Our *friend* just caught her husband sleeping with the nurse assigned to his dying mother. Hours later, our *friend* was arrested for murdering her husband's tramp."

Harris leaned forward and lowered his voice. "This is a nasty mess, Olivia. I'm no fan of Stacy's. What she did was very, very wrong. But she's now a murder victim. You know how the chief insists on treating all parties with respect. Victims. Suspects. Everyone."

Instead of acknowledging Harris's comment, Olivia asked, "How bad is the evidence against Laurel?"

Harris crossed his left foot over his right knee and fidgeted with a loose string on his Converse sneaker. "There are other eyewitness reports in addition to the security guard's statement. Apparently, a couple on their way home from walking their dog saw Laurel yelling at Stacy too. They say Laurel was holding a bottle in her hand. It was too dark for them to say whether or not it was a wine bottle, but they heard the sound of breaking glass moments before they went inside their house."

"Did they call the police?"

"No." Harris shrugged. "They didn't want to get involved. That's the way many people are these days."

Another officer approached the desk. After saying hello to Olivia, he handed Harris a file folder. "Photos. A partial inventory of what was salvaged from the victim's car. Cook is hoping you can sharpen the images of the labels on the glass syringes. Tell us what the letters or numbers say. Mr. Hobbs was able to confirm Ms. Balena's identity using dental records, which he updated two weeks ago. I guess he was her dentist *and* her lover."

Harris frowned in confusion. "Why would Mr. Hobbs be asked to identify the body? What about the victim's parents or ex-husband?"

The officer threw up his hands. "It sounded nuts to me too, but the parents are both dead and the ex-husband says that he wouldn't have a clue what jewelry his former wife wore or that she had a mouthful of fillings. He was of no use. I got the sense that the guy wasn't too broken up about her death. Even when he heard how she died, his main concern was about telling his kids. He certainly didn't shed a tear for their mother."

Harris issued a low whistle. "That's cold. Is Cook having him brought in?"

The officer darted a glance at Olivia, as though trying to decide whether it was prudent to continue discussing the case in her presence, and then nodded. "He asked him to drive over ASAP. We're not picking him up or anything formal. Which is good, seeing as we have so much to do already."

Harris murmured something about how he'd get to the images as soon as he wrapped up the background checks, and the officer turned away. His final glance at Olivia felt censorious, and she realized that he disapproved of her socializing during the most crucial hours of their investigation—the first twenty-four to forty-eight hours following a murder.

Olivia rose to her feet. It had been a long time since she'd felt like an outsider in Oyster Bay. This was her town. She'd grown up here. Her parents had worked here. Her mother had been a librarian and her father a fisherman. After Olivia's mother had died in a freak accident and her father had later abandoned her, her grandmother had whisked her away, fearing Oyster Bay had become a haunted place for her grandchild.

As an adult, Olivia had returned to her hometown. She'd grown weary of traveling the world and sought a place to put down roots. At first, the people of Oyster Bay were reluctant to welcome her back into the fold, but she slowly won them over. As time passed, she became a champion of the community, fighting to preserve the town's history and resources.

Now here she was, all these years later, feeling as though

she didn't belong. Her husband was the chief of police, so she was unaccustomed to this sudden coolness toward her. Not only that, but long before she and Rawlings were married, or even friends, Olivia had supported local law enforcement with her checkbook. It rankled to see how quickly this group of men and women forgot her loyalty.

You're reading too much into one man's expression, Olivia chided herself.

"Stacy's ex-husband sounds like a piece of work," she said to Harris as she moved to leave. "Have you done a background check on him?"

Harris narrowed his eyes. "No. Why? Do you know something?"

"I'm just considering statistics. This type of murder is most commonly committed by the lover or husband. Stacy had one of each." Olivia held up her hands. "I realize that Laurel threatened Stacy shortly before she was found dead. Laurel was also inebriated and witness accounts don't paint her in a very favorable light. Everyone is going to conclude that, after discovering Steve's affair, she went home, confronted him, guzzled wine, and flew into a murderous rage. She then drove around town until she spotted Stacy's car, confronted her, and what? After possibly knocking her enemy out with her wine bottle, Laurel smashes the bottle and then pours gasoline over Stacy's car and sets it on fire? Does that sound plausible?"

Harris closed his eyes for several seconds. When he opened them again, he reached for his computer keyboard. "It's not my job to make those determinations. I'm going to check all the angles, Olivia. I won't just try to wrap this up as fast as possible. You know I won't. We're not on opposite sides just because I have a desk in this room. Okay?"

Though Olivia wasn't certain she believed him, she said, "Okay. Good luck."

"Thanks for the coffee," Harris added, his eyes already locked on his screen. "I'll wash the cup and put it on the chief's desk when I get a chance."

Back in the chief's office, Haviland was laid out on the toddler mattress Rawlings had purchased, much to the amusement of the other cops, for the poodle's visits. When Olivia entered the room, Haviland raised his head, yawned, and then dropped his head again.

"I'm tempted to lie down with you, but I might actually fall asleep," Olivia murmured.

Instead, she pulled out her cell phone and sent a text to Rawlings to let him know that she was eagerly awaiting an opportunity to see Laurel. She then sent a message to Millay, telling her that Laurel was awake and being interviewed. She'd just sent the second text when Rawlings appeared.

His face was drawn. His expression haunted. The interview had been difficult. More than difficult. It had been painful. For everyone involved.

"How is she?" Olivia asked.

Rawlings gave a small shake of his head. "Not well. She was rattled and confused. And those are insufficient terms, to be honest. She looked and behaved like a wounded soldier—a soldier waking up in a field hospital after seeing unspeakable things. We made very little progress. She shivered violently through most of the interview, and when she wasn't shivering, she retched or sobbed. We have a medical doctor in with her now and a psychiatrist is en route." He rubbed his temples. "I know how much you want to be with her, Olivia, but I'm only considering her welfare in seeking professional help. I believe she may have suffered several blackouts yesterday. Her condition is serious enough that even if her attorney hadn't demanded we bring the interview to a halt, I would have made Cook stop."

Olivia's ears pricked at the mention of an attorney. "Was her lawyer present the whole time?"

"Yes. I daresay he was in his car before daybreak." Rawlings studied Olivia. "Who retained his services? It wasn't Steve Hobbs—that's for sure. When one of the foremost defense attorneys in our state presented his card to the desk sergeant this morning, I wondered who might have successfully convinced such an influential man to abandon his other cases in favor of this one."

"Someone desperate to save a friend, I guess," Olivia said. And then, "When can I see her?"

Rawlings took Olivia's hand. "It's likely she'll be admitted to the hospital. The doctor was concerned about dehydration and shock. I think it's a good idea and told Cook as much. I believe the psychiatrist will concur."

Olivia's pulse quickened as her anxiety rose. "Are they going to put her in a padded cell? I know how these things go, Rawlings. Once a person gains a reputation for being mentally unstable—or whatever the politically correct term of the day is—it's nearly impossible to cast it off. It'll hurt her case. It'll be that much easier for everyone to paint her as the crazy scorned wife who murdered her husband's lover."

"The case is secondary. We have to consider Laurel's basic needs first," Rawlings said gently. "And she isn't well. She isn't capable of coherent thought or conversation. We mistakenly believed she was inebriated, but I'm afraid her condition is more serious than that. The case must wait until her mind and body have been restored to the point where she can think and talk lucidly. She can't do either at present."

"Has she asked after the twins?" Olivia wanted to know.

Rawlings nodded. "They've been the focus of her comments. Aside from some derogatory remarks directed toward her husband."

"Which should be considered proof that she hasn't lost her mind," Olivia said. "I haven't been able to utter anything other than derogatory remarks about Steve Hobbs since Millay and I stood in the hallway of Stacy Balena's house and bore witness to Laurel's pain. And I'm not even married to him."

At that moment, someone rapped on the door.

"Come in!" Rawlings beckoned. The same officer who'd delivered the folder to Harris entered the chief's office.

"Mr. Hobbs is here. He's asking to see his wife." The officer glanced over his shoulder as though Steve was within earshot. "He's very agitated, sir."

Rawlings pushed back the cuff of his shirt and looked at his watch. "Where's Cook?"

"Conferring with the two doctors and Mrs. Hobbs's attorney. What should I tell him, Chief?"

"Nothing," Rawlings said. "I'll handle that. Bring him back here, Nuckolls. Thanks."

Olivia planned to make herself scarce while Rawlings spoke to Laurel's husband, so she was surprised when Steve called out to her in the hallway as she and Haviland turned in the opposite direction for the break room.

"Olivia! Wait! *Please!*"

She stiffened, and beside her Haviland echoed the movement. After years of being attuned to her body language, he immediately sensed her anger and discomfort. He responded to her emotions by issuing a low rumble of a growl and pulling back his lips to reveal his teeth.

Olivia did nothing to dissuade his threatening display.

Steve held out both hands in a gesture of supplication. "Please." His tone was high and pleading. "I know you probably hate me. It's okay. I hate me too. I really do. I don't know what I was thinking. I was out of my mind, but I love Laurel. I love my boys. I don't want to lose my family. Please." He shook his laced hands. "I want to help my wife. Please help me help her!"

Flustered, Olivia stared at Steve. His eyes were red-rimmed and puffy from crying and, undoubtedly, lack of sleep. The hands held out in front of him shook and there was a madness to him—he was fixing his gaze on her with the desperation of a man teetering on the cliff's edge. A man pinwheeling his arms. A man on the verge of going over.

It was clear by his words that he was claiming responsibility for his actions, but Olivia's heart remained hard and unyielding.

"I secured the best defense attorney in the state, and my sister-in-law has someone coming to your house in the morning to take care of the twins. Please make her feel welcome," Olivia said, putting her hand on Haviland's neck to calm him. "I believe she can create some stability for the boys, and that will make Laurel feel better."

Steve nodded rapidly. He sniffed and said, "Thank you so much. You're such a good friend. I'm so glad Laurel has you in her corner."

Olivia couldn't tell if Steve was sincere or not. After all, the man was an expert at deceit.

At this point, Rawlings appeared in the doorway of his office. "Mr. Hobbs. Won't you come in and sit down?"

Steve pointed at Olivia. "Could Olivia see Laurel too? I know it would mean so much to my wife. She probably won't want to talk to me anyway."

Rawlings hesitated and then waved for Olivia to reenter his office. She complied and took the guest chair next to Steve's. Haviland returned to his bed. He didn't stretch out, however, but sat on his haunches in an alert posture.

In his gentlest manner, Rawlings reviewed Laurel's fragile condition. As he spoke, Steve's eyes filled and tears ran down his cheeks unchecked. "I did this," he sobbed as Rawlings proffered a handkerchief. "I did this to her!"

Olivia scowled. She believed Steve's tears and self-recrimination were yet another example of his selfishness. Everything was always about him.

"I understand how upsetting this must be, Mr. Hobbs. You've been very cooperative and I know you're anxious to speak with the doctor, but I'd like you to look at these photographs before you do." Rawlings spread out several color photos on his desk. "These were in Ms. Balena's car. Do you recognize any of these items?"

For a second, Steve's eyebrows crinkled in surprise and outrage over being asked to look at photographs when his wife was en route to the hospital. But then, despite himself, he glanced down. Almost instantly, his index finger snaked out and tapped on an image. "That bracelet. It belongs to Laurel."

"Are you positive?" Rawlings asked, watching Steve very closely.

"One hundred percent," Steve said. "A friend gave it to her the first time one of her articles was picked up nationally. I remember because Laurel got flowers from you guys—the Bayside Book Writers—and some coworkers took her out to dinner. I was probably the only person who didn't celebrate her success, so whenever she wore that bracelet, it reminded me that I had failed to do anything for her." He cocked his head. "How did it get in Stacy's car?"

Rawlings avoided not only Steve's gaze, but also Olivia's. "That's a very good question," he said, and gathered up the photographs.

Chapter 7

~~~~~~

Trickery and treachery are the
practices of fools that have not the wits
enough to be honest.

—BENJAMIN FRANKLIN

Olivia and Millay spent several hours in a crowded, ammonia-scented hospital waiting room for a chance to see Laurel, but their wait was in vain. The employee manning the registration desk informed them, quite firmly, that Mrs. Hobbs was not allowed visitors.

"We'll have to find another way in," Millay muttered under her breath.

Olivia shook her head. "This isn't one of those cheesy TV shows where we steal a pair of scrubs from a supply closet and swipe someone's ID badge to get to Laurel. Cook will have assigned an officer to her, so we'll have to find another way to help her."

As the two women headed outside for the parking deck, their steps heavy with defeat, Olivia's phone rang. The caller was Fred Yoder.

"I wanted to tell you that I've made arrangements for the Hummel's repair," Fred said.

It took Olivia a moment for Fred's comment to register, and then she remembered Rachel's damaged figurine and the favor she'd volunteered to complete on Laurel's behalf.

Olivia was struck by the realization that this entire mess began with that offer of help. If she hadn't gone to Rachel's to fetch the Hummel, she wouldn't have overheard Stacy's comment. She wouldn't have driven to Laurel's house to tell her friend of her suspicions.

"Can you hear me?" Fred's voice jerked Olivia back to the present. "It's not like you to go silent at the mention of a murder investigation."

Olivia unlocked her car and she and Millay wasted no time seeking shelter inside the Range Rover. The winters in coastal North Carolina weren't at all harsh, but today Olivia felt as if the damp air had formed microscopic pockets of cold deep in the marrow of her bones.

"What murder investigation?" she asked, turning on the ignition.

"I've been asked to identify objects in a set of photographs," Fred said. He sounded downright jolly. "And seeing as you're married to the chief and you enjoy a good mystery, I thought I'd invite you to play the part of Doc Watson to my Sherlock Holmes."

Olivia turned to Millay and held up her crossed fingers. "Could Millay come along too? She has a debilitating case of writer's block. A change of scenery would be good for her." The look Millay gave Olivia could have frozen a lake in hell, so Olivia barreled on. "Since the two of us got up early, we're hungry. We could show up with a full hamper from the Boot Top Bistro."

"We'll have a picnic in my kitchen!" Fred cried merrily. "See you gals soon!"

Using her voice commands to call the Boot Top Bistro

Olivia spoke with one of the sous-chefs about packing a lunch for three people. After thanking him, she tried to reach Rawlings. Her call went straight to voice mail.

"Try Harris," Millay suggested. "If he answers, let me do the talking."

Olivia complied and Harris picked up on the third ring.

"What's brewing?" Millay demanded without preamble.

Harris stammered out a few phrases about background checks to which Millay responded with a bored sigh. "Sounds like grunt work," she said.

"I'm no grunt!" Harris immediately retorted. "In fact, the chief asked me to sit in on his interview with Ms. Balena's ex-husband."

Millay snorted derisively. "Are they *that* shorthanded?"

"Yeah, they are. And I'm superbusy, so—" Harris snapped.

"I'm sorry." Millay was instantly contrite. "Do you need a caffeine fix? Something to get the blood flowing? It must be insane."

Harris released an audible exhalation, as though he'd been waiting to confide in someone. "You have *no* idea! Reporters are milling about on the lawn and calling on every line. And Laurel's doctors won't let anyone talk to her. They say she's too fragile."

"So, what was Stacy's ex like?" Millay asked, obviously wanting to focus on something other than Laurel's frailty.

After a slight pause, Harris said, "I can tell you that this guy, Gordon Bruce, definitely raises red flags because of his priors. He has a history of losing his temper while under the influence of alcohol."

"Did he go into Hulk mode during the interview?" Millay wanted to know.

"No." Harris sounded disappointed. "And he looks nothing like the Hulk. This guy does *not* work out. He wore a sweater vest and glasses and . . ."

"And what?" Millay prodded.

"I just realized how much he looks like Steve Hobbs. They're almost the same age too. Anyway, he was no Hulk." Harris hurried to continue. "He was pretty calm. Though he did a poor job of hiding how much he hated his ex-wife."

Millay had enough self-control not to leap on this statement. "Oh? How did he express that?"

"Comments. Facial expressions." Harris's terse reply made it clear that he didn't want to divulge any more details.

Olivia made a "slow down" gesture to Millay.

"As long as he didn't lunge for the chief's sidearm or, worse, his coffee, then I guess you guys got what you needed," Millay joked.

Using levity was the right call. Harris's quick laugh was followed by a sigh. "Man, I needed that. Everyone here is wound tighter than a new yo-yo. I wish the four of us could get together and talk. How do I handle this? How can I help her without losing my integrity?"

Olivia's heart went out to Harris. He wasn't on an opposing side. He was caught in the middle. As was Rawlings.

"You can do both, and I'll tell you how," Millay said with a rare hint of tenderness. "You need to get into Stacy's computer. Look at everything, but check out her Facebook messages first. A few weeks ago, Stacy told Steve that she was scared of Gordon. That he'd threatened her. She may have mentioned her ex in e-mails or texts as well. I don't know, but we can't let Laurel take the fall for this just because it's convenient."

"It's not about convenience," Harris argued wearily. "She was seen screaming at Stacy, her bracelet was found inside

Stacy's car, and she had a damn good reason for wanting Stacy dead. I'm not saying she did it. I'm only repeating what's being said around the station. By tonight, I imagine Laurel's fellow journalists will be drawing their own conclusions."

"I hear you," Millay said. "And thanks for not calling her Ms. Balena. I don't think I could take it. But look at those Facebook messages as soon as you can, okay?"

Harris cleared his throat. "I'd ask how you know about their existence, but I have a feeling I'd suddenly be faced with a dropped call."

Now it was Millay's turn to laugh.

Olivia drove to her house to pick up Haviland and then proceeded to the Boot Top to collect their lunch hamper. Michel, her head chef, wanted to go over next week's dinner menu and was flabbergasted when she told him that it would have to wait.

"What?" he cried. Michel was given to dramatic outbursts. "But we also have a *major* event to review! The Shakespeare-themed New Year's Eve party hosted by my supper club. Vendors will *shut down* in a few days, Olivia, and I might not be able to get the specialty items I *must have* for this event."

Giving him a hasty pat on the arm, Olivia assured him that she would acquire anything and everything he needed.

"You promise?" Michel managed to pout and coat the bottom of a frying pan with olive oil at the same time. He then turned the heat on the burner to high and deftly trimmed a salmon filet while he continued speaking. "I might want ptarmigan for that New Year's Eve buffet. There's no point in saying we're having an international meal if we're going to serve ham and pimento cheese biscuits. Everyone should begin a new year by having an unforgettable adventure of the palate." He gingerly laid the filet in the hot pan, describing how each dish on the buffet should create a sense of excitement and curiosity. As he spoke, he sprinkled salt and pepper over the fish and then added a handful of capers to the pan. "And, *bien sûr*, as the one year gives way to the next, we find the person we love most and give her a champagne-laced kiss."

The spell Michel had been weaving over Olivia with his words, his skilled hands, and the scent and sizzle coming from the pan burst like a bubble at the mention of the traditional kiss.

Where will Laurel be when this year dies and a new one begins? Olivia thought.

Grabbing the hamper, Olivia repeated her promise to get Michel the ingredients he desired, thanked the sous-chef for preparing lunch for her, and left.

There were no vacant parking spots in front of Fred's shop, so Olivia slowly drove down the narrow side alley in hopes of squeezing into a space in his tiny rear lot. As she prepared to pull into the small rectangle of asphalt behind Circa, she saw the back door open and three men step outside. Of the three, Olivia only knew Fred.

"Do you recognize any of those men?" she asked Millay. There was something about the first man that seemed familiar.

Millay's brow was furrowed. "No, but that guy reminds me of Steve," she said, referring to the first man. "Remember how Harris described Gordon Bruce?"

"But why would Stacy's ex-husband be at Circa?" Olivia wondered aloud. "And why would he be leaving Fred's shop through the rear?"

Olivia studied the second man. He was several inches shorter than his companions and had dark, close-cropped hair. He wore a black leather jacket, wool dress slacks, and Italian loafers. Of the three, he was the best coiffed, but he had the air of a used-car salesman about him.

As the two women watched, Fred and the man they assumed was Gordon Bruce embraced. Fred then shook hands with the man in the leather jacket with noticeable stiffness and went back into his shop. The other two men walked the length of the building, turned the corner, and disappeared from view.

Once again, Olivia experienced a knife-twist sensation in her belly. "We should examine the photographs before we ask Fred about those men," she said to Millay. "If he has something to hide, he might not tell us why Stacy's ex-husband was here." She sighed. "Is no one what they seem?"

"Don't go all Virginia Woolf melancholy on me now," Millay said. "As my second-grade teacher, Mrs. Rudolph, used to say, 'You'll feel better once you've eaten.'"

Olivia released Haviland from his canine seat belt, grabbed the hamper, and knocked on Fred's back door.

"Maybe I should call you Mrs. Hudson instead?" Fred teased, his blue eyes twinkling as he eyed the hamper.

"Millay will be your Watson," Olivia said with a smile.

Fred beckoned for the women to come inside. To Millay, he said, "I hope you don't mind if Duncan sniffs your ankles for a solid thirty seconds."

"Sniff away, sir." Millay looked on in amusement as Duncan gave her silver-studded boots a thorough inspection, his black nose quivering with interest, before he abruptly snorted and turned away to greet Haviland.

In the kitchen, half a dozen photographs were spread out in a neat row along the counter. Olivia wondered if Fred's two male visitors had been asked to the shop specifically to view them.

Unable to come up with a solid reason as to why Fred would do such a thing, she studied him closely. He didn't seem the least bit nervous or troubled. He seemed as relaxed and congenial as ever.

Fred pointed at the hamper. "May I?"

"Dig in," Olivia replied.

Fred unpacked a veritable feast of belly-warming food. All the items were labeled, and Fred delighted in reading the name of each menu item as he placed it on the table. "Tomato and lentil soup. Watercress salad. Cheddar, apple, and pastrami grilled cheese. Pear and cherry clafoutis." He gave Olivia a puzzled look. "What is that?"

"It's one of Michel's favorite winter desserts. Of French origin, it usually features cherries. The cherries are placed in a buttered dish and topped with a batter not unlike flan. The whole thing is then baked and covered with powdered sugar, cream, or both prior to serving."

Fred rubbed his hands together. "I'm starting with dessert."

Olivia's stomach still hadn't settled down, so she selected a container of soup. "What have you researched so far?" she asked Fred.

Pivoting in his chair, he grabbed the photograph at the end of the row and held it up so both women could see the image. "Eighteen-karat-gold ear clips in a rather inelegant square shape. Care to guess the stones, Olivia?"

Olivia studied the gems. "Carnelian and diamonds?"

"Very good!" Fred exclaimed. "Your turn, Millay. What do you suppose these are worth? I'll give you a hint by saying that they were made by Cartier in the early nineteen seventies."

Millay shrugged. "I wouldn't give you twenty bucks for them, but since they were made by Cartier, I'll guess a thousand."

"Try twelve thousand," Fred said.

Olivia whistled. "Who owns this jewelry?"

Fred shrugged. "No clue. I was only told to provide as much detail as possible about each item. These earrings were the first. Next, we have a set of men's art deco cuff links."

Millay squinted at the photo. "Are those diamonds in the center?"

"Yes indeed," Fred said. "Octagonal-shaped, platinum with onyx edging, and a full-cut diamond in each piece. There are nine pieces in the entire set with a net worth of around fourteen thousand dollars."

"Seriously?" Millay was stunned. "I've seen nicer bling at the county fair."

Fred reached for the next photograph. "It's a matter of taste. And supply and demand. One couldn't walk into a store and buy these antique cuff links. If you wanted them, you'd have to hunt for them. Often, the rarer an item is, the more desirable it is."

"In other words, people want what they can't have?" Millay grumbled.

"Oh, antiques aren't quite that cynical," Fred replied with a smile. "Most of the collectors I know like their homes to reflect their personalities. They want their possessions to be unique. The conversation pieces are important because these objects can represent a person's taste, style, passions, and hobbies. Olivia can back me up on this one. You've seen her living room. She has all kinds of treasures on her bookshelves from French porcelain figurines to English tortoiseshell tea caddies."

Olivia made a noise of assent. During Fred's monologue, her focus had been entirely fixed on the photographs. As she stared at them, her thoughts continued to circle back to the same questions. What had Stacy Balena been doing with such valuable antique jewelry? Had her patients given her these items as gifts? Or had she stolen them during her tenure as their caretaker?

"Why don't I record what you've found so far?" Olivia suggested to Fred. "As we proceed, I'll add to the list."

Fred readily agreed. While he and Millay ate their sandwiches, Fred brought over his laptop and showed them the reference sites he used most frequently to identity antiques he wasn't familiar with and to ascertain current market values.

"We don't need to research the item in the next photograph because I sold it last spring," Fred said, looking troubled for the first time since Olivia and Millay had arrived. "I'll just give the police a copy of the sales receipt."

Feeling like a cad, Olivia touched Fred on the arm. "Is the victim one of your customers?"

His gaze slid from the photographs to his Westie. Olivia knew Fred was using the sight of his dog as a source of comfort. She'd done the same thing hundreds of times herself. "I pray not," he said in a near whisper. "My customers seem like good people. I don't get to know all of them, of course. In many cases, I only meet them once. Or I deal with them online and never get a sense of what they're really like. But for the most part, I become familiar enough with them to be able to call them acquaintances." He smiled at Olivia. "Or friends."

"So when you look up the receipt for that ring, then you might discover the identity of the victim?" Millay asked.

"I know exactly who bought it." Fred's fingertips hovered over the image of a ring with a cluster of diamonds and pale gemstones. "I don't deal in fine jewelry anymore, but back when I did, a local lady asked me to keep an eye out for a ring fitting this description. You see, her favorite novel was *The Moonstone*, and she collected moonstone jewelry."

Fred's eyes lost focus as he went back in time. "She was an elderly lady. And frail. When I found this ring for her, she was in declining health, but she still wanted it. For a small fee, I brokered the deal for her and delivered the ring to her home. It cost forty thousand dollars, and she lit up like a star when she slid it on her finger. She's gone now, but I'm positive that she meant to leave this ring to her sister or daughter."

Olivia didn't want Fred to fixate on the notion that a relative of one of his most memorable customers—the lifelong Wilkie Collins fan—could be the murder victim. Fred was obviously aggrieved by the thought, and Olivia believed she could disabuse him of the notion without giving herself away.

"We can text Harris asking for the victim's name," she said soothingly. "The police will have to make it public anyway. In the meantime, what else do we need to find?"

Distracted, Fred moved on to the next photograph. As he described the basic search criteria for a Tiffany tennis bracelet, Millay pulled out her cell phone and pretended to send a message. She then glanced at Fred and said, "The victim's name is Stacy Balena. Was she related to the moonstone lady?"

Fred showed no sign of recognition, despite the fact that he'd embraced Stacy's ex-husband less than an hour ago. He sat quite still and seemed to be concentrating hard.

Finally, he said, "Neither the sister nor the daughter was named Stacy."

"Harris says she was a hospice nurse," Millay continued, glancing at her phone screen for good measure. "Isn't it weird that she owned all of these rare antiques and you've never met her?"

Fred shook his head. "No. There are plenty of area collectors who don't shop at Circa. What I'd like to know is how this woman came to possess these items. They're all unique, valuable, and"—his eyes scanned the row of photographs again—"portable."

"As in, they may have been stolen?" Olivia asked. "From patients?"

"I couldn't say unless I knew which objects belonged to which patients," Fred said. "And who knows? Maybe patients left these treasures to the nurse in their wills."

Olivia grunted. "Come on, Fred. The total value of the pieces I've recorded so far is nearly a hundred thousand dollars. This woman would have cared for her patients for a month or two at most and she would have shared that responsibility with other team members—other nurses, doctors, aides, volunteers. Why should she be singled out by so many patients to receive costly gifts?"

"When you put it that way, it doesn't seem very likely," Fred said. "I just hate the thought of someone stealing from the old or infirm. That's as low as a person can go."

Recalling some of Stacy's lewd messages to Steve, Olivia thought, *Trust me, Fred. She was as low as a slug trail.*

However, Stacy's complete and utter absence of morals might end up being Laurel's ticket to freedom. If the hospice nurse had been stealing precious antiques, then she was undoubtedly pawning them off.

If so, what was she doing with the profits? Olivia wondered, recalling the decrepit state of Stacy's house and car.

As Fred turned to the last photograph, Olivia suddenly realized that he might not recognize Stacy because she must have reverted to her maiden name. Taking a big chance, she looked at Millay. "Did the victim have any other aliases? Was she married?"

Millay understood at once. "I'll ask."

She sent another text and then turned her attention to the

pocket watch featured in the last photograph. When her phone chimed, which Olivia assumed was merely Millay using the sounds function in the settings menu of her phone, Millay briefly gazed at her screen and said, "Stacy was married four years ago. She was Stacy Bruce then. Her ex-husband's a chiropractor named Gordon. They have two kids together."

Fred reacted instantly. He pushed back from the table and cried, "Gordon? No! I just saw the man! He didn't say a thing about his ex-wife being murdered. It couldn't possibly be him!" His eyes went wide. "Unless . . . Is there a chance he doesn't know?"

"I suppose," Olivia lied. "They're not married anymore, so the police might not have contacted him yet. Are you and Gordon friends?"

Fred stood up and began clearing the lunch things off the table. A veil had fallen over his features and even though Duncan gazed up at him with adoration, Fred ignored his beloved terrier. "Let's just say that we've known each other for a long time."

Olivia and Millay exchanged perplexed glances and then Olivia thought of another question. "Is he a collector?"

At this, Fred barked out a laugh. "Of antiques? Not at all! Gordon thinks a framed *Matrix* movie poster is as valuable as an original van Gogh, and he'd rather have a race program autographed by Dale Earnhardt Jr. than a painting by Rembrandt."

"He *would* be aware of Stacy's financial status," Olivia persisted. "I don't understand the nuances of divorce and custody arrangements, but I assume that Gordon has to make regular child support payments."

Fred paused in the middle of wiping off the table with a

damp paper towel. Again, he looked aggrieved. "*I* can't speak to that, but the police will undoubtedly want to talk with Gordon. I should try to be there when they do—to lend him support."

Olivia cocked her head. "Gordon isn't a collector and you said that you and he aren't friends, but you're obviously concerned about how he'll take the news of his ex-wife's death. I must be missing something."

Fred leaned over and scratched the fur behind Duncan's ears. He then put his hand in his pocket, pulled out a coin, and spun it like a top on the table in front of Olivia.

It was impossible not to track its movement, but as soon as it began to slow and wobble from side to side, Olivia saw that it wasn't a monetary coin. It was some kind of decorative token.

"That is my twenty-year chip. I got it about six months ago and I've been carrying it in my pocket ever since," Fred said quietly. "I know Gordon from Alcoholics Anonymous."

Olivia was astonished. She thought she knew Fred Yoder well, but apparently, she was mistaken. "Twenty years. That's amazing." She pointed at the token. "May I?"

He smiled and made a "go ahead" gesture.

Picking up the bronze coin, Olivia brought it closer to her face. The front held a triangle and the words TO THINE OWN SELF BE TRUE. A single word ran along each side of the triangle, and Olivia read these aloud. "'Unity. Service. Recovery.'" She then flipped the coin over and studied the poem on its reverse.

"God grant me the serenity to accept the things I cannot change, courage to change the things I can, and the wisdom to know the difference," Fred said. "That's the Serenity Prayer. It's used by Twelve-Step programs."

"Good for you, Fred." Olivia returned the coin. She felt guilty for not having known this significant part of her friend's life and admitted as much to him.

He waved off her confession. "It's not as though you asked me to go out for a cold one after work. We take our dogs to the park. We have chats over coffee in my shop. The subject didn't come up and I didn't bring it up. That's not your fault."

Millay, who'd silently listened to this exchange, now raised her hand and said, "Um. I write young adult novels. But I'm also a bartender."

Fred stared at her for a long moment and then laughed. "You're not my enemy. Bartenders can actually save people's lives. During my heavy-drinking days, more than one bartender kept me from doing some seriously stupid things."

"What about Gordon?" Millay asked. "Did he need the same kind of rescuing?"

"It's not for me to share another man's journey," Fred said. "I can attest that Gordon's come a long way since I first heard his testimony. He's battled some serious demons. Fallen off the wagon a few times, but he gets back on and keeps fighting."

"When did he last fall off the wagon?" Olivia asked very softly.

The implication of her question hit Fred full force and he sank down into his chair with slumped shoulders. "Do you think . . . ?" His eyes strayed to the police photographs and to the bronze anniversary coin in his hand. "No. It couldn't have been Gordon."

Olivia reached over and covered Fred's hand with hers. "Did it happen recently? Gordon's slip?"

Fred gave a single slow nod as though it pained him to move his head.

"Last night?" Olivia asked.

"How did you . . . ?" Fred began, and then it dawned on him that she'd known about the murder all along. "I think you should go now," he said.

Olivia opened her mouth to explain, but what could she say? That she'd manipulated one friend to save another? Instead, she apologized for her duplicity and told Fred that one day, she hoped he'd understand her motives. And be able to forgive her.

When her apology was met with stony silence, she picked up the hamper, called Haviland, and held open the back door for Millay.

Outside, a light rain had begun to fall.

"I was supposed to write two thousand words today," Millay said, squinting up at the gray sky. "I won't write anything, though. Just like yesterday. How can I write when I feel like this? When the sky is like this? When everything comes down to one word?"

"Bleak," said Olivia.

"Yeah. That's the one," Millay murmured. "Bleak."

Chapter 8

*Bitterness is like cancer. It eats upon
the host. But anger is like fire. It burns
it all clean.*

—MAYA ANGELOU

Olivia called Rawlings from the car to tell him what she and Millay had learned about Gordon Bruce.

"I don't know what kind of alibi he gave you," Olivia said. "But you need to talk to Fred and then call Gordon back in for questioning. If Stacy's ex was already mad at her before he started drinking, the alcohol could have eliminated his inhibitions entirely. Who's to say he didn't come along after Laurel threatened Stacy? He could be the murderer. After all, Laurel drove away. No one *saw* her lay a hand on Stacy."

"Olivia, we're chasing every lead," Rawlings said. "Cook has every intention of conducting a follow-up interview with Mr. Bruce, but he wants to collect more information first. This is how cases are built. You know this. And I know this is frustrating, but please trust us. Trust me."

Olivia took a moment before replying, "Haven't some of your most challenging cases gotten solved because we all worked together? Not just the cops, but the five of us? The Bayside Book Writers. Puzzling things out on the side. Can't the remaining four still be a team?"

"Yes, but the police work must come first. We have to be the ones to gather the facts, conduct the interviews, and examine the evidence without interference." There was a hard edge to Rawlings's tone.

Feeling her anger rising again, Olivia quickly ended the call.

She then dropped Millay off at her car.

"Are you going to try to write?" she asked her friend.

Millay smirked. "Am I going to open my laptop and pretend to write while I listen to music, surf Etsy, and see if there's anything else I can find floating around in cyberspace on Stacy or Gordon? Then yeah, sure. I'm going home to write."

Olivia hated feeling so inept when it came to helping Laurel, but it also pained her to see Millay's slumped shoulders and to know that with each passing day, her friend's deadline was growing closer and closer and the number of words she needed to write was increasing by the thousands.

Putting down her window, Olivia called out, "You write about wyverns, right? Wyverns burn things."

Millay, who'd just unlocked her driver's-side door, paused with keys in hand. "And?"

"You and I know that Laurel didn't kill Stacy. She isn't capable of burning another human being—dead or alive. Who is? Imagine the rage such an act would require? You write fire scenes so well. Why not try an exercise? Without having any idea who the killer is, put yourself in his shoes and describe this murder."

Tiny sparks ignited in Millay's eyes. "Yeah. I could do that. And later, I could turn that exercise into a death scene for one of my minor characters. There's a ruling female in the Gryphon clan whose treachery has caused dozens of deaths. Tessa has suspected her from the beginning of the book. By this point in the narrative, she's caught her and must decide her punishment. Maybe I'll have Tessa put the traitor inside an upturned carriage or something. That way, she can see the wyvern coming. Her own death coming in a whir of wings and flames." Millay's body radiated energy. "And I could totally describe what that fire would look like. The acrid smell. The burning and crackling. The charred wood of the carriage. The metal wheels melting. All of it. Because Tessa would watch."

Olivia smiled. "Sounds like you won't be on Etsy this afternoon after all. Good luck."

Millay gave her an absent wave and got in her car, clearly eager to get home and start writing. Olivia could almost see the words dancing inside her friend's head.

Despite Haviland's presence, Olivia felt keenly alone without Millay.

I feel adrift because I don't know what to do, she thought.

She had no interest in working at the Boot Top Bistro or the Bayside Crab House, and, unlike Millay's manuscript, Olivia's work in progress could sit in a drawer gathering dust for the next twenty years. She had deadlines other than the ones she gave herself. Because she was a realist, Olivia knew that a collection of short stories featuring characters from her childhood would never be in high demand from a commercial publisher, so she took her time with each story. At this point, she'd painted ten portraits with words. Colorful characters who, from the outside, might not seem complex or fascinating, but upon closer inspection were as deep as the ocean. People like the lighthouse keeper, the woman tending the roadside fruit stand, the shrimp boat captain, the one-armed grocer, the all-knowing postmistress.

Like Millay, Olivia knew she'd benefit from some kind of writing exercise. Her anger kept bubbling up inside her. Any moment now, the pressure would become too great and she would explode. The release of her fear and frustration wouldn't be the fun, loud pop of a champagne cork. Olivia didn't need a psychologist to tell her that her anger had originated long before Steve cheated on Laurel. It could be traced back to the night Olivia's father abandoned her in that dinghy. When he motored off in the fog to make a new life for himself on Ocracoke Island.

And that event had occurred decades before Olivia learned that Willie Wade wasn't even her biological father. She'd only recently discovered that Willie had a twin, Charles, and that *he* was her biological father.

Since then, she and Charles had formed a tentative connection. After Olivia's marriage to Rawlings, Charles had tried to cultivate that relationship. And just when Olivia had been prepared to let him into her heart, Charles had fled Oyster Bay, leaving his newly acquired bookshop, Through the Wardrobe, within days of its grand reopening.

Once again, Olivia felt abandoned by a father. She and Charles had barely spoken over the past few months.

"So I have trust issues when it comes to men," Olivia murmured to her poodle as she pulled up in front of her house.

Opening the car door, she told Haviland to get some exercise. She watched him disappear over the dunes and wished she could also trot over the sand, as content and carefree as her dog. She longed to return to summer—to long evening strolls filled with endless daylight, ocean air, and warm sand under her feet.

On this gray afternoon, her poodle would come back into the house smelling of salt spray and adventure—his only concerns being his next meal and where to take a nap—while Olivia would struggle to find an outlet for her agitated thoughts.

Olivia opened her laptop and began to research Gordon Bruce. She wasn't Harris, however, and other than discovering the location of his chiropractic office, his corporate sponsorship for a Little League baseball team, and a Google street view of his modest but attractive house, Olivia's time online was wasted.

Closing her laptop with a rough snap, she fished in her desk drawer for a notebook and a pen.

Olivia had never written about her mother. She'd always put Camille Limoges on a pedestal. Canonized her. Preserved her in a series of golden memories in which she was always smiling, singing, baking, reading, or doting on her only child. Olivia held on only to recollections of being loved, cherished, and comforted by her mother.

The truth was far more complex. Camille had loved one man but married another. She had given birth to Charles Wade's child, though it was Charles's brother, Willie, who had provided for that child. Willie had never been able to love Olivia, and she'd felt that absence of love throughout her childhood. She now felt anger toward her mother too. Camille had married someone she didn't love for the sake of propriety and then died, leaving Olivia with a man who was only her father in name.

"Even if you hadn't died in that hurricane, things still wouldn't have ended well," Olivia said, her fingers curling around the starfish pendant nestled in the hollow of her throat. "Willie knew you didn't love him. He was drinking more and more every night. He was always going to leave."

It came to her then. She wasn't only angry with Steve Hobbs because he'd hurt Laurel deeply, and Laurel was

Olivia's friend. There was more to it than that. Steve's behavior reminded Olivia of Willie's weakness.

"You both tried to escape when things got tough," she muttered, her pen flying over the page. "Cowards. Both of you."

Laurel's pain also reminded Olivia that while no marriages are perfect, some are better than others. And the marriage Olivia knew best—that of her parents—was built on a foundation of desperation and deception. Willie and Camille shared the same house, but theirs was no partnership. They were friendly, but they were not friends. For the most part, they lived separate lives. It was a lonely existence for them all.

Olivia wrote and wrote. She'd never blamed her mother for her unhappiness. It had always been Willie's fault. Or Charles's. But there was something extremely freeing about taking Camille off her pedestal.

When the phone rang, Olivia was so absorbed in her work that the sound startled her.

"Were you taking a walk?" Rawlings asked. "It's already getting dark."

Olivia glanced out the window overlooking the ocean. The gloom had spread from the sky to the water, and the remaining light was seeping away. "I was writing," she said, surprised by the time. "I decided to do a story about my mother."

"I'm glad. On both counts," Rawlings said. "I'm calling from the hospital. I've just spoken with Laurel and I knew you'd want to hear how she's doing."

Olivia felt a tightening in her chest. "And?"

"She's okay. Considering the circumstances," Rawlings added. "She's tired and still confused. I assured her that the twins are being cared for, but she wouldn't calm down until I let her call the house and speak to the woman Kim hired to help out with the boys. Luckily, Laurel knows her and the two of them had a nice chat."

The tightness in Olivia's chest eased a little. "Good."

"After that—and yes, her attorney was with her the whole time—Laurel told me that she has significant memory gaps from last night. Blanks that she couldn't fill in. She remembers being on Steve's computer. She remembers reading messages between him and Stacy. She remembers drinking wine. She does not recall driving to her mother-in-law's house."

"Do you believe her?"

Rawlings grunted. "I don't think she's fabricating these holes in her memory. Neither does her doctor. He also doesn't think they're alcohol-related. They may indicate that Laurel has suffered a trauma. It's too soon to tell."

"Did you ask her what she said to Stacy?"

"No," Rawlings said. "I saw no point. She doesn't even remember getting in the car, let alone driving to her mother-in-law's condo. I did ask her what the next thing she remembered after reading her husband's messages was, and she began to weep. She said that she walked out to the end of the pier because that's where Steve proposed. She doesn't know how long she stayed out there, but she believes she may have thrown her wedding ring into the ocean."

Olivia made a sound that caught between a laugh and a sob. "She's not sure?"

"No. All she knows is that it's not on her finger," Rawlings said sadly. "We don't have it either. She also has no recollection of where she last saw the bracelet we discovered in Ms. Balena's car."

Olivia closed her notebook. "Is she allowed visitors?"

"Laurel refused to speak with Cook or her husband. She agreed to see me and, naturally, she'd dearly love a visit from you if her doctor grants her permission." After a pregnant pause, he continued. "Olivia. The medical professionals have presented the possibility that Laurel is suffering from PTSD. Though I've never heard the diagnosis used in conjunction with marital infidelity before, I'm not discounting their theory. Laurel's attorney, on the other hand, was quite happy to fill me in on the nuances of this condition. He also felt the need to repeatedly caution me that our department should treat Laurel with the utmost care."

At any other time, Olivia would have derived some satisfaction from hearing that Rand was living up to his reputation as a tenacious bulldog of an attorney, but at this moment she was too focused on Laurel—alone in her suffering—to feel anything but anxiety. "So? Can I see Laurel?" she asked, making no effort to tamp down her impatience. "I'm not a member of the police department, and Laurel *needs* a friend. Probably more now than at any other time in her life."

"I'm sure that's true," Rawlings said. He sounded tired and altogether miserable. "However, I don't think it'll be possible today."

Olivia lowered her voice to a dangerous whisper. "Are you forbidding me to visit?"

"It's not up to me. Or Cook. The physicians are calling the shots, though I have a feeling they're being strongly influenced by Laurel's attorney, and what they think she needs most is fluids and undisturbed rest," Rawlings explained with no small amount of exasperation. "Like I said before, you and I are on the same side. If I could get you five minutes with Laurel, I would. As it stands now, I don't see that happening until tomorrow morning."

"I hate this," Olivia said.

"I know."

The silence stretched between them for several seconds before Olivia spoke again. "You must be exhausted."

"I am. I'm coming home. Cook is handling Mr. Bruce's second interview."

Olivia sucked in a sharp breath. "Is there a chance . . . ?" She couldn't seem to get the rest of the question out.

"That Mr. Bruce could also be considered a suspect?" Rawlings finished for her. "There's a chance. Will he be arrested? I don't know. All I can say is that everyone needs sleep tonight. The last twenty-four hours have been hell. I just want to come home, eat something, and curl up in bed with you. Can we comfort each other, Olivia? Can we build a wall around us? Just for tonight?"

Olivia said that yes, they could.

When Rawlings finally called it a day and entered the house, he looked so weary that Olivia refrained from hammering him with questions about the case. Instead, she made sandwiches, which they ate on the sofa in front of the fire. Later, they went upstairs and spooned on the bed. They didn't speak. They simply pressed themselves together and let the warmth from their bodies envelop them in a protective cocoon.

Eventually, they fell asleep—their breath mingling and their limbs entwined—and when Olivia woke the next morning, Rawlings had left her a note by the coffeemaker. She recognized the lines, which had been written by one of Rawlings's favorite poets, Pablo Neruda. Olivia didn't know much about poetry and didn't consider herself a romantic, but she slid the note into her shirt pocket so that it would remain close to her heart throughout the day. It said:

so I wait for you like a lonely house
till you will see me again and live in me.
Till then my windows ache.

She was just finishing her breakfast of oatmeal mixed with fresh blueberries when the phone rang.

"Laurel has been given permission to check out of the hospital," Rawlings said. "She'd like you to pick her up."

Olivia was so stunned that it took her a moment to reply. "How did this come about?"

"Multiple factors contributed to her release. First, the prosecutor doesn't think he has enough hard evidence to survive a preliminary hearing, especially considering Laurel's lack of criminal history and her standing in the community. Not only that, but I think he's also more than a little intimidated by the defense counsel."

"Good," Olivia said with a trace of smugness.

"Also," Rawlings continued as though she hadn't spoken. "The medical professionals can't predict if or when she'll recover her memory from the night of the murder. And while they believe her condition is genuine, we have no choice but to submit her to a polygraph."

This came as a surprise to Olivia. "I didn't know that you even owned one."

"We use them to test applicants," Rawlings said. "And we're well aware that the machines have limited accuracy, but they do tend to promote truth-telling. If Laurel is creating a nonexistent case of amnesia to avoid a murder charge, the lie detector will help us identify the falsehood. And before you get angry with me, I doubt very much that she is. She knows that she'd only be delaying the inevitable."

Having rinsed her bowl while Rawlings was talking and loaded it into the dishwasher, Olivia now collected her coat and car keys. "Am I supposed to take her from the hospital to the police station or can she go home first? I'm sure she needs to shower and change."

"She needs to come in," Rawlings said. "It won't take long and when she's done, she can go home and rest."

After ushering Haviland out into the cold so he could do his business before getting in the car, Olivia asked, "What happened with Gordon Bruce?"

"I can't go into detail right now, but he's been elevated from a person of interest to a suspect."

Olivia felt a rush of triumph, but it was short-lived. After all, it wasn't as though Laurel was off the hook. And Gordon wasn't under arrest, which meant Cook didn't possess enough evidence to paint Stacy's ex-husband as the murderer.

"Look, I know that Gordon has priors for assault," Olivia said. "Fred Yoder told me that Gordon could be a mean drunk. He also told me that Gordon fell off the wagon the night Stacy was killed. But what got him so mad? They've been divorced for four years."

"According to Mr. Bruce's statement, Ms. Balena planned to sue for joint custody," Rawlings said. "When the couple first divorced, Ms. Balena didn't feel she could handle raising two kids. She was too broken up. So she focused on herself and her career. It was only recently that she decided she was ready to accept the responsibility of equal custody and she was preparing to take her former husband to court to prove that she was capable of supporting the children and of being a good parent and provider."

Olivia grunted in disbelief. "I don't see how she would have accomplished that while fooling around with a married man." Recalling Stacy's texts and messages, Olivia wondered what game Stacy had been playing with Steve. She'd alternated between acting submissive and being completely self-absorbed in those messages. Hardly mother material. But she wouldn't want Steve to view her in a maternal light, would she? She'd want him to see her as a sexy, unattached, young woman—a woman he couldn't live without. And when she was sure he was thoroughly obsessed, she'd ask him to leave his wife. Which was exactly what she'd done—right before she was murdered.

Rawlings interrupted her ruminations by asking, "What's going on in your head? I can practically hear your wheels spinning."

"I'm wondering about Stacy's motives. What did she ultimately want from Steve? Or from Gordon? Because I don't think she wanted to take Laurel's place and become stepmom to the twins. I think she wanted money. But to get her kids back? Really? Did she have photos of them in her wallet? In her house? Because there weren't any on her Facebook page. And what's with the antique jewelry you had Fred research? Was she given those pieces or were they stolen?"

"All excellent questions," Rawlings said with evident approval. "But the answers will have to wait, because Laurel is waiting."

Olivia nearly jumped. "Yes! See you later."

Slamming the phone into the cradle, Olivia ran outside and whistled for Haviland.

At the hospital, Olivia was suddenly nervous. She wasn't sure she'd know what to say to Laurel and wished she could take Haviland inside for moral support. Instead, she paid the valet to keep the Range Rover idling with the heat on while she retrieved Laurel.

Laurel looked like a ghost. Her skin was pale, her cheeks were hollow, and her eyes were empty.

When Olivia moved to embrace her, Laurel barely returned the hug. It was as though the effort was just too much for her.

"I'm so sorry," Olivia said. "I wanted to be with you when you woke up at the station. I didn't want you to be alone."

"It's not your fault." Laurel clasped a plastic water cup bearing the hospital's name against her chest. "You did all you could for me. And for the boys."

Olivia led Laurel down the hall toward the exit. "I called your house on my way here. The twins got off to school on time. They're doing fine." She hesitated. "I hate that I can't take you straight home. But I'll be with you the whole time."

"I don't blame them for doing the test." Laurel's voice was subdued. Resigned. "I'm not trying to be dramatic. I wish none of this were true, believe me. I wish I could wake up in my bed at home and have this all be some horrible nightmare. But the life I knew is over. My husband is a stranger. The woman he was sleeping with is dead. And though I don't remember what happened, I threatened her at her house—the day I caught them together. I told her I wanted her to burn. Well, she burned, didn't she?"

By this time, the two women had reached the exit doors. Olivia waited until they'd slid shut behind them before turning to Laurel. "Did you actually see Stacy's car on fire?"

"If I did, I don't remember," Laurel said. "But I know what happened because I watched a news report on TV while I was waiting for you. I learned that Stacy's car had been doused in gasoline while she was still belted into the driver's seat. Preliminary reports indicate that she was unconscious when the fire started. Cause of death was probably smoke inhalation."

Olivia wasn't surprised by Laurel's ability to discuss Stacy's death with such detachment. Laurel was dialing into her journalistic side as a survival mechanism. If she allowed herself to think of her husband or children, she'd likely fall apart.

Outside, she did bury her face in Haviland's neck for several seconds, and the poodle responded to Laurel's need by covering her cheeks with sweet canine kisses.

The ride to the police station seemed interminably long. Olivia couldn't fill the silence with the usual small talk, but when she turned on the radio and holiday music streamed out into the cabin, Laurel's face crumpled.

"Christmas is ruined," she said, beginning to cry. "There's nothing I can do to save it for the boys. For the rest of their lives, they'll have flashbacks to this time of year. They won't remember family dinners or church pageants, but that their mother was arrested for murder and their father had an affair with their grandmother's nurse. They're going to be in therapy for years."

"Try not to think that far ahead," Olivia said. "Just make it through one ordeal at a time. Your first ordeal for today is this polygraph. You'll handle that and then deal with the next thing. And your friends will stand with you through everything."

At the station, Laurel walked with a steady, even gait and kept her chin raised and her eyes locked on some point in the distance. She didn't acknowledge the local journalists or other members of the media, with their cameras and barrage of shouted questions. She simply marched on, her hands trembling violently, until Rawlings came outside to escort her into the building. He shooed the reporters away and led Laurel inside, a protective arm wrapped around her shoulder.

After searching in vain for Harris, Olivia and Haviland waited for Laurel in the chief's office. Olivia had brought her writing notebook along and tried to work on the story she'd started the day before, but she ended up jotting down questions about the murder case instead.

Why was Laurel's bracelet in Stacy's car?

Did Stacy steal those valuable antiques or were they given to her by grateful patients or their family members?

If Stacy was planning on taking her ex-husband to court, why hadn't she sold the valuables? Wouldn't she need the money to cover legal fees?

Had she gotten anything valuable out of Rachel Hobbs?

"You seem lost in thought," Rawlings said quietly.

Olivia closed her notebook and got to her feet. "How did she do?"

Rawlings gave Olivia a reassuring smile. "Very well. In fact, the only time her response reflected a significant change on the graph—and you know this type of test isn't completely accurate—was when Cook showed her the photograph of her bracelet." He held up his hand. "I can't say anything else. I just came in to tell you that Laurel's more than ready to go home. Let's walk her out through the rear exit."

By the time the media realized that they'd been duped, Olivia already had the Range Rover in drive and was accelerating out of the parking lot.

When a reporter and his cameraman blocked her path, Olivia stuck her head out of her window and yelled, "I *will* run you over!" She then laid on her horn and revved her engine until the two men scurried out of the way.

"Was it hard?" she asked Laurel at the next stoplight.

"Only when they asked me about my bracelet. A friend from college sent it to me the first time one of my stories went national. It has such sentimental value that I became furious when I realized that it had been found in *her* car." Laurel's lips tightened into a thin line. Forcing herself to relax, she continued. "I don't know how it got there, and I can't remember the last time I put it on. If Steve gave it to her—"

Olivia was quick to disrupt Laurel's negative train of thought. "I was with Steve when Rawlings asked him about the bracelet. He seemed genuinely surprised to learn that it had been in you-know-who's car. I don't think Steve would be foolish enough to lie to the chief's face."

Laurel laughed. It was a terrible, heartbroken laugh. "He's been nothing but a fool. And I know I'm not supposed to act angry because I'm a suspect. But I'm angry, Olivia. Every cell in my body is filled with anger. Anger and grief. That's why I don't think I killed her. Because if I had, I think I'd feel better. I think I'd feel a tiny bit of peace."

Olivia didn't subscribe to the belief that murder brought anyone peace, but she held her tongue.

Several minutes later, Olivia pulled into Laurel's driveway. There were two TV vans parked along the curb, and Olivia saw the occupants scrambling to shoulder cameras and turn on microphones.

In front of her car, the garage door opened and Steve waved for Laurel to hurry inside.

"Do you want me to come in with you?" Olivia asked.

Laurel shook her head. "I may hate it, but this is my life now. Thank you for everything. I don't know what I'd do without you."

The women exchanged a brief hug and then Laurel hurried into the garage, ignoring her husband's outstretched hand.

As Olivia put her car in reverse, she thought of how tempting it would be to back over one of the vultures' cameras, but she had better things to do than mess with journalists.

She needed to have a frank talk with a dying woman.

Chapter 9

This particular nurse said, Cancer
cells are those which have forgotten
how to die.

—HAROLD PINTER

Though Olivia had met Rachel's nurse Wanda the day she'd accompanied Laurel to the meeting at Tidewater Hospice, she reintroduced herself at the door of the Hobbs condo.

"I remember you. I've been answering the door so I can chase away those pushy reporters. They keep pestering poor Mr. Hobbs about his son and daughter-in-law." Wanda stepped back. "Anyway, come on in. Mrs. Hobbs is resting, but Mr. Hobbs is in the kitchen."

Steeling herself for a battle, Olivia passed through the living room into the kitchen, where she found Milton sitting at the table, drinking black coffee and reading the newspaper.

Seeing Olivia, he gave his paper a rough shake. "What are you doing here?"

"I'm trying to figure out if you had a thief in your midst,"

Olivia said and, without waiting for an invitation, sat down across from him.

"What are you talking about?"

Olivia lowered her voice. "Has any of your wife's jewelry gone missing since the various staff members from Tidewater Hospice began visiting your home?"

Milton was instantly affronted. "Of course not. Don't you think I'd know if people were stealing from me? I'm not blind."

"No, but you can't watch them all the time," Olivia said. "And despite the fact that you and Rachel never bonded with Laurel, I know you don't want the mother of your grandchildren to end up in jail for a crime she didn't commit. Your wife's former nurse, however, may have been a thief." Olivia went on to tell Milton about the photographs she, Millay, and Fred Yoder had researched.

When she was done, Milton stared at her in shock. "That Stacy sure had Rachel fooled. My wife talked to her like they were old friends—told her things I didn't think she should tell a stranger." He glanced at his hands. "But she's sick, so I let her do what she wants. At this point, I can't deny her anything."

Again, Olivia was reminded that she was speaking with a man who truly loved his wife—a man whose main goal was ensuring that her final days were as peaceful and painless as possible. "I can't imagine how hard this must be on you," she said. "Rachel is lucky to have such a caring husband."

Milton shot her a suspicious glance, but when he realized that she was sincere, he gave her a self-conscious nod. "It's not hard. I could handle hard. It's hell. But I'm trying my best."

Olivia could understand how witnessing the slow and

agonizing decline of the person one has shared the better part of one's life with could easily be described as hell. "I don't mean to create strife," she said softly. "But Laurel is also tormented. Like you, she has always tried to do what's right for her family. Like you, she has been the victim of circumstance. So I'm asking for your help. All I'd like to know is whether or not Rachel gave Stacy an expensive gift of jewelry or if your wife is missing something valuable. The answer may help exonerate your daughter-in-law."

Suddenly remembering his coffee, Milton put his hand around his cup and frowned. "Gone cold." He then looked at Olivia. "Would you like a cup? I make it real strong."

Interpreting this as a peace offering, Olivia said that she would and Milton surprised her by serving her coffee in a bone china cup along with a plate of cookies. He even folded a napkin into a triangle and set a teaspoon squarely in the center of it before resuming his seat.

Olivia took a sip of coffee and moaned appreciatively. "This is very good."

Pleased, Milton drank some of his own and then held up his hand. "Okay. I'll ask Rachel. If she gets the slightest bit upset, however, I won't push her."

"I wouldn't dream of upsetting her," Olivia lied. If it were up to her, she'd question Rachel on the subject regardless of the distress it caused the dying woman. In Olivia's mind, Rachel owed Laurel restitution. She'd treated her daughter-in-law unkindly for years and had likely done her best to turn her son against his wife.

Yes, thought Olivia. *Rachel Hobbs has been a toxic influence on her son's marriage, but she has a chance to make up for her behavior before she dies. Will she, though? Will she even tell the truth?*

Emboldened by anxiety, Olivia blurted, "May I come

with you? I'd like to tell your wife about her Hummel figurine. Before all the chaos, I took it to a friend of mine to be repaired."

Sensing he was being tricked, but unwilling to lose face, Milton grunted and waved for Olivia to follow him. "Let me talk to her first," he commanded before he tiptoed into the bedroom.

Treading as quietly as she could, Olivia entered the room behind Milton. She took in the hospital bed, the IV stands, the pill bottles on the dresser, the half-drawn shades, and the close air, and instantly she felt claustrophobic. She avoided staring at the figure in the bed. Instead, she retreated to the far corner of the room and fixed her gaze on Wanda. The nurse sat in a chair near Rachel's right hand. She had a magazine open on her lap and appeared to be reading Rachel an article on holiday gift giving.

At the sound of their entry, Wanda looked up from her magazine and smiled. "She's awake."

Milton smoothed his wife's hair. "How's my girl?"

"She's having one of her better afternoons. She drank her whole milk shake," Wanda said brightly. "She's feeling strong. A good day for a visitor."

Rachel murmured something and Milton bent over her, placing his ear near her lips. He then turned and whispered to her before straightening again.

"Wanda?" Milton had his hands pressed together as though in prayer. "Would you work your magic on my wife's feet? You know how much she loves it when you massage them and then wrap them in hot towels."

Wanda gave Rachel's calf a gentle squeeze. "That's why I'm here, Mrs. Hobbs. To work my magic. I even brought special lotion for you. It's an organic, hypoallergenic goat's-milk-and-honey lotion. It's incredibly gentle, and when I'm through, your feet are going to feel as soft as your pillow. Be right back. I'm going to heat your towels in the microwave."

As soon as Wanda had left the room, Milton leaned close to Rachel again. "Honey, I need to talk to you before Wanda gets back, so listen to me, okay? I know how much you liked Stacy," he continued. "I know that you two had a special connection."

Rachel groaned and Olivia couldn't stop herself from wincing. Even though most of Rachel's body was tucked inside the bedding, it was clear that she had progressed from painfully thin to downright skeletal. The hands resting on top of the duvet cover were nothing but skin and bone and the nails appeared brittle with a yellow cast.

"Sweetie, did you give Stacy a gift? A piece of jewelry, maybe? As a show of gratitude?" Milton ran his fingers along his wife's cavernous cheek. "I could see you doing that. You're so generous when it comes to the people you care about. Look how much you love buying things for the boys."

Olivia assumed that Milton was referring to his grandsons, but before she could dwell on the thought, Rachel grew agitated. Olivia wanted very much to hear the dying woman's words, but they were too faint for her to hear from across the room.

"It was Laurel's?" Milton asked in obvious surprise. "How did it end up here?"

Olivia saw Rachel's chest rise and fall and then she sank deeper into the pile of pillows on her bed. The brief conversation with her husband had taxed her.

Milton shot Olivia a plaintive glance. "Would you tell my wife about her Hummel? Don't worry if she doesn't say anything. She can hear you. She's just tired from talking to me."

"Of course." As Olivia passed through a beam of winter sunshine and dust motes on her way to Rachel's bedside, she wondered if Rachel looked out her window anymore or if she'd lost interest in anything beyond her four walls.

"I have good news. Your Hummel can be repaired," Olivia said with as much enthusiasm as she could muster. "The work is already under way and the gentleman doing it understands the importance of getting the figurine back to you as soon as possible."

Rachel said nothing. However, she did raise the thumb of her right hand.

"She says 'thanks,'" Milton explained just as Wanda re-entered the room.

She carried a mixing bowl filled with steaming towels and was humming in a low, rich voice. Olivia saw Rachel's face relax and the corners of her mouth turn ever so slightly upward.

"She loves humming," Wanda said. "Yesterday, she told me that she was practically raised by a black housekeeper called Maisie. She said Maisie was big as a house, made the tastiest lemonade and molasses pie, gave the world's best hugs, and had the voice of an angel. Whenever young Rachel was upset, this woman would gather her up in her arms and rock her, humming until she fell asleep."

Milton gazed at his wife, tears standing in his eyes. "She never told me that story."

"She said she's been hearing Maisie's songs," Wanda continued. "Like Maisie's calling to her."

Now Milton looked scared. "Do you think that's true?"

"Somctimes they know better than we do when they're getting ready to go," Wanda said, and then shrugged. "Sometimes they just get lost in their memories. I just hum to relax her. When she's relaxed, she feels less pain. I've been humming to her since I got here."

"Thank you," Milton said. His voice was hoarse. Turning to Olivia, he gestured at the door. "I'll walk you out."

Olivia remained silent, respecting Milton's grief. He accompanied her all the way to her car, and it was only when she was settled in the driver's seat, with Haviland sniffing her neck and shifting back and forth on his paws in an effort to get attention, that he elaborated on his whispered exchange with his wife.

"The only thing Rachel intentionally gave Stacy was a bracelet that originally belonged to Laurel." Milton gazed at the ground and shook his head. "It sounds cruel, I know, and I wish she hadn't done it. It must have fallen off Laurel's wrist the last time she came to visit. I think she was adjusting pillows or something on the bed and the clasp got caught on Rachel's blanket. Anyway, the bracelet came off and Stacy noticed it when she showed up for her shift. When she admired it, my wife told her to keep it. That was wrong because it wasn't hers to give, but there you go. My wife doesn't know if any of her jewelry is missing. It's not likely, seeing as we put her valuable items in our safe-deposit box months ago, but I'll check."

Olivia grabbed both of Milton's hands and squeezed, doing her best to convey her gratitude through her touch. "You did a good thing today. I'll never forget it. Thank you."

And though Milton Hobbs was a man weighed down by the sorrow of his wife's impending death, Olivia felt a momentary lightening in him. He gave her a brief smile and she released his hands and drove away.

"Oh, Captain!" Olivia cried, happy for the first time in days. "Laurel's bracelet wasn't in Stacy's car because Laurel is a killer! Laurel's bracelet was in Stacy's car because Laurel's mother-in-law is a mean and vindictive woman. Stacy was *wearing* the damn thing!"

As Olivia headed into the business district, she got caught at one of the longer stoplights and decided to call Rawlings while she waited for it to turn green. She was about to use her car's voice command system when she noticed the poster announcing Oyster Bay's Christmas flotilla. This year's nautical parade, which would take place in two days, was to have a literary theme. The committee in charge of the event had decided to use Dr. Seuss's *The Grinch* as an example of the theme and had put a stylized version of the cartoon creature on every poster.

Maybe Rachel's heart grew too, Olivia thought, looking at the Grinch's red eyes and malicious smile. *Maybe the sound of humming, which brought back the memory of a woman who once loved her, was all it took. Rachel's heart softened in the nick of time.*

"Olivia? I can't really—" Rawlings began when he came on the line.

"Rachel Hobbs gave Laurel's bracelet to Stacy," Olivia cut in. "That's why it was in her car. It's *not* a piece of evidence against Laurel. You can call Milton and hear the story directly from him. Rachel is too exhausted to repeat it now, but she might be able to by tomorrow. Though I don't know how many tomorrows she has left."

Rawlings made a sympathetic noise. "That whole family . . . Jesus. There doesn't seem to be any respite for them."

"There could be for Laurel," Olivia said. "A tiny break anyway. If she didn't have to worry about being a murder suspect, she might be able to begin the process of healing. She could deal with one trauma instead of two. One is enough for any human being."

"Yes," Rawlings agreed. "I'll tell Cook. Now go home, Olivia. Pour a drink. Kick off your shoes. Eat something. Watch TV. Take a break. I'll see you soon."

Olivia took his advice. After a supper of salad and spaghetti Bolognese, she curled up on the living room sofa and covered her legs with a chenille blanket. Haviland stretched out on the part of the rug closest to the fireplace. The gas logs were set to high and the room was cozy and warm. Olivia flipped through channels until a familiar cartoon visage appeared on her screen. Go figure, it was the Grinch.

Setting the remote control down, Olivia watched the holiday special.

When it was over, she stared up at the ceiling, observing the shadow play created by the flames, and thought of Rachel Hobbs. She wondered if Rachel was awake. And if so, did she hear her beloved Maisie humming to her?

"That would be a lovely way to go," Olivia murmured drowsily, recalling her own mother's soothing lullabies.

And that was the last coherent thought she had before she was pulled down into sleep.

"I've been writing like a fiend," Millay exclaimed over pancakes at Grumpy's the next morning.

"I'm very happy to hear that," Olivia said.

Millay pushed a forkful of pancakes around on her plate. "Really? Because I feel like a total jackass. Laurel is in the darkest pit of despair and I'm holed up in my apartment, pecking away on my laptop like my book is *so* important. What kind of crap friend can do that?"

"Do you think Laurel would want you to quit on this book?" Olivia asked. "If anything, she'd want you to focus even harder and do what she won't have a chance to do—at least not for a long time."

Millay frowned. "Which is what?"

"Chase your dreams. That first book wasn't the end of

your aspirations. It was just the beginning. You hope to be a career novelist, right?"

Millay nodded.

"Then you need to write. Nearly every day. Even when you don't feel like it." Olivia pretended to type midair. "You need to find your rhythm. Like you did yesterday. Don't worry about what will happen after the book comes out. Keep your focus on your characters. What does Tessa want? What's going on inside her head?"

"Do you seriously think I can concentrate on my book with what's going on with Laurel?" Millay glared at Olivia. "And Harris is acting weird too. He's always been straight with me. I mean, seriously, we used to *date*. We're *supposed to be* friends and fellow struggling authors, but even before Laurel's arrest, he started dancing around certain subjects. Did you know that he invited Emily to visit for Christmas? I think he's going to pop the question. He hasn't been able to convince her to move here and he's tired of the whole long-distance thing, so the only way to get her to commit is to put a ring on it."

Olivia couldn't imagine Harris asking his Texas-based girlfriend to marry him in the midst of a murder investigation—especially an investigation involving a close friend—but she kept her opinion to herself. "Maybe he just needs to know where he stands. There comes a point in every relationship where both partners have to determine their level of commitment once and for all. Harris loves Emily and he loves his life in Oyster Bay. He tried living in Texas. It didn't work for him, so I hope Emily will give North Carolina a shot."

"See? These kinds of complications are *exactly* why I don't want a serious relationship," Millay said. "Ever. And if Emily moves here and becomes Mrs. Williams, what does that mean for our Bayside Book Writer meetings?"

"Harris isn't going to cease being a writer just because he's happy," Olivia said.

Millay grunted. "Come on. How many contented, well-balanced, highly functioning people write novels? Let alone get them published? Writers are damaged. We have haunted pasts. We either eat or drink too much. Our sleep is constantly interrupted by wacko imagery and snippets of dialogue." She paused to wipe some maple syrup off her lower lip. "Harris has struggled for two years to pen three-dimensional characters. He's come such a long way and done so many revisions, but you and I both know that he should be submitting his manuscript to agents. So why hasn't he?"

"Fear of rejection? He wants to wait until after the holidays?" Olivia shrugged. "He still has to write the dreaded query letter, remember? Some people say that composing that document is more challenging than finishing a full-length novel."

Millay considered this. "It was rough. But I could help him." She pulled out her phone. As she typed a text message to Harris, she continued to talk to Olivia. "We should all keep focusing on our projects. Laurel would want us all writing. What about the chief? Has he had any rest or does he look like an extra from *The Walking Dead*?"

"Everyone we know is losing sleep because of this murder." Olivia looked around for Dixie and, after spotting her preparing to have a nice, leisurely chat with a local couple dining at the *Cats* booth, signaled for a coffee refill. "Rawlings is no exception. And when he tries to sleep, he flails around like a child with night terrors. I just hope the lead he and Cook are following this morning pays off."

Olivia had told Millay about her visit to the Hobbs condo when she called to invite her to breakfast. Because of the late hours she kept, Millay rarely rose before noon, and

Olivia knew that she'd have to dangle a pretty big carrot to coax her friend to meet her at Grumpy's at what Millay would consider an ungodly hour.

Dixie skated over to their table, refilled their mugs, and sat down next to Millay. Haviland, who'd been gazing out the window, turned to her, gave her a toothy grin, and wagged his tail.

"I'll be sure to tell Grumpy how much you enjoyed your meal." Dixie grinned at the poodle. To Olivia she said, "My patience is really bein' tested today. People I've known for years are believin' everything they hear on TV about Laurel. Some anchorman with too much foundation and lots of hair gel speaks and they take what he says as gospel. Can't they think for themselves? Laurel is one of their own, for heaven's sake!"

"Laurel's story probably scares the crap out of them," Millay said. "From the outside, her life looked perfect. And these people are either living similar lives or wishing they had her life. Successful career. Husband. Two kids. Nice house in the suburbs. Country club membership. Learning that Laurel's white-picket world is flawed makes them feel better about their own situation, but it freaks them out too. What will they dream about now?"

Olivia stared at her younger friend. "When did you get so cynical?"

"I've been this way since birth," Millay replied.

Dixie suddenly jumped to her feet. "Well, if my customers were runnin' their mouths before, their tongues'll be waggin' double time now. Here comes the chief, and he looks like he's carryin' the weight of the world. I'll grab him a clean cup. If ever a man needed coffee, it's him."

Rawlings entered the diner and headed for the window booth. If he sensed curious eyes following him, he didn't acknowledge them.

"I'll scoot over," Millay offered. "I wouldn't dream of displacing Haviland."

Rawlings thanked her and sat down with a heavy sigh.

"Is it Rachel Hobbs?" Olivia asked. "Is she worse?"

"Yes," Rawlings said in a leaden voice. "Cook and I were permitted to see her, but it was clear that we wouldn't be asking her any questions. I'm afraid she's had a dramatic decline since you saw her yesterday. Her breathing has become labored. It sounds wet. And she's very weak. She's been drifting in and out of consciousness."

Without realizing it, Olivia had reached out for Haviland while Rawlings was talking. The poodle licked her hand, comforting her as he'd done for years.

"I'm sorry to hear that," Olivia said. "It's as though Rachel's cancer infected two people, but will only kill one of them. Milton will have to keep on living, which is probably even harder than watching his wife die." Removing her hand from Haviland's back, she placed it over Rawlings's. "You went through this with Helen," she said, referring to the chief's first wife. "Did this morning's visit bring up painful memories?"

At that moment, Dixie skated over with the coffee carafe and a mug. "Grumpy's fixin' you a breakfast sandwich," she said. "You might not be hungry, but you need protein. Just holler when you want more coffee."

Rawlings thanked Dixie and she zipped off to deliver the check to the couple at the *Tell Me on a Sunday* booth.

"Seeing Milton's anguish brought it all back," Rawlings said, answering Olivia's question as he added a splash of cream to his coffee. "But I had to put the feelings aside, do my job, and focus on the next task. Which is what Harris and I were going to discuss over coffee." He looked at Haviland. "You'll have to move now, Captain."

Olivia arched her eyebrows. "You're going to let us in on the investigation?"

"We're just four friends having coffee." Rawlings waved at Harris. "Besides, I was never shutting you out. It's just this isn't my case. It's Cook's. And people will be watching to see if I do anything that compromises it out of loyalty to Laurel."

Harris had barely settled in the seat next to Olivia when Dixie arrived with Rawlings's breakfast sandwich. "Don't worry, honey," she said, addressing Harris. "I'll tell Grumpy to make you one too. Coffee?"

"In the biggest cup you've got," Harris said.

Millay gave him an assessing stare. "Did you pull an all-nighter?"

"Yep. I passed out on a pile of photos. Sorry, Chief, but I drooled on at least four of them." He put an expanding file folder on the table.

"Photos of what?" Olivia asked Rawlings.

"The contents of Ms. Balena's apartment. Can you spread out the jewelry images so we can all see them, Harris?"

Harris pulled out a group of familiar photos and displayed them in a fanlike pattern stretching from the salt and pepper shakers to Olivia's coffee cup.

"You saw these at Fred's shop. Ms. Balena had these pieces of jewelry hidden in a shoe box in her closet. Cook and I were both curious about why they were stored there and whether or not they were valuable. When Fred confirmed just how valuable they were, we had to ask ourselves if her murder was related to these pieces," Rawlings said. "Harris ran a search on all the lost and stolen jewelry claims for the last five years in every county that Tidewater Hospice serves, and he discovered an interesting fact."

"Nerds love their facts," Millay said, and flashed Harris one of her rare smiles.

Rawlings pointed at the file folder. "Can you divide the printouts among us?"

Harris distributed a stack of papers to each person at the table.

"In reviewing these reports, we expected to find additional connections between Ms. Balena and these missing items," Rawlings said. "However, that didn't pan out. Some of these reports were filed before she worked for Tidewater. That means another team member must be involved. Someone who already had an eye for valuable pieces of antique jewelry. Someone who recruited Ms. Balena. We might be looking at a larceny ring preying on the old and terminally ill."

"That is seriously messed up," Millay muttered in disgust.

Olivia examined the report detailing the loss of a pair of antique diamond earrings. "Have you been able to trace any of these pieces?" she asked Harris.

"Not yet," he answered. "Only that they weren't resold online. I couldn't find a single match."

"Which means they're being sold to shady dealers who don't care about provenance," Olivia said.

Millay, who'd shuffled through her packet fairly quickly, gestured for Harris to hand over his packet.

"You haven't read all the details in your pile yet," he protested.

She gesticulated with more force. "Humor me."

Everyone else fell silent and watched as Millay quickly examined the images of the lost or stolen items detailed in the second group of reports. She repeated this with Olivia's pile. She was midway through Rawlings's stack when Dixie skated over with Harris's breakfast sandwich.

"You're an angel!" Harris cried before taking an enormous bite of his sandwich.

The smell of eggs and bacon brought Haviland to attention

and he stared at Harris from the end of the booth. Harris shielded his plate from the poodle's eyes and ate faster.

"I don't know if this means anything, but the majority of these items have something in common." Millay put down the last set of reports.

"They do?" Rawlings and Harris asked in unison.

Millay nodded. "Ninety percent of this jewelry is set with diamonds."

Olivia recalled the items found in Stacy's apartment. Millay was right. Every piece of jewelry included diamonds. She looked at Rawlings. "Do you think that's relevant?"

"It could be," he replied. "Especially since Gordon Bruce recently invested a large amount of money in his brother-in-law's jewelry business. I'm referring to his second wife's brother, of course." Rawlings fell silent for a moment, and the rest of the group let him think. "I don't really think that the ill will between Mr. Bruce and Ms. Balena centered on their children. The murder may be entirely connected to the jewelry and to the possible existence of a larceny ring. Either Mr. Bruce, his brother-in-law, or both of these men could be involved in this mess."

"What's the brother-in-law's name?" Olivia asked. She doubted she knew the man, but she wanted to research his jewelry store.

"Hold on, there's more," Harris interrupted. He'd finished his food and had pushed his plate away. "These reports weren't the only thing I was working on. I've been using every program known to man and gamer trying to clean up one of the crime scene photos. There was so much smoke damage that it was almost impossible to read, but the more I zoomed in, the more it looked like a label from a pill bottle or something. As it turned out, the label was from a preloaded syringe."

"Were you able to identify the drug?" Rawlings asked.

Olivia didn't move. She hardly dared to breathe. She didn't want anything to detract from Harris's revelation.

"Yep." Harris took a sip of coffee, drawing out his triumph. "That label came from a preloaded syringe of morphine."

Olivia thought of all the pill bottles and syringes she'd seen in Rachel Hobbs's room. "You said this was found at the crime scene. Where?" She directed her question at Rawlings.

"Inside Ms. Balena's car," Rawlings said, pulling out his wallet. "Harris, we need to go."

Rawlings had just removed a bill from his wallet when his phone rang. He answered the call and Olivia could tell by the look on his face that he'd received bad news.

When he lowered his phone again, his eyes were dark and somber. "It's Rachel Hobbs," he told the rest of his companions. "She's dead."

Chapter 10

*Ships that pass in the night, and speak
each other in passing, Only a signal
shown, and a distant voice in the
darkness; So on the ocean of life, we
pass and speak one another, Only a look
and a voice, then darkness again and a
silence*

—HENRY WADSWORTH LONGFELLOW

To Laurel's immense relief, Lynne Chester and some
other church ladies volunteered to assist Milton with
the arrangements for Rachel's memorial service.

"I'd be of no use to Milton," Laurel said to Olivia the
next day over the phone. "And Steve isn't much better. Neither of us has slept much since I caught him in bed with
her." Laurel paused, collected herself, and began again. "If
Kim hadn't found Mrs. Bartlett, who's like our own Mary
Poppins, I don't know how we would have survived the last
few days. When I can think straight, I'll have to tell her how
grateful I am."

Olivia was pleased to hear that one thing had gone right
for Laurel and her boys and told her as much.

"They're too young to realize exactly how bad things
are," Laurel said. "They don't know about my overnight stay
in jail and they have no idea about their father's extracur-
ricular activities. I told them that he and I are working on

some problems that have nothing to do with them. Still, I need to get them out of the house this weekend, so we're going to the Christmas parade. I feel like we can all wear baseball caps, hide in the crowd, and avoid the news crews. Will you and Millay come with us? If you're there, I might be able to hold myself together."

Normally, Olivia would have balked at the thought of sitting on a noisy, crowded dock on a cold winter evening to watch illuminated boats float past, but she couldn't refuse Laurel.

"We'll be there," she promised.

"What about the case?" Laurel asked. "Can you give me any hope?"

Olivia hesitated. Cook and his team must still have been questioning Gordon Bruce and his brother-in-law, for Rawlings had yet to phone saying that they'd made an arrest. His silence made her nervous and she was reluctant to mislead Laurel. However, Laurel was a journalist. Because of this, Olivia believed that her friend could hear the facts without getting carried away by her emotions, so she told her about the theory of a ring of antique jewelry thieves preying on the sick and elderly.

"Do the cops have evidence to back this up?" Laurel asked. She sounded excited, as though she'd shed her lethargy and depression for a precious moment. "A paper trail? Cash deposits? Big-ticket purchases by Stacy, Gordon, or the brother-in-law?"

Olivia hated to burst her friend's bubble. "It's just a theory right now. Cook will have to get permission to take an in-depth look at Bruce's and his brother-in-law's finances, and at this point I don't think a judge will grant it to him."

"Maybe I can do some snooping," Laurel said. "What's the brother-in-law's name?"

Olivia had asked Rawlings the same question last night before she and Rawlings went to bed. "Arnold Vonn of Vonn's Fine Jewelry. He has two shops. One in New Bern and one in Bayboro. I already read up on his business. He does deal in antique jewelry, but only minimally. Judging from the Web site and customer testimonials, people patronize his shops because of the large selection and reasonable cost of his wedding and bridal jewelry."

"Which means he deals in lots of diamonds!" Laurel cried.

"But not antique diamonds," Olivia gently pointed out. She heard the sound of a computer being booted up and glanced at the pile of work she'd barely made a dent in since arriving at the Boot Top Bistro hours earlier. "I'll call you if I hear an update from Rawlings," she said, and Laurel, who was now clearly distracted, promised to phone if she was able to discover any promising leads on her own.

Olivia forced herself to order a slew of requested inventory items and to balance the budget. After that, she padded her employees' checks with a surprise holiday bonus, which required some finagling. Finally, it was time to review the menu for the Shakespeare-themed New Year's Eve bash.

She'd barely started on the appetizer list when her mind drifted to a college class she'd taken on Shakespearean tragedies. She recalled how often the theme of betrayal came up in the Bard's works: *Othello*, *Macbeth*, *The Tempest*, *Julius Caesar*, *Hamlet*, *Antony and Cleopatra*, *Romeo and Juliet*, *King Lear*, and so on.

"Betrayal always led to death in your work," Olivia mused aloud as she made notes on the menu. However, she was unable to concentrate on the food.

Was Stacy's murder the result of a betrayal? she wondered. *Had she been romantically involved with someone in addition to Steve? Someone who taught her which jewelry to steal?*

Olivia wrote Arnold Vonn's name and Stacy's name and then drew an arrow and a question mark between them.

"And is Steve Hobbs in the clear?" Olivia added his name below the first two and decided to ask Rawlings whether or not Steve had provided the police with a cast-iron alibi for the time of Stacy's murder. Because if not, Olivia couldn't see why he wasn't being considered a suspect.

"Are you drooling yet?" Michel asked from the doorway of Olivia's office. "Can you picture the magnificence of it all?"

Olivia glanced at the scribbled names on the menu and moved to cover them with her forearm. "I'm sorry, Michel. I know you're looking for enthusiasm right now, but I'm too worried about Laurel to respond as I normally would. I'm going to take this with me and look at it when I can give it the attention it deserves."

"Oh, *mon Dieu*." Michel balled his hand into a fist and pressed it against his lips. "I am the one who should be apologizing. I become so wrapped up in these events that it is possible for me to forget all about the outside world. But I care about Laurel and I do not believe—not for a tiny second—that she did this thing. And that husband of hers! I would like to hit him with my biggest pan! And then, after I'd trussed him up like a holiday roast, I'd give Laurel my meat tenderizer. How I'd love to watch her—"

"Yes," Olivia interrupted. "Many of us feel as you do. But we aren't in Laurel's shoes. She isn't just part of a couple. They are a family. I believe that makes things much more complicated than any of us realize."

Michel leaned against the doorframe and released a mournful sigh. "What will she do once the police catch the real killer?

Will she leave her husband or will she stay and try to make things work?"

"I don't know," Olivia said. "But my main priority is making sure that she's free to make that decision."

The Boot Top Bistro's head chef returned to the kitchen and Olivia finished up answering a dozen e-mails and tidied her desk before reaching for her coat. She'd barely taken it off the hook before Haviland was on his feet, his tail wagging in anticipation. He'd napped long enough and was ready for some fresh air and exercise.

"Let's walk down to the docks, Captain."

Rawlings met them there a little later, bearing cappuccinos from Decadence. "Shelley sends her best," he said, handing Olivia a take-out cup. "Have you seen her create designs in the foam? She made me an angel. And I thought the display window was magical." Glancing out at the boats moored in the harbor, he went on. "We'll have to take your niece and nephew and Laurel's kids to the shop before the Christmas flotilla. Buy them a few treats and some hot chocolate."

Olivia, who'd yet to sip from the cup Rawlings had given her, frowned. "I have a feeling you're trying to distract me. Were there no arrests, then?"

Meeting her eyes, Rawlings shook his head. "The problem is that no one has a solid alibi for the time of Ms. Balena's murder. Cook is requiring that Laurel see a psychologist for intensive daily sessions in hopes that she'll recover her memory from that night. As for Steve Hobbs, we found no witnesses to corroborate his story that he stayed home after Laurel drove off following their talking-and-yelling session."

"So he should be a suspect," Olivia blurted.

"Gordon Bruce was inebriated," Rawlings continued without reacting to Olivia's interruption. "And while he contacted Fred Yoder by phone to confess that he'd fallen off the wagon, he can't account for his movements. During his previous interview, he claimed that he didn't drive to the bar and had used Uber instead. We've since checked on that claim. He did use Uber to take him to a bar on the outskirts of New Bern shortly after six and back home again close to midnight. However, the bartender doesn't think Mr. Bruce was there for six hours. More like three. So where was he the rest of the time?"

"What was his answer to that question?"

Rawlings growled in frustration. "He fed us some baloney about leaving to grab a bite to eat at the fast-food joint down the street, where he conveniently paid in cash. After that, he thinks he wandered around for a bit in an attempt to clear his head and fight the temptation of returning to the bar, but he failed."

"Why did he start drinking again in the first place?" Olivia asked. "Did it have something to do with Stacy?"

"Stacy told him that Steve was going to divorce Laurel in order to marry her. She also said that she was saving money to take her ex to court with the sole purpose of suing for joint custody of their children. Mr. Bruce was shocked because his ex-wife hadn't shown much interest in parenting before. She'd always focused on herself and hadn't seemed interested in caring for her kids the two weekends a month she had them." Rawlings grew quiet for a moment. "Both Cook and I believe that Mr. Bruce has a very close bond to his children and was very upset over the idea of having them raised by his ex-wife. He claimed she was too narcissistic to look after a goldfish, let alone his son and daughter."

Olivia, who already knew this information, stared at Rawlings. "Sounds like Gordon Bruce had a strong motive for eliminating Stacy."

Rawlings conveyed his irritation with a frown and a brief shrug. "So there you have it. No alibis. Four motives."

"Four?"

"Steve's motive is arguably the weakest, but he could have killed Ms. Balena to keep her from spreading the news of their affair around town. He also could have murdered her out of a deep sense of shame and guilt."

Olivia, who'd finally taken a sip of cappuccino, wiped a bead of froth from her upper lip and scoffed. "I doubt it. I bet he sat home and waited for Laurel to clean up his mess. He's let her shoulder the heavy burdens for years, so I have no doubt that he expected her to sort this out too. Deal with Stacy. Explain things to the kids. Line up therapists. Fix their marriage. She's the strong one, after all."

Suddenly realizing that she was actually painting Steve as an unlikely suspect by pointing out the weaknesses in his character, Olivia pressed her lips together and faced the harbor.

"Though I tend to agree with your line of reasoning, we can't rule Steve out," Rawlings said. "Lastly, there's Mr. Bruce's brother-in-law, Mr. Vonn. Mr. Vonn treated a female companion to dinner at the Bayside Crab House of all places. When asked why he dined so far from home, seeing as he lives in New Bern, he surprised us by saying that he sometimes comes to town to eat and to attend AA meetings with his brother-in-law. He hasn't gone through the program himself, but he supports Gordon's efforts to stay sober. Mr. Vonn met his dinner date at one of these meetings. This was their first date, and according to both Mr. Vonn and the lady in question, there was no chemistry. They parted after the meal with no hard feelings."

Olivia frowned. "What kind of man picks up women at AA meetings?"

"I wondered about that too, so I asked Mr. Vonn exactly how often he comes to town with his brother-in-law," Rawlings said. "When pressed, he claimed that it was less than once a month and that Fred Yoder could back up the veracity of his statement."

"Fred?" Olivia repeated. Suddenly, the memory of Gordon Bruce and a third man leaving Fred's antique shop by the back door surfaced in her mind. Had the third man been Arnold Vonn? "What does Vonn look like?"

Rawlings raised his hand to his chin. "He comes up to here on me. Late forties. Dark hair. Close-cropped. Conservative attire. Nice wool slacks. Ironed dress shirt. Expensive watch. Gold pinkie ring. A bit too much cologne."

"Was he wearing a black leather jacket? Olivia asked.

Rawlings's gaze turned sharp. "What do you know?"

"Nothing. But I think I saw Arnold and Gordon together." She told Rawlings about the scene she and Millay had witnessed. "It could be nothing," she said when she finished. "Maybe Arnold was supporting his brother-in-law following his slipup by taking him to a friend from AA. But my gut feeling is that Arnold was the odd man out of the trio, and that Fred wasn't entirely comfortable in his company."

"It's worth looking into," Rawlings said. "I can ask Fred casually. He doesn't need to know the tip came from you."

Olivia dismissed that idea with a shake of her head. "He'll know, and it won't matter, as he's already upset with me. I'm going to have to repair things with him when this is all over if he'll let me."

"It's Christmastime." Rawlings slid his arm around Olivia's waist. "We should all try to believe in miracles."

The next day, the Bayside Book Writers met at Through the Wardrobe to spend a little time together before the Christmas flotilla began.

The bookstore was mobbed. Patrons were picking up

last-minute gifts and purchasing books from the large table at the front of the store.

"Smart idea." Rawlings pointed at the table. "Encouraging customers to buy the books that the decorations for the boats are being based on. Way to capitalize on tonight's event. I bet that was Emmett's doing," he said, referring to Olivia's friend and the new manager of Through the Wardrobe.

Harris frowned. "I don't know. Doesn't it spoil the surprise? Take all the magic out of wondering which literary themes the participants have chosen?"

"No," Millay said. "There's a disclaimer on the table sign. See? It says these books would make great flotilla themes. Other than *The Grinch*, which is definitely going to be in the lineup based on the event posters, any of these books or book characters could be out on the water tonight. Your magic is intact, Harry Potter."

The group moved deeper into the store, where they found Laurel and the twins in the children's area. Laurel was talking to Kim while Olivia's niece, Caitlyn, read a book on a beanbag chair, and her nephew, Anders, played in the puppet theater. Laurel's sons were sprawled out on the alphabet rug, each flipping through the pages of a Marvel comic.

Olivia noticed that the other moms stood apart from Laurel and Kim, as though the pair had a contagious disease, and were engaged in bouts of animated whispering. They kept ogling Laurel and her boys until Olivia didn't think she could stand it for another second.

"I got this," Millay said, giving Olivia a coy wink.

Olivia nodded. There was no one she trusted more to address a slight.

"Could I help any of you ladies?" Millay asked the group of women in a bright singsong voice. "Maybe I could recommend a few titles for you?"

The women eyed Millay's black-and-blue hair, pierced brow, black clothing, and spiky leather thigh-high boots and demurred. They'd already begun turning away from her when she flashed them a dangerous Cheshire cat smile.

"No, really, I have some great suggestions for all of you. How about a book called *Judging Another Person When I Have No Idea What's Really Going On*? Or how about this one: *Let's Gossip About a Good Person Who's Going Through a Hard Time to Make Myself Feel Better About My Own Imperfect Life*?" Millay threw out her arms. "Any takers?"

The women, uncomfortable now, started gathering their children in an attempt to escape Millay's accusatory gaze and maniacal smile.

"Okay, I can see I'm missing the mark." Millay tapped her chin, feigning deep thought. "How about *Shallow Suburbanites: The Art of Deserting Your Friends When They Need You Most*?"

"Mommy?" a little girl asked a woman in jeans and a Christmas sweater. "What's the lady with the blue hair talking about?"

Instead of answering, the woman grabbed her daughter by the arm and led her out of the children's section.

Millay shot Olivia an apologetic look. "Sorry. I might have cost you a bunch of sales just now."

Olivia waved her off. "I haven't really thought of the bookstore as partially mine since Charles took off for New York. I didn't even realize I've been avoiding coming here until I walked in tonight." She grinned at Millay. "But I wouldn't have missed *that* performance for the world."

"Me either." Harris beamed at Millay. "Can I treat you to coffee for coming up with the best on-the-fly titles I've ever heard?"

Millay laughed. "Let's all get something hot. It's almost time to head down to the docks."

Laurel, who'd been too focused on her conversation with Kim to catch what Millay had said to the other women, now joined her friends. "What was that about?"

"I'm practicing being a bookseller in case my author career doesn't pan out," Millay said.

"Not going to happen," Rawlings argued. He then turned to Laurel. "Would the boys like hot chocolates for the road?"

She smiled. "Naturally. With tons of whipped cream and chocolate drizzles. I told Kim we'd get some for Caitlyn and Anders too. Afterward, we can all walk down to the harbor together."

The five friends left the bookshop side of the newly renovated store by passing through a massive wardrobe made of steel. When they entered the café section, it became apparent that they'd be waiting in line for a long time.

"We're going to be watching the flotilla from the lighthouse at this rate," Harris grumbled. After a few minutes of waiting, he gave Rawlings a nudge. "So, do you get a better viewing spot for this event because you're the police chief?"

Rawlings shook his head. "Temporary viewing platforms have been erected only for those with disabilities. Besides, I'm off duty. I'm just an average citizen enjoying an evening out with his friends and his best girl."

Though Rawlings's reply sounded genuine enough, Olivia couldn't help wondering if his willingness to fraternize with Laurel would have changed had he been on duty. Though he wasn't in charge of Stacy Balena's murder investigation, he was still very much involved with the case. Then again, so was Harris. Were both men really seeing her purely as a friend or were they studying her—on the sly—as a suspect?

This is what lack of trust does, Olivia thought. *It drives wedges between people. Creates fissures. And over time, relationships crumble like a sand castle in a storm.*

"Don't worry, Harris," Olivia said as the Bayside Book Writers took their place at the end of the line. "I might not have an official title, but I've arranged a special viewing spot for all of us. We'll have to pile in our cars and drive closer to the water, but you won't be disappointed."

When her friends stepped out onto the upper deck of the Bayside Crab House to the welcome blast of outdoor heaters and the inviting sight of a row of cushioned chairs, they burst out into spontaneous applause.

"I fixed a light supper," her half brother announced. Hudson appeared on the deck wearing an apron emblazoned with the text: YOUR OPINION WAS NOT ON THE MENU. "Chowder and homemade bread. It's being served in take-out containers so we can eat outside and toss everything in the trash can when we're done. There's beer in the cooler in the corner and I've got a big thermos of coffee and another with hot cider on the far table. Kim's going to make some of her famous white hot chocolate for the kids to go with the peppermint sticks Olivia has for them."

Olivia swatted her half brother. "That was supposed to be a surprise!"

"Oh, so I shouldn't tell them about the *other thing* either, should I?" he asked in a false whisper.

Dallas was immediately intrigued. "What other thing?"

"Ms. Limoges put together flotilla gift bags for all the kids," Kim explained. "Caitlyn and Anders, would you show the boys to my office? Your aunt hid them somewhere back there."

"Cool, a treasure hunt!" Dermot exclaimed, and the four kids raced back inside the restaurant.

When Olivia saw that Laurel had tears in her eyes, she raised a warning finger. "Don't do that. I want you to try to savor a few moments of happiness with your sons. Do you hear me?"

"Aye-aye, Captain," Laurel said, performing a mock salute.

Olivia was delighted by the gesture, for it showed that Laurel hadn't lost her spunk.

"Where's the real captain, by the way?" Harris asked, glancing around the deck. "It's so weird to see you without him, Olivia."

"I called the organizers and asked if there would be fireworks or anything like that," Olivia explained. "Haviland's grown sensitive to loud noises, and while the people in charge wouldn't tell me exactly what kind of pyrotechnics to expect, they dropped enough hints that I decided to leave my oldest friend at home."

"I left my husband at home. You left Haviland at home," Laurel said to Olivia. "I know who we'll miss more."

Millay, who'd helped herself to a bottle of beer from the cooler, paused in the act of opening it. Though she seemed momentarily paralyzed by Laurel's remark, she quickly recovered when Laurel gave her a thumbs-up sign. Using her key chain, Millay gestured to the east. "Good thing you made that decision, Olivia. The first ship is heading our way, and if my eyes aren't deceiving me, the lead boat appears to have a *Polar Express* theme. I bet they'll broadcast some kind of shrill whistle. Dogs all over Oyster Bay will be howling their lungs out."

"I'd better call the kids," Laurel said as the enormous schooner leading the flotilla came closer.

Traditionally, all kinds of vessels were enlisted to form Oyster Bay's Christmas flotilla, but the general rule was the bigger the better. After all, each boat was decorated with thousands of lights strung together to form recognizable shapes. These shapes were often animated. And while the theme changed every year, one thing didn't, and that was the creativity of the participants.

The children burst out onto the deck with a chorus of gleeful shouts and quickly pressed the binoculars Olivia had put in their gift bags to their eyes.

It was magical to see a train made entirely of lights moving around a circular track in what seemed like the middle of the air. In truth, the track was built along the ropes erected between the bowsprit, masts, rigging, and booms.

"It looks like it's floating!" Anders cried breathlessly.

In addition to the train, pale blue snowflakes glittered against a background of sails covered by thousands of white lights. This picture was reflected in the water so that it looked as if there were two trains on a field of snow—all made of dazzling light.

When the schooner reached the midway point of the docks, the audio portion of the show began. As Millay had correctly predicted, the *chug-chug* of a steam engine hard at work reverberated across the harbor, followed by a high-pitched whistle.

"I thought *The Grinch* was supposed to be first," Caitlyn said, looking to her mother for an explanation.

"Me too," Kim replied, handing her daughter a cup of soup. She then pursed her lips and whispered, "Do you think his boat sprang a leak?"

Caitlyn's mouth curved into a reserved smile. "I hope not. He's the best character in that story."

"Other than his dog, of course," Olivia added.

Following *The Polar Express* schooner came four boats representing Charles Dickens's *A Christmas Carol*. The first vessel, a luxury powerboat, portrayed the Ghost of Christmas Past. Victorian figures—made completely of lights—danced on the deck or trimmed a giant Christmas tree. The second ship, the Ghost of Christmas Present, featured more Victorian revelers. This time, the figures of light were scattered around the deck of a barge. The scene was set up as an outdoor market, and the various merchants and animals delighted the children.

"I love the pig!" Anders shouted.

"Yeah, he'd make lots of bacon," Dallas said.

At the very back of the barge, Tiny Tim rode on his father's shoulders. He held a crutch in one hand and waved his cap with the other.

The next boat looked as though it had come from the salvage yard. Its mast was broken and there were several holes in its hull. The Ghost of Christmas Yet to Come was more like a Halloween display than a Christmas scene. Ghosts drifted out of the cavities in the hull, and tombstones bobbed up and down in an eerie floating graveyard tended by a spectral undertaker. The sounds of haunting cries and wails, along with the rattling of chains, echoed across the water, and when Olivia shot a worried glance at Laurel, she could see that her friend seemed hypnotized by the horrifying noises.

Finally, the last boat of the *Christmas Carol* scene went by, and it showed the merry meal shared by Ebenezer Scrooge and the Cratchit family. Olivia had no idea where the decorators of this boat had found outdoor light displays of so many different kinds of food, but she was particularly fond of the wine decanter that constantly refilled itself as well as the tiered cake plate. The cakes and buns on the plate seemed to vanish one by one, only to reappear seconds later.

"Now, that's Christmas magic," she whispered to Rawlings.

After the *Christmas Carol* group came boats showcasing *Miracle on 34th Street*, "The Gift of the Magi," *Olive, the*

Other Reindeer, and *The Mitten*. Last, "'Twas the Night Before Christmas" was represented by a magnificent tall ship. In the bow, children slept while a light show of various candies danced above their beds. Santa's sleigh, complete with animated reindeer, flew from the highest mast while the father in his nightcap gazed out of an open window.

"Is it over?" Anders asked.

Rawlings shook his head. "Not quite. Look! Here comes the star of the show!"

The Grinch—or a man wearing an illuminated Grinch costume—zipped in and out of the tall ship's wake as he piloted a sleek speedboat. Suddenly, he accelerated, and when his boat passed by the tall ship in front of him, the sparkling candy canes hanging from the hull winked out.

The crowd booed.

The Grinch repeated this behavior along the length of the flotilla until all the Christmas lights on every ship went dark and the crowd was shouting and hissing at the green creature spinning his boat in circles on the water.

And then the famous chorus of the Whos of Whoville rang out. The Grinch eased his throttle back and listened. For a long moment, he didn't move. Suddenly, he reached into a sack and pulled out a Santa hat. Donning the hat, the Grinch raced back down the flotilla line, relighting the lights and signaling the launch of the grand finale: a burst of red, green, and yellow fireworks.

"That was awesome!" Laurel's twins declared in unison when the show was over.

Olivia and Laurel exchanged smiles, and for that moment, Olivia did believe in the possibility of miracles.

The feeling was short-lived, however. After thanking Hudson for the delicious food, the Bayside Book Writers began to disperse. Laurel needed to get the boys home to bed, and Millay had to start her shift at Fish Nets.

"Why don't you pull up a stool at my bar?" Olivia heard her ask Harris. "You can tell me how things are going with Emily."

"They're going nowhere," Harris answered in a hushed voice. "I told her this wasn't a good time for her to visit. And even though I tried to assure her that it had nothing to do with our relationship, she got really upset. She's not speaking to me right now."

Millay clapped him on the back. "The holidays bring out the best in people, don't they? Come on, first round's on me."

Olivia and Rawlings said good night to their friends and headed for the Range Rover. They hadn't made it very far when a familiar figure emerged from the shadows and latched onto Rawlings's arm.

"Chief!" Fred Yoder could barely get the word out. With his hands on his knees, he sucked in great gulps of air before continuing. "I don't have my phone, but when I saw Olivia's car . . ." He stopped and began again. "There's a body. It's Gordon. He's in the water by the fishing docks. God, I think he's dead!"

"Show me," Rawlings said.

Fred turned away from the twinkling parade of boats and led them into the darkness.

Chapter 11

The ocean and the sky, at one and the same time: the one is a tomb; the other is a shroud.

—VICTOR HUGO

*O*ne suspect down, was Olivia's unfeeling thought as she and Rawlings followed Fred to the fishing docks.

"What were you doing here, Fred?" Rawlings asked. "Watching the Christmas flotilla?"

"No. I haven't been feeling the holiday spirit lately." Fred's voice was low and heavy with sorrow. "Between worrying about Gordon and dealing with Duncan's diabetes, the last thing on my mind was bundling up to spend a December night with a bunch of families. I don't need a Christmas flotilla to remind me that all I have in this world is my dog and a few people I call friends." He paused, and in a near croak added, "And now one of them is dead."

Guilt made Olivia's cheeks grow warm. She considered herself to be one of Fred's friends, but she wasn't focusing on how he was feeling at this moment. Even now, as she silently followed Fred and Rawlings toward Gordon Bruce's body, she hoped that Gordon's death would somehow exonerate

Laurel—that perhaps Gordon had felt compelled to take his own life because of what he'd done to Stacy. It was a terrible and cruel thing to wish, but Gordon Bruce wasn't her friend. Laurel was.

As they walked, Olivia thought back on all the times she'd read and critiqued Laurel's writing, listened to her musings and worries, met her for lunch, gone shopping with her, and witnessed the shenanigans of her twins. Though Laurel's boundless energy and optimism could get on Olivia's nerves, it was also what Olivia admired most about her. In short, she loved her friend, and her freedom meant more to her than the pain Gordon Bruce's death might cause Fred or Gordon's family.

By this point, the three of them were the only people on the street running along the edge of the harbor. Though the night was quiet, their footfalls were muffled by the sound of the water lapping against the dock pilings, and none of them spoke. It wasn't until they reached the dock where the shrimp boat captains tied their trawlers that Fred's step faltered.

Rawlings put a hand on Fred's shoulder. "If this is too difficult, you can just tell me where Mr. Bruce is and I'll find the way. I don't want to cause you more grief."

This is why he's a better person than me, Olivia thought, looking to Fred to see how he'd respond to Rawlings's kindness.

"I'm man enough to admit that it's a shocking sight," Fred said hoarsely. "And I don't want to see him again—not like that—but I can get you close enough to the place. It's the least I can do. Especially since I wasn't there for him when it mattered. I wasn't there . . ."

"Are you referring to the night Mr. Bruce consumed alcohol after he'd managed to maintain his sobriety for such a long time?" Rawlings asked.

Fred said nothing.

"Did he reach out to you? And you were unavailable?" Rawlings persisted. "Is that why you feel responsible?"

Again, there was no answer from Fred.

"Were you his sponsor?" Olivia asked gently.

"I used to be" was Fred's laconic reply.

"I only have a basic understanding of how AA works, but if Gordon had another sponsor, isn't that who he's supposed to call when he's in a bad way?"

"Yes, but you don't have to be a sponsor to be a friend!" Fred snapped. "I get what it's like to want to drink until you go numb, okay? Gordon wanted to speak with me because his sponsor wasn't answering his phone. I was the backup. The thing is, you have to be in a good place to have the patience and clarity to talk an alcoholic down from a ledge, and I wasn't in a good place when Gordon called. Because of that, I let him leave a message on my voice mail instead."

As Fred's feet struck the uneven boards of the fishing docks, his step faltered.

"This is far enough. You can direct me verbally from here," Rawlings assured him, and then gave Olivia a stern look. "You stay with Fred."

Fred pointed to a trawler tied at the end of the dock. "He's in the water. By the stern. He told me that he was bringing his family to watch the show tonight—that he had to do something to take his mind off being questioned by you and your men. I know about alcohol blackouts. About losing chunks of time. I knew why Gordon was so scared, but I also knew that he wasn't the same guy who'd once been arrested for assault. He'd put his house in order. He'd found faith and sought treatment for his anger issues. He'd married a good woman. He became a great dad. Gordon worked hard at his practice, coached a Little League team, and joined a bowling league. He'd gone for years without a drink and for years without losing control of his temper. I don't believe—not for a second—that he murdered his ex-wife."

Olivia swung around to face him. "Do you think Laurel killed her?"

"She had a damn good reason," Fred retorted defensively. "Gordon was used to Stacy's crazy behavior. To her bad parenting decisions and her selfishness. If he hadn't changed, he would have murdered her years ago!" He made a visible effort to calm down. "The truth is that no, I don't believe Laurel killed anyone. She just doesn't seem capable of such an act. No matter how justified she might have been. I can't make sense of what happened, but I guess no one can. Merry Christmas, eh?"

Olivia would have liked to explain that Laurel also suffered memory loss—though her blackouts were a symptom of trauma instead of alcohol—as a way of reconnecting with Fred. But she suspected Rawlings might react unfavorably to her sharing this information.

As Rawlings walked farther down the dock toward the trawler, Olivia turned to Fred and said, "I should have trusted you. I haven't been this frightened since I was a little girl, and I don't know how to handle it. Whenever I try to help Laurel, I hurt other people I care about. Like you. And Harris. And I've been pushing Rawlings away too. I'm really sorry."

Fred hung his head. "I'm the one who should be apologizing. I had my doubts about contacting Arnold Vonn to repair Rachel's Hummel. Still, I try to avoid dealing with Vonn. I've been in the business a long time and I know which dealers are fair and which ones are legalized crooks. Vonn fits the latter category."

"Is Arnold Vonn involved in Stacy's murder? Or Gordon's?" Olivia asked, recalling the day Gordon and Arnold left Fred's shop. There'd been genuine warmth between Gordon and Fred, but Fred had been noticeably reserved with Arnold. "Fred," Olivia prodded. "What were Gordon and Arnold doing at Circa the day Millay and I came to help you research the antique jewelry?"

Olivia tried to read Fred's expression, but the docks were poorly lit and Fred's face was cast in shadow.

"Vonn plans to open a third jewelry store and they wanted to know if I'd be an investor," Fred said. "I turned them down. Even if I liked and trusted Arnold, which I don't, I wouldn't have said yes, because it's not a good idea for AA sponsors to be financially involved with their sponsees. And though I'm Gordon's former sponsor, he continues to view me as a mentor—probably because I'm nearly two decades older."

Rawlings was using the flashlight mode on his smartphone to examine something on the dock. He abruptly stopped and both Fred and Olivia stared in silence as Rawlings's camera flash momentarily lit up the darkness.

"Did you have any idea they were going to approach you about investing?"

"None," Fred said. "In fact, it's been months since Gordon and I attended a meeting together. The last time we did, he seemed really preoccupied, and though we chatted a bit, we didn't really *talk*."

Olivia had yet to understand why Fred's connection to Gordon and Arnold meant that he owed her an apology.

"The cavalry's here," Fred said, pointing toward the street.

After turning to see two police cars and an ambulance heading their way, Olivia was grateful that they'd opted not to use their sirens. Their flashing lights were bad enough.

When the vehicles came to a sudden halt, the rotating lights made the scene instantly surreal, as if they were all trapped inside a nightclub with an oversize disco ball. Except there was no music. Only the rhythmic slap of water against wood. And there were no people dancing. Just rows of boats bobbing gently in the current.

The night's quiet was swiftly violated. Radio crackles, raised voices, the wheels of a gurney going *thump, thump, thump* over the dock planks filled the air with a frenetic energy that felt incongruent with the surroundings.

Fred shrank back from the incoming tide of personnel, but Olivia craned her neck, hoping to catch a glimpse of a clue or a piece of evidence that might indicate what or, more important, who had killed Gordon Bruce.

Without consciously thinking about it, she moved forward, following the last policeman. It was only when Rawlings caught her by the arm that she realized she'd made it as far as the trawler's bow.

"You can't be here," Rawlings said sternly.

Olivia shot a quick glance at the still-unoccupied gurney and then pivoted her body. "I know. Sorry." She pointed to where Fred stood, huddled against a tall piling. It looked as though he was seeking refuge in the shadows. "He's in shock. We should get him a warm blanket and some coffee."

"He'll have to wait until we get to the station," Rawlings said. "You can drop us off and then go home. I'll get a lift home from an officer when I'm done, and I expect to be very late, so don't wait up."

Rawlings was angry. And while Olivia didn't believe that his anger was primarily directed at her, she knew that a good bit of it was. After all, she'd deliberately withheld information from him. Even so, she was unaccustomed to being the target of Rawlings's ire and she didn't like how that made her feel. Her innate reaction was to be defensive, but she quelled her instinct and mutely nodded.

After pausing to confer with Cook at the street end of the dock, Rawlings returned with Olivia's car. He put the Range Rover in park and signaled to Olivia.

"You sit in the front," Olivia told Fred. "The chief will blast the heater and warm you up." She noticed that he'd taken on that glassy-eyed, slack-jawed look of shock she'd seen far too often as of late.

The trio rode to the station in silence. At one point, Rawlings turned on the radio, but the Christmas music was so painfully cheerful that Olivia instantly asked him to switch it off.

"I used to dread this season," Fred said. "Back when I drank, it was always the worst time of the year. I'd try to hide from my loneliness at the bottom of a bottle, but it only made things worse. Being sober doesn't make life magically better, but I can find positives about the holidays now. My business booms between Thanksgiving and Christmas. I'm invited to friends' parties as the charming, witty bachelor with the cute dog. And on nights without parties, I often go to meetings and listen to other people who feel the same way I feel. We have cookies and coffee, and for a few hours we keep each other company."

Olivia was surprised by Fred's admission. Before falling in love with Rawlings, she'd been content living alone. She'd had Haviland, her friends, and her businesses to occupy her time, and her life had felt both rich and full. She also hadn't known how incomplete her existence was until Rawlings came along, but Fred was clearly more in touch with his feelings than Olivia had ever been with hers.

If I don't hear Fred's story now, I'll have to wait until

tomorrow, she thought, and wondered just what question to ask to keep him talking.

"I haven't been the friend that you deserve," Olivia said from the backseat. She leaned forward so that Fred could hear her clearly. "I haven't made enough time for you lately, and then when I did come visit, I immediately begged a favor. I brought you that stupid Hummel. You would have told any other customer that it absolutely had to be shipped out, right? But you knew that I wanted to get this done for Laurel, so you tried to make it happen for me. Did I put you in a compromising position? Did you end up owing Arnold Vonn a favor in return for a quick repair job on Rachel's figurine?"

Rawlings kept his eyes on the road, but Olivia knew that his ears were pricked.

"I owe him, but not because of the Hummel." Fred was clearly struggling to get the words out. "Years ago, he covered for me when I made a mistake. I'm not a jewelry guy, okay? I've never really dealt in it because it's not my area of expertise. I can identify what's an antique and what's not and do a decent job of appraising antique pieces, but gems and jewelry aren't my cup of tea. I've always avoided dealing in the stuff because dealers are incredibly susceptible to fakes, robberies, and swindlers. Thanks, but no, thanks."

Fred shook his head and stopped talking. He was quiet for so long that Olivia feared he wouldn't continue. Eventually, he resumed his narrative. "However, there were instances when I'd buy entire estates. Sometimes I did this to acquire a few killer pieces of furniture or valuable pieces of art. In general, I'd cherry-pick certain items to sell in the shop and give the leftovers to a local auction company to sell. Typically, I made out nicely with this plan."

"I sense an exception coming," Olivia said.

"Yes, indeed. And it came in the form of a gold charm bracelet." Fred seemed relieved to be sharing his story. "This piece was part of an estate I purchased. There wasn't much jewelry and most of it was vintage costume stuff, which I sold directly to a friend of mine in Chapel Hill. I held the bracelet back because I thought it was from the Victorian era and that I could probably ask a couple thousand dollars for it."

Rawlings whistled.

Fred responded with a caustic snort. "If I'd been correct, that would have been nice. But I wasn't correct. The bracelet was wrong. Only some of the charms had a hallmark I recognized. The chain itself wasn't stamped. I didn't find this too unusual because antique jewelry isn't always marked and I'm not familiar with all the hallmarks. I recognize the standard fourteen- or eighteen-K symbols and other common stamps, but that's it. I did some basic research and came up dry. So I based the price on a similar bracelet that had sold at Skinner's in Boston, and a judge from New Bern bought it for his wife as a Valentine's gift."

"Oh dear," Olivia murmured.

"Exactly," Fred said. "The wife brought the bracelet to Arnold's to be resized. It took his repairman all of five minutes using one of those gold testing machines to conclude that the chain and half of the charms were made of gold fill instead of solid gold."

Rawlings cast a puzzled glance at Fred. "What does that mean?"

"Gold fill is gold that's bonded to a base metal such as sterling silver or brass. It's a durable material but not nearly as valuable as solid gold," Fred explained. "And it also meant that the bracelet wasn't Victorian. Some of the charms were, but the piece was *wrong*, to use the vernacular of my world.

I should never have offered it for sale. And because I sold it as a genuine gold Victorian bracelet, I broke the law."

"And Arnold Vonn deduced that the bracelet came from your shop?" Olivia guessed.

Fred nodded. "He immediately called to tell me what a huge mistake I'd made and how this judge was going to string me up if I didn't make amends. So I contacted the judge, confessed my error, and returned his money. All I know is that I owed Vonn for giving me the chance to put things right. He could have told that judge's wife that she'd been swindled and left it at that."

"Very gentlemanly," Rawlings said without conviction. "But what of the judge's wife? Did Vonn's repairman complete the work on her bracelet or did he refuse to work on the piece because it was, as you put it, *wrong*?"

"I don't know," Fred replied after a lengthy pause. "I was so preoccupied with staying out of jail that I never asked. After I returned the money to the judge and he assured me that he didn't plan on pressing charges because he believed I hadn't intentionally cheated him, I felt so grateful to Arnold that I sent him a fruit basket and a thank-you note. As for me, I tried to forget about that damn bracelet and I vowed never to deal in jewelry again. If it's part of an estate, I just send it straight to auction. That way, it's not my problem."

Fred's tale had taken up the entire ride. By the time he was done, Rawlings was pulling up to the police station.

"What does this have to do with your owing me an apology?" Olivia asked softly. "My takeaway from your story is that this mistake, for which you made amends, put you in Vonn's debt. And despite the fact that he saved your reputation and possibly helped you avoid criminal charges, you dislike and distrust the man. I don't get it. I also don't understand where I, or Rachel's Hummel, fit into the narrative."

Rawlings put the Range Rover in park but kept the engine running. Fred unclicked his seat belt and pivoted to face Olivia. She tensed, wondering what sort of blow he was about to deliver.

"When I called Vonn to ask about repairing the Hummel, I explained the urgency of the situation," Fred said. "He told me to bring the piece to his New Bern store, but that he couldn't make any promises because his jewelers were already overbooked. When I was in the back room talking to the man who could repair the Hummel, I noticed a familiar-looking pendant. I couldn't remember where I'd seen it, but I had this strong feeling that it had been in the local paper or in one of my antique journals or what have you."

"Was it stolen?" Olivia asked in a near whisper.

Fred spread his hands. "It was just a niggling feeling at the time. It wasn't until I got back to my shop that I remembered where I'd seen the pendant. The *Gazette* had run a short piece about items taken from Mrs. Bertrie's home during her illness. A woman working for the cleaning service Mrs. Bertrie used was arrested after authorities discovered that she'd stolen several bottles of Mrs. Bertrie's prescription drugs. However, they never found any of the missing jewelry in her possession, and those items remained at large."

"What made the pendant so memorable?" Rawlings asked. "You said that you weren't interested in jewelry."

Fred laughed. "I might not want to deal in it, but I still appreciate beautiful or unique pieces. Any item that has a story to tell is of interest to me. And this piece had a story to tell. It was a 'lover's eye' pendant." Seeing the blank look on Rawlings's face, Fred went on to elaborate. "It was a popular fad during the Georgian period to have the eye of a loved one—usually, a lover—painted on a pendant, ring, or brooch. The idea was that the lover would always be close—a likeness captured in the jewelry. Often, a lock of hair was added to the piece as well."

Olivia grimaced. "Sounds a little gruesome. Like mourning jewelry."

"That was the custom of the times." After casting a quick glance at the façade of the police station, Fred hurried to complete his narrative. Turning to Rawlings, he said, "In retrospect, I should have called you to report my suspicions, but I was beholden to Vonn. Plus, I wasn't positive that the lover's eye was Mrs. Bertrie's. When you sent me those photographs, however, I started to get a bad feeling that the rumors about Vonn weren't just rumors—that *someone* in our area was responsible for stealing antique jewelry from the elderly." He focused on Olivia again. "If I'd spoken up about that lover's eye pendant earlier, Laurel might have avoided a night in jail. I'm so sorry."

Olivia squeezed Fred's shoulder. "You had a hunch, but you knew nothing for certain. If you falsely accused Vonn and ended up being wrong, you'd have made a powerful enemy." She looked at Rawlings. "You interviewed Vonn and didn't have enough evidence to hold him. Could Fred help you find a way to link Vonn to these robberies? What about to the murders?"

Rawlings made a "slow down" motion with his hand. "The investigation into Mr. Bruce's death is just beginning, Olivia. After I speak with Fred, I'll be driving to New Bern to inform Mrs. Bruce of her husband's passing. Like I told you before, it's going to be a long night. Please go home. It'll make me feel better to know that you're getting some rest."

The image of Rawlings waiting on the Bruces' front stoop to deliver his earth-shattering news to Gordon's wife completely derailed Olivia's burgeoning theories on Vonn being a thief and murderer.

After giving Fred a brief hug and making him promise to pick up the phone when she called the next day to see how he was doing, she took Rawlings's place behind the wheel and watched the two men walk into the building.

At home, she fed Haviland and then took a hot shower. She wanted to wash the last hour away, but the effort proved fruitless. Sleep evaded her as well, and it was only when she was finally drifting off that she remembered what was on her calendar for the next day.

Tomorrow was Rachel Hobbs's memorial service.

Olivia didn't hear Rawlings come to bed, but she found him asleep beside her the next morning. Though Olivia wondered if he'd made any headway into Gordon's murder, she wouldn't wake Rawlings just to satisfy her curiosity. He hadn't moved a muscle when she slipped out from under the covers, and he remained as still as stone the whole time she showered and dressed.

When she went downstairs to make coffee, she saw that he'd left her a note saying that he'd gotten home very late and needed to go back into the station the next morning.

Leaving Haviland behind to snooze with Rawlings, Olivia drove into town to breakfast at Grumpy's.

"I saw your car," Millay said, sliding into the seat opposite Olivia. "Thought I'd fortify myself with a pot of coffee before we're subjected to an hour's worth of depressing music and rose-colored memories of Laurel's monster-in-law."

Olivia cracked a smile. "At least we don't have to participate. All we have to do is sit in the back."

"Our presence is our present?" Millay quipped. "I hope

you have something more creative to put under the tree for the chief."

"We don't exchange gifts," Olivia said. "We don't need anything. Instead, we bring things to Caitlyn and Anders and to Rawlings's sister and her family."

Millay seemed surprised. "You don't wrap up anything? Not even a trinket? A little joke present?"

"Well, we *do* give each other one thing. This won't come as much of a surprise, but we mark all occasions with books. We gift-wrap a favorite book, write a personal note inside, and leave it somewhere for the other person to find."

"I like it." Millay nodded in approval. "What did you get Rawlings this year?"

"John Updike's *Rabbit, Run*."

Millay snorted. "That's a heavy read."

"Yes, but a good one. With some beautiful lines too."

Later, when Milton proceeded to the front of the church to give Rachel's eulogy, he stood next to a poster-size photo from his wedding day. The photographer had captured a laughing Milton and a radiant Rachel holding hands on their way to a car festooned with tin cans and a hand-painted congratulations banner.

Olivia's gaze moved from the photograph to where Laurel and Steve sat. Steve clung to Laurel's hand as tears rolled down his cheeks. Laurel's free arm was draped around one of the twins. The other boy was fidgeting with something on his lap. Laurel's face was void of expression.

The only other guests Olivia recognized were Wanda Watts, the hospice nurse who'd cared for Rachel until the bitter end, and the people Olivia had met the day she accompanied Laurel to the meeting at Tidewater Hospice. She remembered Haley, the young aide who'd been doodling for most of the meeting; Jonathan Zemmel, the palliative care doctor; and Lynne Chester, the plump, pushy matron who'd rubbed Olivia the wrong way by implying that Laurel hadn't been a devoted daughter-in-law. Now, however, Olivia felt she might have misjudged Rachel's church friend. After all, Lynne had gone out of her way to assist Milton with the memorial service.

Lynne caught her looking and bobbed her head in solemn greeting. Olivia returned the gesture, doing her best to instill a bit of warmth into it by adding a smile. Lynne had spared Steve, and therefore Laurel, additional stress by organizing this service. Not only had she helped out in that regard, but she'd also been a shoulder for Milton to cry on. At least, that was what Laurel had told Olivia.

"I always thought Lynne was a total shrew," she'd whispered outside the church prior to the service. "But she sacrificed hours of her time to make sure Rachel's final wishes were fulfilled. That's really given Milton a measure of peace. It's the only silver lining I can come up with right now, and it's all thanks to Lynne. Pastor Rhodes has been wonderful too. And I can't believe how many of the hospice people came. I figured, considering how the media have presented me as the scorned woman who killed their coworker, that they'd stay as far away from this service as possible."

"None of the legitimate papers read like that," Millay had said. "Only the rags. And you can't pay attention to them. Next they'll say you were abducted by aliens or that Elvis whispers to you in your sleep."

Laurel had managed a dry laugh. "I might actually get a book deal out of that one. Speaking of which, how's your writing coming along?"

"Better. I'm still going to be late turning it in, but not scary late. I finally told my editor what the deal was last night," Millay had admitted a trifle sheepishly. "It felt good to get it off my chest. She said things slow to a halt in the publishing world over the holidays, so if I needed a little extra time, I could have it. It was such a relief to hear her say that. I should have just been honest with her when I started falling behind, but I felt like a failure. I wanted to just fix things quickly so I'd never have to tell her how much I'd messed up."

"That's not how relationships work," Laurel had said in a leaden voice. "You need to communicate. Trust me, I've learned that the hard way."

Olivia had touched her friend's arm. "Did you hear about Gordon Bruce?"

"Yes, from a colleague at the *Gazette*. One of the few who still speaks to me. Does Gordon's death have anything to do with what happened to *her*?" Laurel's eyes were both hopeful and fearful.

"I don't know," Olivia had said. "Rawlings was still asleep when I left this morning. Has anything come back to you from that night? Anything at all?"

"Only one flash," Laurel had whispered as the mourners began to file into the church. "I saw her car and I pulled my van behind her so she couldn't back out of her spot. I yelled at her. I can't remember exactly what I said, but she got out of her car and I got out of mine. But I made her retreat. Because I remember throwing an empty wine bottle at her car. When it shattered against her window, which was closed, she was back in her car. I remember the expression on her face. She was scared. For the first time since I caught her and Steve in bed, I felt like I was in control. I think . . . I think I laughed. I know I'd had too much to drink, but I think I was really losing it."

Alarmed, Olivia had taken hold of Laurel's arm. "Have you told anyone else about this?" When Laurel shook her head, Olivia said, "Forget about it again, okay? This memory serves no purpose."

"But if I pretend that I haven't remembered, I'll be lying to the police."

"They have the Gordon Bruce investigation to focus on." Olivia had gestured for Laurel to enter the church. "You've already suffered a trial by fire. Let someone else have a turn."

"No more talk of fire," Millay had whispered once Laurel was inside. "We both heard what Laurel said that day in Stacy's house. She wanted to see Stacy burn. She wanted to douse her in gasoline. While she watched. And laughed."

Chapter 12

*There's a convention that one doesn't
speak ill of the dead. That's stupid, I
think. The truth's always the truth.*

—AGATHA CHRISTIE

A select group of mourners had been invited to the Hobbs
condo for refreshments following the service, and though
Olivia had had her fill of whispers, tears, and melancholy
reminiscing, she and Millay felt compelled to attend. Not
only did they want to support Laurel, but they also wanted
to subtly question the other Tidewater Hospice personnel
just in case the Oyster Bay Police Department failed to pin
Stacy's murder on Arnold Vonn.

"Is it common for patients or their families to bestow
expensive gifts on their hospice nurses, doctors, or aides?"
Olivia asked Wanda as the two women sipped hot tea in the
kitchen.

Wanda looked at Olivia as if she had two heads. "Not in
my world. Don't get me wrong. Folks have been grateful.
I've been mentioned in obituaries, and from time to time
the family will give me a token of appreciation. But I'm
talking about a scented candle or a gift card to Applebee's.

That sort of thing. When you say expensive, what exactly are you talking about?"

"Jewelry," Olivia said flatly. "Gold and diamond jewelry."

Wanda guffawed and then, seeing that Olivia was serious, gaped at her. "Honey, we don't save anybody's lives, remember? We just help them pass as peaceably and as painlessly as we can. No one is thanking their Lord and Savior that they'd had to call on us. By the time we show up, there's only one outcome. The question is only how long. Folks don't lavish us with jewels for helping the people they love die. They know we're just there to make things easier on everyone, but seeing somebody you care about leave this earth is hard. No matter what we do, we can't spare the family members pain."

"Your job is so important. And extremely challenging," Olivia said. "I believe we all wish to die well. With dignity. We don't want to tremble in fear. Or cry. Or be petty or vindictive. But who can predict how we'll act? And yet you can take a stranger's hand and offer comfort and reassurance when it's most needed. You also counsel and console the family and friends who will be left behind. All I can say is that you deserve diamonds and gold. Whatever you're being paid, it can't be enough."

Wanda threw her head back and laughed. "I really need to get you to talk to my boss. But come on, now. Tell me what this is all about. Do you know a nurse who got nice jewelry as a thank-you gift? Because I need to find out how they did it!"

"Stacy Balena owned quite a bit of antique jewelry," Olivia said casually. "Expensive stuff. Almost every piece was set with real diamonds too."

"Where'd she get it?" Wanda frowned in confusion. "I've been working way longer than she has and I can barely save up enough to take a decent vacation when my two weeks come due." Suddenly, an idea came to her and she glanced into the living room and whispered, "Was it him? The dentist she was sleeping with? Did he give it to her?"

Olivia shook her head. "Steve didn't buy her gifts. I think he only wanted one thing from Stacy Balena, and she was willing to let him have that without him having to buy her so much as a steak dinner in return."

After shooting a disgusted glance in Steve's direction, Wanda shrugged. "Well, in that case, I can't figure out where she'd get her hands on fancy jewelry. Her folks didn't leave her money and her ex only paid her what he had to for the kids. She wasn't a saver either. She liked to party. Buy clothes. Go to concerts. The girl didn't have a lick of sense. I hate to talk ill of the dead, but for someone who had two kids, she acted like a child. A selfish child." Wanda jerked her thumb in Steve's direction. "Guess that's why she wanted him. A sugar daddy to take care of her."

"But why not just sell the jewelry?" Though Olivia spoke the question aloud, she didn't expect an answer.

"Maybe it wasn't hers to sell," Wanda suggested. "Aren't you married to the chief of police?" Her gaze turned shrewd. "If she stole these things from her patients, it'd be tough to unload them, wouldn't it?"

Olivia nodded. "It would. But you'd think she'd have a bigger problem than that. Patients or their families would file complaints or police reports about the missing jewelry. Have you heard rumors about stolen jewelry at work?"

"Not since I've been with Tidewater," Wanda was quick to say. "At the place I worked before, I heard talk of pills going missing. Never jewelry, though. That's awfully risky. Folks tend to notice when their gold rings disappear, and our director always recommends that anything of value be put away so nobody has to worry about that kind of thing and we can all focus on what's important, which is taking care of the patient."

Having said her piece on the subject, Wanda finished her tea and excused herself. Millay entered the kitchen and reported on her conversation with Haley, the nurse's aide.

"She didn't know squat about the stolen jewelry," Millay grumbled. "The girl is very sweet and as strong as an Olympian—I'll grant her that—but she doesn't seem particularly observant. She just showed up when she was supposed to, did her job, and moved on to her next patient."

"Out of all the staff, you'd think Haley would take note of the most details," Olivia said. "Her tasks require such intimacy. The bathing, the dressing, the range-of-motion exercises, et cetera."

Millay shrugged. "Maybe it's because she doesn't want to be an aide much longer. That's why she's going to nursing school at night. Before she started school, Haley actually hung out with Stacy. They weren't BFFs, but they'd hit the mall or go out for margaritas—that kind of thing. They were close enough that Haley felt confident swearing that Stacy didn't own any diamond jewelry other than the engagement ring Gordon had given her five years ago. And she supposedly sold that for cash."

Olivia started. "I wonder where. At one of Vonn's stores, perhaps? Didn't he once run newspaper ads claiming that he paid more than any other jeweler for used diamonds? That wasn't how it was worded, but that was the gist of the message." She looked around, wondering if there was any reason to linger. Laurel was preoccupied with the twins, who didn't seem particularly sad, but more tired and ill at ease, and Millay was obviously itching to go home and work on her novel.

"You should get going. You have writing to do. I'll stay a little longer," Olivia told Millay. "Maybe Lynne knows something."

Lynne Chester, who'd played the part of the gracious hostess at both the church and here at the condo, was discussing fine art with Pastor Rhodes and Milton.

"Rachel was the real connoisseur," Milton was saying. "I just signed the checks and tried not to think about how many zeros were on them."

Lynne waved her hand around the room. "But you and Rachel chose such beautiful things—what a wonderful legacy to pass on to your grandchildren."

Milton's face clouded over. "My legacy. My legacy is supposed to begin with my son. The man who made Hobbs a household name because of his shameful behavior? I don't know who that person is anymore. I used to. He used to be a good boy. A fine boy. He worked hard. He told the truth. We raised him better than this, Rachel and I."

Pastor Rhodes put his hand over Milton's. "He isn't a bad person, Milton. He's a man who made a mistake. No doubt, he's in great pain over his actions and could use your support and your forgiveness."

"He hasn't asked for it," Milton said gruffly.

The pastor made a noise of understanding. "He needs to ask for his wife's forgiveness first. And he needs to earn it before it can be granted." He gave Milton a patient smile. "Steve and Laurel have a long, rough road to travel, but their family is worth the challenges they'll have to face. Isn't staying together worth it? You and Rachel were married for many, many years. Didn't you experience peaks and valleys?"

Milton nodded. "Sure, but neither of us cheated. And neither of us got arrested for murder. I'm glad Rachel doesn't have to see the fallout from her son's choices. Her passing was a true blessing. She doesn't have to bear the physical or the emotional pain now."

While the pastor murmured words of assurance and comfort, Lynne got up from the table and began to collect the dirty dishes. Seeing a chance to speak with her in private, Olivia jumped in to help.

"You've been very generous with your time," Olivia said to Lynne. Deciding to lay the praise on thick, she continued. "It was so kind of you to lend a hand with the arrangements. I wouldn't know where to start, but it seems like second nature to you."

Puffed up with pride, Lynne said, "I'm a deacon at the church. It's one of my responsibilities to assist with funerals. I also visit the sick and the homebound. It's been my calling since I retired from teaching."

"That's not a call most people would be capable of answering. I can't stand hospitals, for example. Or any place resembling them. And I have no bedside manner at all," Olivia confessed. Abruptly, she switched subjects. "Were you and Rachel close before she became ill?"

"No," Lynne replied honestly. "We didn't see each other regularly enough, because she and Milton didn't live here full-time. I only got to know Rachel after they made this condo their permanent residence."

Olivia proceeded to ask Lynne if Rachel had ever mentioned missing pieces of jewelry.

"Not to me," Lynne said, leaning over to load plates into the dishwasher. "But we mostly spoke of spiritual things. And about her family. Whenever Rachel was down, I just asked her about those grandsons of hers and she'd light up like the sun. She adored those boys, and who could blame her? I wish I had grandchildren of my own. They give a person purpose."

Following Lynne's gaze over the counter and into the living room, Olivia could see that Dallas and Dermot were more than ready to go home. They were both on the sofa, snuggled up against Laurel, and all three were the picture of exhaustion.

"You should tell her to go on home," Lynne said gently. "They're all done in. I can clean up here. I'm going to stop by next week to help Milton box up Rachel's clothes. She had so many lovely things and she was very clear that she wanted to donate everything to the church thrift shop."

"Wow," Olivia said. "Everything? Even her jewelry?"

Lynne looked nonplussed. "Maybe her costume pieces. I'm not sure what will happen with her good things. Since Rachel only had one son and she and Laurel never really got along—"

"That wasn't Laurel's fault," Olivia couldn't keep from blurting. "She's a nice person. Ask anyone. It's almost impossible *not* to get along with Laurel Hobbs." She balled her hands into fists. She was getting off track. It was the jewelry that lay at the heart of Stacy's murder. Olivia was certain of it. This was not the time to defend Laurel's character.

Still, it didn't appear as though Lynne knew much about Rachel's valuable pieces, so Olivia thanked her and walked into the living room.

Squatting in front of Laurel, she put her hands on her friend's knees and whispered, "You look ready to collapse."

"We're going," Laurel said, rousing herself. "Thank you so much for being here. Not just today. Through all of it. These are my roughest seas and you're my lighthouse."

Olivia didn't want to tear up while the twins were watching

her, so she blinked several times until her emotions were in check, tousled the boys' hair, and told Laurel she'd talk to her soon.

Luckily, Milton was just saying good-bye to another guest when Olivia went to the front hall to retrieve her coat.

"Ms. Limoges," he said. "I've been waiting for a chance to speak with you in private. Do you have a minute?"

Olivia felt her blood quicken. What was this about? "Of course," she said.

"I want to show you something in my office," Milton said, and turned toward the hall leading to the bedrooms.

It took a moment for Olivia to fall into step behind Milton. After all, she'd stood in that hallway admiring the Picassos the day she overheard Stacy's strange remark about Steve Hobbs. The memory was not a pleasant one.

Milton's office was a masculine space filled with books, a plump reading chair, and an executive desk. Unlike Steve's desk, it was tidy and uncluttered and held framed photographs of his wife, his son, and his son's family. Opening the top drawer, Milton pulled out an envelope and handed it to Olivia.

"This is an inventory of Rachel's jewelry, complete with photographs and market values at the time. I made this for insurance purposes years ago, but with all that's happened, it completely slipped my mind. I was digging around for another document on the computer when I saw it. I printed out a copy for you."

"Thank you. I appreciate your entrusting me with this," Olivia said.

Though she couldn't wait to rip open the envelope, Olivia had to contain her eagerness until she was back in her car. She was just working her index finger under the flap when someone knocked on her passenger window.

She looked up to see Rawlings pointing at the lock button, signaling for her to let him in.

"This is the last place I expected to see you." Olivia waited until he'd closed the door and settled into the seat before continuing to tear the envelope.

"I knew you'd be here," Rawlings said. "What are you opening with such urgency?"

"A clue, I hope." Olivia pulled out a sheaf of stapled papers. She unfolded them, on top of the center console so that Rawlings had a clear view. "These belonged to Rachel Hobbs," she explained, slowly flipping through the images of necklaces, rings, bracelets, earrings, and watches.

"Where are these pieces now?"

"In a safe-deposit box downtown," Olivia said. "According to this cover sheet, which is addressed to an insurance company, I'd say that Rachel's good pieces were transferred to the bank when she and Milton made Oyster Bay their permanent residence."

Rawlings examined the cover letter. "It's unlikely there was any antique jewelry for Ms. Balena to steal from the condo, then."

"No," Olivia reluctantly agreed. "So it looks like my investigating has brought me to a dead end. Was yours more successful?"

"Successful? Heartrending is more like it. Mrs. Bruce is absolutely devastated. Last night, when Gordon told her that he had to go meet a friend, she feared that he was sneaking off to drink. She said that he'd been acting secretive as of late, which isn't at all like him, and that he seemed troubled. She asked him to talk to her about what was on his mind, but he assured her that it was merely work-related issues at his practice that he'd iron out after the holidays."

Olivia shook her head. "I doubt issues at a chiropractor's

practice led him to a fishing dock on a cold December night. What did his office staff say?"

"They're stunned by his death. Everyone liked and respected Mr. Bruce, but when we took a close look at the books, it appeared that Gordon had recently taken out a substantial loan, borrowing heavily against the practice."

"What was he doing with the money?" Olivia asked.

"Gambling," Rawlings said. "Specifically, online sports betting. It seems that Mr. Bruce exchanged one addiction for another."

Olivia gazed out the windshield. "That's so sad."

"It is," Rawlings agreed solemnly. "Even more so because Mrs. Bruce didn't know."

"She will soon enough," Olivia said, feeling a rush of pity for Gordon's wife. "Did Gordon invest in his brother-in-law's new jewelry shop or was that a lie as well?"

Rawlings grunted. "No, no. He paid his way, fair and square. I guess his teams were winning when he wrote that check to Arnold Vonn."

"Arnold Vonn," Olivia mused aloud. "So many roads lead back to him. Fred spotting that stolen pendant in Vonn's shop. Vonn deals in wedding jewelry, which is almost exclusively diamonds. And Vonn knew at least one of the murder victims. He may have known Stacy too. Or at least known of her. After all, Vonn's sister married Stacy's ex-husband."

"I agree that he appears to be a central player in this drama. Unfortunately, we need concrete proof of his role, and we don't have anything substantial." Rawlings sounded angry. More than angry. He was furious. Tired, frustrated, and furious. "We have no prints, no witnesses, no one admitting to having bought or sold stolen jewelry from Mr. Vonn. We don't have enough to hang a hat on, let alone a murder charge."

Olivia closed her eyes. Two murders within days of each

other. The first threatened to tear Laurel's world apart. The second caused Fred anguish. And now the greed and wickedness of the vile person or persons stealing from the elderly were infecting the lives of Olivia's friends like a debilitating virus.

"Gordon lied to his wife the night of his murder because he needed to get away in a hurry." Olivia turned to Rawlings. "But who would he agree to meet in such a dark and isolated place? It had to be someone he knew and trusted."

"Even if he knew the person, it was a foolish decision. He placed himself in a very vulnerable position, which speaks to me of desperation," Rawlings said. "Mr. Bruce's cell phone isn't helpful either. He received no calls the day of the Christmas flotilla, and his two outgoing calls were to his wife. Of course, Mr. Bruce had spent a number of hours with the Oyster Bay Police as of late, so that might explain his lack of calls." He drummed his fingers on the dashboard. "His killer must have contacted him another way. Harris is looking through Mr. Bruce's e-mails as we speak."

An elderly woman, who Olivia surmised must have been one of the last guests to leave Milton's condo, shuffled over the front lawn to the street. She was bundled up in a floor-length parka, a pink knit hat, and purple mittens. As she made her way to a condo three doors down, another neighbor appeared and hailed the woman. The two exchanged a series of friendly shouts followed by a burst of raucous laughter before disappearing inside their homes.

Those jewel thieves can't take away what matters, Olivia thought. *When these two women are on their deathbeds, they won't care about rings and bracelets. It's their human connections that will have retained the greatest value. The memories of a smile, a touch, a lullaby, a fragrance, a kindness—these things cannot be stolen by another person, no matter how diabolical.*

As much as Olivia wanted to hold on to the feeling the exchange between the pair of old women had filled her with, she couldn't keep the haunted look on Fred's face as he'd stood in the gloom near the fishing dock from surfacing in her mind.

"How did Gordon die?" she asked Rawlings quietly.

"He was struck from behind." Rawlings touched the base of his head. "Here. With a cleat. There's a whole pile of rusty cleats in a wood crate at the end of the dock. The killer somehow coerced Mr. Bruce to kneel, brought the cleat down hard on his skull, and then watched as he pitched forward into the water. The official cause of death was drowning."

Olivia experienced a sudden chill. "That's awful. And cruel. If it's the same killer, then he likes to let the elements do the actual killing for him. Stacy died from smoke inhalation and Gordon died by drowning. Do you think there's anything to be read into a death by fire followed by a death by water?"

"I believe Ms. Balena's killer used fire in order to destroy evidence," Rawlings said. "I'm not ruling out the possibility that we're dealing with a cruel and vindictive individual. However, to take the time to douse the car with gasoline and set it ablaze put the killer at risk. So why do it? Because you've left fingerprints or DNA in that car or on Ms. Balena's person. And the most effective way of eliminating those is with fire."

Olivia considered the phrase "on Ms. Balena's person" and grimaced. "Are you referring to Steve?"

"Yes, but he's not the only possibility. Ms. Balena's killer most likely incapacitated her by injecting her with the morphine from those preloaded syringes we found in the backseat of her car. Imagine my taking you by surprise and injecting the contents of one syringe into your neck." Rawlings pressed a pen against the back of Olivia's neck. "There. You didn't even see that coming. But you'd be ready for the second. You'd put up a struggle. By the third, however, you're going to be too doped to fend me off."

Though this theory made sense to Olivia, she couldn't understand how the murderer had slipped into Stacy's car, injected her with morphine, set the car on fire, and escaped without notice. And how did Laurel fit into this picture? Had the killer snuck into the car while Stacy was watching Laurel wobble back to her minivan?

Unless Laurel remembers more about that night, she won't be able to help, Olivia thought.

"As for the water," Rawlings said, returning to the subject of the elemental theme, "I think the murderer chose the docks because of the event. It gave him or her the chance to hide among the crowd beforehand. They were just a regular person watching the Christmas flotilla until it was time to meet Gordon Bruce."

"Gordon must have been a truly desperate man," Olivia said. "But if he was deep in the hole from gambling debts, and the killer was offering him a way to dig his way out, then I guess he'd have gone anywhere."

Rawlings looked at his watch. "I have to get back. I just needed fifteen minutes to get out of the station. And I wanted to see you." He reached for Olivia's hand. "These cases are hard. Not only because they involve our friends, but because they remind me what people are capable of—the good and the ugly. Being with you helps settle me. Helps me think." He grinned at Olivia and gave her hand an affectionate squeeze. "Now, if I could only learn whether Stacy Balena actually met Arnold Vonn in person, I'd be golden. I'll ask Mrs. Bruce, of course, but if she doesn't know, the lead might be another dead end."

"I might have a theory." Olivia squeezed his hand in return. "Haley, the nurse's aide who cared for Rachel, was friendly with Stacy outside of work. She told me that Stacy pawned the only diamond she ever owned, which was the engagement ring Bruce gave her."

"None of our local businesses buy jewelry with cash, do they?" Rawlings asked.

Olivia knew of only one jewelry store in Oyster Bay. "No," she said with confidence. "They've had so many radio commercials coaxing men to buy their ladies jewelry for Christmas that I could practically recite their policies. They'll accept trade-ins toward a more expensive item. Like deducting the price of your used car against the cost of the new one at a car dealership."

Rawlings gave her an absent nod, his gaze fixed on some point in the middle distance. "I believe it's time for us to question Mr. Vonn's employees, especially while he's tied up with Cook at the station."

"Maybe Millay and I should go on this errand," Olivia suggested. "Harris too. He and Millay could pretend to be a couple shopping for engagement rings while I could be looking for the perfect Christmas gift for my husband. Something expensive. Harris and Millay could visit Vonn's shop in Bayboro and I could pop into the New Bern location."

"How will you raise the subject of a woman who pawned her engagement ring for cash?" Rawlings was clearly dubious. "Who's to say any of the salespeople will remember her? She probably pawned that ring years ago."

Olivia smiled. "I'll ask to work with the clerk with the most experience. I'll also find out who handles the cash trades. When I know that I'm chatting up the right individual, I'll work Stacy into the conversation and see if there's a flash of recognition from the salesperson. That will be enough for us to confirm that Stacy visited the shop to pawn her ring, at the least. At best, one of us will learn that she dealt directly with Arnold Vonn."

Rawlings contemplated this in silence for a full minute. Finally, he seemed to come to a decision. "How will you work Ms. Balena into the conversation when you're supposed to be Christmas shopping?"

"If I've learned anything from Dixie, it's that most people are keen to be in the know when it comes to juicy gossip," Olivia said. "Millay, Harris, and I are from Oyster Bay. All we have to do is act like we have inside knowledge about the murders—maybe dangle an irrelevant detail or two that hasn't appeared in the papers or on TV—and Vonn's employees will be eating out of our hands. Not all of them will lack discretion, but we're still in the South. He who shows up at the holiday party or family gathering with the best story wins."

This elicited a hearty laugh from Rawlings. "All right. I'll ask Cook to give you three the green light. We can't spare Harris for long, so he and Millay will have to work fast."

Recalling Millay's theory that Harris had intended to propose to his girlfriend during her Christmas visit, Olivia said, "Trust me, he is *not* going to want to linger over engagement rings."

Chapter 13

Christmastime ... a kind, forgiving, charitable, pleasant time; the only time I know of, in the long calendar of the year, when men and women seem by one consent to open their shut-up hearts freely.

—CHARLES DICKENS

If Harris balked over being asked to shop for bridal jewelry, it was nothing compared to Millay's reaction.

"Find someone else!" she snapped. "Why should I stop writing to chase some needle-in-the-haystack lead in Bayboro?"

Olivia, who hadn't expected Millay to turn her down, didn't know how to respond. "I need someone smart, crafty, good at reading people, and able to maintain a pretense under pressure. Where am I supposed to find a woman like that in the next five minutes?"

"You have a bounty of waitresses and hostesses at your disposal," Millay said. "Use one of them."

Hearing the anger in Millay's voice, Olivia waited a long moment before speaking again. "Do you feel like I'm using you to help Laurel? That I don't care about you or your work, and that I'd sacrifice both if it meant seeing her exonerated?"

Millay didn't answer.

"Because I can understand why you'd think that," Olivia continued. "Look how I've treated Fred. But I want you to succeed. Maybe more than anyone. More than your parents. More than your other friends. More than your agent, your editor, or your fans. I want you to fly as high as you can fly. I want you to be like Daedalus."

"Wasn't he the Greek guy who got too close to the sun and died because the wax on his wings melted?" Millay was now offended and annoyed.

"That was Icarus, his son," Olivia explained. "Daedalus created the wings to help them escape an island prison. Their only way out was to fly over the ocean like birds, so Daedalus used his inventiveness and courage to fashion wings. He was fearless and brilliant—just like you. And if you need to stay home and write, I get it. But I'm not using you. You want Laurel's freedom as much as I do."

"Of course I do." Millay sighed. "I'm sorry. Honestly, I've been a total wreck lately. Not just about Laurel." Millay was silent for a long moment. "My parents are splitting up. I've known for weeks, and I don't know why I even care," she said defiantly. "It's not like we're close. I guess it just makes me mad—after the endless lectures my mom gave me on being a proper lady—and she's the one who had a boyfriend behind my dad's back for the past *seven* years! Having to deal with this while worrying about Laurel and my deadline has really sucked."

"No wonder you had writer's block."

A strangled laugh echoed through the phone speaker. "Exactly. Tell Harris to pick me up in fifteen minutes. If I'm going to look like his fiancée, I have to dig around in my closet for a hat and some prepster clothes. And, Olivia? Don't tell anyone about my parents. It's Christmas Eve tomorrow and I think we've had enough downers for one holiday season, don't you?"

"Definitely," Olivia agreed.

If the customers entering Vonn's Fine Jewelry in New Bern weren't already in the holiday spirit, the sales associates did their best to put them in the mood.

The shop was festooned with a tasteful display of lights, bows, and greenery, and instrumental holiday music played in the background. Glass jars stuffed with candy canes had been placed on top of every display case, and urns with coffee and hot chocolate had been set out on a side table by a grouping of comfortable chairs.

Olivia hadn't been in the store long before a slim, fresh-faced redhead approached her. "May I help you, ma'am?"

"I'm looking for an associate who worked with a friend of mine," Olivia fibbed. She scrunched up her eyebrows as though trying to remember. "Someone who has been here since the shop first opened. Or else, it was the associate in charge of buying jewelry with cash. Do you know if that would be the same person?"

The redhead pursed her lips. "Kat's been around since we opened. She's the only original employee. She knows more about this place than anyone but Mr. Vonn, but he's off-site, reviewing the plans for our third location."

"I heard that you were expanding." Olivia did her best to sound impressed. "So, is Kat available?"

"She's just finishing up with the couple by the David Yurman counter. I'll get her for you."

The redhead raised her hand in a graceful gesture and Olivia saw a tall, elegant woman with silver hair wave good-bye to a cute couple in their early thirties. The couple walked toward the exit, and Olivia seized her opportunity to catch Kat's eye.

"Happy holidays!" Kat greeted Olivia with a broad smile. "May I assist you?"

"Well, I've never shopped here before," Olivia began doubtfully. "I prefer to buy locally, but our jewelry store doesn't have the selection yours does. I'm from Oyster Bay."

Kat smiled proudly. "We're known for having twice the inventory of other area stores. And you couldn't have picked a better time to stop by. We're offering a special interest-free payment plan just for the holidays."

Olivia gave this a disinterested wave. "I don't use payment plans."

This had the desired effect. Kat gave Olivia a nearly imperceptible nod of respect while subtly noting her wedding band. "Are you shopping for someone in particular?"

"I'm looking for a gift for a friend. Someone who has been through a difficult time," Olivia said. After casting a covert glance to her left and right, she whispered, "Have you heard about the two suspicious deaths in our town?"

Kat's smile slipped a fraction. "Yes. Horrible."

Olivia realized she'd broached the subject too abruptly. "Please forgive me. That was very insensitive. I'd forgotten that Mr. Vonn's brother-in-law was one of the victims. You must have known him."

"He wasn't in the jewelry business, but I'd met him several times," Kat said. "He was a nice man."

"Mr. Vonn must be incredibly upset. I imagine this holiday season will be very difficult for him." Olivia feigned concern. "I hope he has other family or close friends to turn to for comfort."

"Luckily, he has both," Kat said in a voice that made it clear that the subject was now closed.

Taking the hint, Olivia focused on the closest display case, which was filled with men's watches. "My friend is also a victim of this tragedy. It's caused her immense pain and stress. I want to get her something to remind her that she's a wonderful person. I want her to wear this piece of jewelry and, every time she glances at it, remember that she is capable of incredible feats. That nothing in the world can diminish her."

Kat must have sensed the sincerity behind Olivia's speech, because the smile she gave Olivia was replete with warmth. "You and your friend must share a unique bond. Are you thinking of a ring, bracelet, or necklace?"

Olivia pictured Laurel's charm bracelet. It now sat in a police evidence bag, but even when it was returned to Laurel, would she want to wear it again? Olivia doubted it. That bracelet would forever trigger horrible memories for Laurel. It was likely she would simply ask Rawlings to dispose of it for her.

"A bracelet," Olivia said. "I'd like to replace one given to her by another friend. It had special meaning, but it's gone now. I don't want any charms. Something simple, elegant, beautiful, and strong. Just like my friend."

"Lovely," Kat said, her attention fixed on the items in the display case. "Do you have an idea what you'd like to spend?"

Olivia shook her head. "That isn't how I shop. Finding the right piece is paramount over cost."

Again, she received a nod from Kat. "Is your friend a yellow gold or white gold wearer?"

"Neither. She prefers platinum."

"And her eyes?"

Olivia wasn't sure why Laurel's eye color was relevant, but she deferred to Kat's expertise. "Blue. Like a summer sky."

"And your friend has been through a time of trial. She needs to get back on her feet—to believe in herself again. So we're looking for a piece that speaks of courage, fortitude, hope, self-love, peace, and wisdom, and it sounds like a dose of power wouldn't hurt either. Did I hear you correctly?"

All Olivia could do was murmur in amazed assent. This woman was good.

"In that case, might I suggest a bracelet set with aquamarines? It's said that each gemstone has a meaning. The words I just used describe the aquamarine. It's one of my favorite gems because of its connection to the sea."

Olivia liked Kat more and more by the minute. "I love the ocean too. Can you show me some examples with aquamarines?"

"We have an impressive selection across the room." Kat waved at the far side of the store. "If you'd care to help yourself to a cup of coffee, I'll take out the pieces that I have in mind."

Sensing this was how Kat worked best, Olivia meandered over to the coffee urn. Instead of pouring a cup, she sent a text to Harris to see how he and Millay were doing. When he didn't reply, Olivia headed back to Kat.

The veteran saleswoman had placed three bracelets on a black velvet pad. The first was a bangle covered in tiny square-cut aquamarines. It was dainty, but underwhelming. The third piece was set with oval aquamarines and natural pearls. It was very classy, but a bit old-fashioned. The middle bracelet, however, was exactly what Olivia wanted. Five bezel-cut aquamarines in the same shade of blue as Laurel's eyes were perfectly spaced on a delicate platinum chain. The bracelet was timeless elegance.

"This is it," she said to Kat. "May I have it gift wrapped?"

"Certainly." Kat beckoned to the redhead, who darted forward to collect the bracelet.

After Olivia handed Kat her credit card, she said, "We

can settle up for my friend's gift now, but I'd also like to take a look at the men's watches if you have time."

"I'd be delighted to continue assisting you." Kat rang up the bracelet, chatting with Olivia as though they were old friends throughout the exchange.

Taking advantage of their newfound camaraderie, Olivia made a sweeping motion around the store and asked, "Do most people take advantage of the payment plan or do some of your customers trade in old pieces toward the price of new ones?"

"A bit of both," Kat replied amiably.

"Do you pay cash for their pieces?" Olivia continued. "Even if they don't wish to purchase any jewelry from the store?"

Kat presented Olivia with the credit card slip to sign. "We used to, but we don't do that anymore. Mr. Vonn felt that the practice created a pawnshop atmosphere, and his goal was to establish the most tasteful and refined jewelry-buying experience in all of coastal North Carolina." She smiled. "Shall we head over to the watch case?"

"We should. But first, I want you to know exactly why I'm asking you these odd questions," Olivia said. "Normally, I wouldn't be this blunt, but I really appreciate the assistance you've given me today. You did more than sell me a piece of jewelry. You listened to me so attentively. Please listen to me for a little longer."

Though Kat looked dubious, she said, "All right."

"Mr. Vonn's brother-in-law, Gordon Bruce, is the ex-husband of the first murder victim, Stacy Balena. I'm sure you know what happened to her. Of her death, I mean." Olivia waited for an acknowledgment from Kat, and was relieved when the saleswoman inclined her head. "Back when Vonn's Jewelry paid cash for jewelry, did Stacy come into this store to sell the diamond engagement ring Gordon gave her?"

Kat gave a nervous laugh. "That is a *very* odd question."

"I'm asking because I'm trying to help the friend I bought the bracelet for. I'd do anything for her, and she's in a heap of trouble. Maybe you have a friend who's like a sister to you. If so, you might do exactly what I'm doing." When Kat stared at her, unmoved, Olivia felt utterly defeated. Though she wasn't ready to surrender just yet, it seemed prudent to drop the subject for the time being. "How about we focus on the watches now?"

The watch counter seemed to be of less interest to the current group of shoppers than the other displays, so Kat and Olivia had the area to themselves.

Olivia stared down at the men's watches. They all seemed far too big, shiny, and ostentatious for Rawlings. He preferred function to designer names and had worn the same Timex since she'd known him.

"I do have a friend like that," Kat said, speaking in a low murmur. "And she's the only reason I'll tell you that I took in Ms. Balena's ring. I don't remember exactly what I paid her for it, but I'm confident that it was a better offer than she would have received anywhere else within a hundred miles because Mr. Vonn paid well for any diamond of decent size and quality, but Ms. Balena wasn't satisfied. The next day, she came back to lodge a complaint with Mr. Vonn about how I'd cheated her."

Olivia adopted a pained expression. "How insulting."

"Yes," Kat agreed. "Anyway, Mr. Vonn met with her in his office—probably to avoid having her cause a scene in front of the other customers—and when she left nearly thirty minutes later, I knew she hadn't gotten what she wanted. Her diamond was only decent. Nothing more." Kat smirked at the memory. "She pretended otherwise, of course. Sashayed across the store like she owned the place. Head held high, flicking her hair over her shoulder, and wearing a haughty expression—as though no man could resist her—but she wasn't fooling me. I have to be able to read people in my line of work. And that girl was a phony. She felt as small as an apple seed inside. And just as toxic."

"You should work for the police," Olivia said. "Or as an FBI profiler. You're incredible."

Kat thanked Olivia, smoothed her hair, and cleared her throat. "Now, did any of these watches catch your eye?"

"I wish they did, but they're all too flashy for my husband. He's more of a—wait." Olivia leaned over the case. "What's the story with that one in the corner?"

"Oh!" Kat tittered in embarrassment. "That piece is a manufacturer flub, I'm afraid. It's supposed to be an East Carolina Pirates watch, but though the pirate was added to the face, the ECU logo was omitted. Also, the hour markers are meant to be purple, with a yellow second hand, the school colors. Unfortunately, the hour markers on this watch are black and the second hand is red. Therefore, none of our ECU fans are interested in this watch, but we're hoping an individual who likes the pirate emblem might purchase it at cost."

"You've found that customer," Olivia said. "I'm going to put this under the tree for my husband, along with a beautifully illustrated copy of *Treasure Island*. I was going to give him a different book, but I've changed my mind. You helped me to remember that gifts can be powerful. Magical." Reaching into her handbag, Olivia pulled out two tickets for the Shakespeare Supper Club event. "If you're free on New Year's Eve, I'd love for you and a guest to join me at the Boot Top Bistro in Oyster Bay."

Kat blushed. "How lovely. Thank you." She accepted the tickets and moved off to ring up the pirate watch.

Ten minutes later, Olivia took her purchases out to her car and called Millay.

"That was a total waste of time. We got nowhere." Millay sounded extremely cross. "We're almost home. Where are you?"

"Just leaving New Bern," Olivia said. "And guess what. Your lead panned out. Stacy did sell her ring here, and that experience led to her being closeted with Arnold Vonn for over thirty minutes. I think he spent that time assessing her—determining if she'd make a good thief, seeing what kind of mettle she was made of."

"The pliable kind, apparently," Millay mumbled. "Hold on a sec. Harris is talking to me at the same time." There was a slight pause. "He says that Vonn might have had dirt on Stacy—something he found out from Gordon and used to force Stacy into joining the merry band of thieves."

"It's possible that Vonn blackmailed Stacy," Olivia said. "But I doubt he coerced her into initiating an affair with a married man. She was no naive girl. However, she paid for her sins. It's Vonn's turn now. I only hope that Rawlings can use what we discovered today." When Millay didn't respond, Olivia said, "I'm sorry to have wasted your time. And Harris's. Is he doing okay?"

There was a shuffling noise and then Millay said, "You're on speaker now. Harris, Olivia wants to know if you're okay."

"Yeah. Why wouldn't I be?"

Millay released an irritated sigh. "Come on. I don't know when we all started keeping secrets from each other, but look where it's gotten us. We're all screwed up. Well, maybe not Rawlings. But the rest of us? Definitely. My parents are splitting up and the shock of my mother's double life nearly gave me permanent writer's block. Laurel caught Steve with another woman and then became a murder suspect. Olivia's father ran back to New York because he thought he'd be blamed for the bad things that happened last year in the bookstore. And, Harris, your dream girl won't move to Oyster Bay, so you have no idea what the hell to do next on the relationship front. Am I warm?"

"Totally," Harris admitted grudgingly. "Until we found out the body in that burned car was Stacy Balena, I had this stupid plan to propose to Emily on Christmas."

"Why stupid?" Olivia asked.

Harris barked out a humorless laugh. "Because I'd be asking her for the wrong reason. I was doing it to coerce her into moving here. Not because I want to spend the rest of my life with her. I haven't looked that far ahead. I'd like to try being together in the same town for six months—see how that goes. The more time we're apart, the harder it is to close the distance growing between us."

Olivia heard the heartache in her friend's voice. "Do you love Emily?"

"Yes!" Harris exclaimed without a second's hesitation. "Absolutely."

"Then tell her everything you just told us. Maybe she's feeling exactly what you're feeling," Olivia said.

Harris groaned. "What if she isn't? What if she doesn't want to give this town a try? What if she doesn't love me enough to take that risk?"

"Then you have to let her go," Millay said. "From this point, either you go forward together or you separate."

"Just be honest with yourself and with Emily," Olivia advised. "And for what it's worth, I think she loves you too, Harris."

There was a momentary lapse before Millay's voice came through more clearly than before. "You're not on speaker anymore. Harris just dropped me off, but he says thanks for the advice. As for me, I need to get to work, but this was *not* a waste of my time. I want to help Laurel any way that I can. Besides," she added, turning flippant again, "there was grade A people-watching in that jewelry store. I took pages of mental notes for the market scene I'm planning to write tomorrow. I can't decide whether all the fake, greedy, oppressive characters should be mowed down by gryphon riders or flambéed by wyvern fire. It's a tough call."

Olivia laughed. "Are you going to your mom's or dad's for Christmas?"

"Are you kidding?" Millay scoffed. "I would prefer less drama, not more."

"In that case, join the chief and me for dinner," Olivia said.

Millay grunted. "Because every couple dreams of spending a Christmas evening with their stressed-out, cynical, holiday-hating friend. Thanks for the invite, but Harris and I are going to celebrate an anti-Christmas this year by catching a double feature at the theater. Nothing says peace and love like an explosion-filled action film followed by the latest bloodbath of a horror flick."

"As long as you have each other and a big tub of buttered popcorn, then you'll have everything that matters."

The next day, Christmas Eve, Olivia and Rawlings sat together at the kitchen table, drinking coffee and reviewing Olivia's conversation with Kat once more before Rawlings left for work. Haviland sat on his haunches behind Olivia's chair. This was his way of letting her know that he was ready to take a walk on the beach.

"I'd hate for Kat to get in trouble because of what she told me," Olivia said. "I liked her."

"We can worry about protecting her identity from Mr. Vonn if the information ends up building a stronger case against him," Rawlings said. "Cook and I need to review everything the man has previously stated. If we can catch him in a lie, we'll have just cause to bring him back in. We might even be able to obtain a warrant to search his premises—something the judge has not yet been willing to grant us."

Olivia crossed her first two fingers. "Here's hoping for a little Christmas magic. Call me if you learn anything new. In the meantime, I'm going to head into work. I also want to see if Laurel can meet me for lunch or coffee."

"I saw the bag from Vonn's Jewelry on your bureau," Rawlings said. "Did you find a gift for Laurel?"

Olivia nodded. "Something to replace the charm bracelet. She'll never want that back. It's completely tainted." She touched her wrist. "But I want Laurel to remember how she felt when she wore that other bracelet. The reason it was given to her. To celebrate her triumph. Her personal success. What she was able to accomplish by sheer strength of will and persistence."

Rawlings leaned over and kissed Olivia. It was a long and tender kiss, and when he pulled away, he stared at her lovingly, his fingers tracing the line of her jaw. "Every day with you is a gift," he whispered.

He then kissed her softly on the forehead and shrugged on his coat. After scratching Haviland once more behind the ears, Rawlings collected his travel mug and headed into the chilly morning.

Olivia finished her coffee and called Laurel, who was glad for an excuse to get out of the house.

"Don't get me wrong. I'm so grateful to be at home with my boys and not in a jail cell," she told Olivia once they'd ordered their food. "But it's incredibly hard to maintain this facade of normalcy—to smile at the twins, to stand at the stove and make them chocolate-chip pancakes, to keep all the rage I feel toward Steve inside until after the boys have gone to bed. It's exhausting."

"I can't begin to imagine."

Laurel gave her a funny look. "It's strange. Of all my married friends, you've been married the shortest amount of time. And yet you've shown me the most empathy. Because you understand the pain of betrayal better than most. Also, you're the truest friend I've ever had."

Olivia had driven Laurel to a seaside café twenty minutes south of Oyster Bay. She'd chosen the café not for its food, but for its location. Olivia didn't want people whispering about Laurel or shooting her sideways glances. For an hour or so, she wanted Laurel to simply be a woman enjoying a meal with another woman. If it was possible for Laurel to truly enjoy anything while she was still hurting so deeply.

"I like this place," Laurel said, taking in the cozy dining room with its red plaid tablecloths and centerpieces of white tulips. Gold ornaments hung from the ceiling, reflecting the soft light from the chandeliers, which were festooned with fresh greens and pinecones.

"Me too," Olivia said. She liked it even more when their waitress arrived with steaming bowls of chicken and barley soup. The soup, which was loaded with fresh herbs, vegetables, and tender pieces of chicken, warmed Olivia's body right down to her toes.

Though Laurel seemed to like her soup, she was unable to finish it.

"I'm just not hungry these days," Laurel said when she caught Olivia looking at her soup bowl. "I can't sleep. Can't eat. Apparently, I'm still traumatized." She fiddled with her flatware. "I haven't remembered anything more from that night either, but my therapist wants me to stop taking my sleeping pills before I become addicted. Tonight's my last dose. Considering I barely sleep *with* those pills, I can't imagine what the nights will be like without them. Still, the last thing I want is to become dependent on drugs."

"I expect the nights will be really rough for a while," Olivia said. "Nighttime is when we're the most vulnerable. Images and memories may come to you even though you don't want them to. Even when you try to fight them off."

Laurel nodded in misery. "That's what I've read in my self-help books too."

Olivia waited for the waitress to clear their soup bowls and deliver their salad plates before grasping Laurel's hand. "Your husband betrayed you. You did not deserve to be cheated on. Lied to. To have your trust and your heart broken. You are worth such better treatment than you were shown, Laurel Hobbs. You are smart, hardworking, kind, generous, and beautiful. You're an amazing mother, writer, and friend. Anyone who has you in their life is lucky." When Laurel dropped her eyes, Olivia gave her hand a shake. "Don't you do that. Don't you let what happened make you believe anything else but what I've told you. Other people's actions do *not* define you, Laurel Hobbs. You are *still* you. Don't let their mistakes bring you down. You might feel depleted of strength, courage, and determination, but they're in you. Keep showing your sons—and the rest of the world—what you're made of. And whenever you forget, let this serve as a reminder."

Laurel gasped as Olivia fastened the aquamarine bracelet around her wrist. "Oh, Olivia! You shouldn't have!"

"People are always saying that to me," Olivia said with a playful smile. "As if I'd ever pay a bit of attention." She held up a warning finger. "No tears. We're just two ladies having lunch, remember?"

This made Laurel laugh. "Right. Of course. Two regular gals out for a holiday meal. We should talk about what normal women would talk about, like what we bought our husbands for Christmas." She flashed an impish grin. "I didn't buy squat for Steve, but I got myself a T-shirt that says: IF YOU MISS YOUR CHEATING HUSBAND, RELOAD AND FIRE AGAIN."

It took a moment for Olivia to realize that Laurel had actually made a joke. The waitress, who'd stopped by to check on them, heard the comment and nearly doubled over with laughter.

"Laurel, you're going to be okay," Olivia said after the waitress had recovered enough to move on.

Glancing down at her bracelet, Laurel whispered, "I have to be. There's no other choice."

Laurel seemed like her old self until Olivia turned in to her subdivision. A heaviness descended upon her and the glint in her eyes faded like the stars being chased away by the dawn light.

"Remember who you are," Olivia said when Laurel moved to exit the Range Rover.

Before Laurel could answer, Olivia's phone rang. Rawlings's name appeared on the dashboard screen.

"Talk to your husband," Laurel said softly. "And thanks again. For everything."

Olivia pushed a button and Rawlings immediately asked, "Are you still with Laurel?"

Laurel paused in the act of shutting the car door.

"Yes," Olivia replied. "Why?"

"Because I wanted to give her a Christmas gift a day early. Put her on speaker." Rawlings couldn't contain the excitement in his voice. "We've arrested Arnold Vonn for the murder of Stacy Balena. Laurel, you are no longer a suspect. It's over. You can concentrate on reclaiming your life now. All of it. Your job, your reputation, your writing, your memory. You earned these. Don't let anyone take them away. And if people give you grief as you try to return to a sense of normalcy, remind them that you're close personal friends with the chief of police and I won't tolerate the harassment of my friends. Got it?"

Tears streamed down Laurel's cheeks as she whispered, "Yeah. I got it."

Chapter 14

*Christmas waves a magic wand over
this world, and behold, everything is
softer and more beautiful.*

—NORMAN VINCENT PEALE

"I've been waiting all day to hear how this came about,"
Olivia said the moment Rawlings sat down in one of the
leather club chairs opposite her in the Boot Top Bistro's bar.

As Christmas Eve was not a busy time at the restaurant,
they practically had the lounge area to themselves. Gabe,
the best-looking and most gregarious male bartender in
Oyster Bay, had only one other customer. However, like the
rest of Olivia's staff, he was in a jovial mood, as he'd received his holiday bonus check, and was polishing a glass
tumbler with extra verve.

Rawlings took a sip of beer and scooped up a handful of
snack mix from the bowl sitting in the middle of the table
before answering Olivia. "Sorry, but I'm famished. Lunch
seems hours ago."

"We'll order something, but not until you start talking."

"I like it when you get bossy." Rawlings tossed the handful

of nuts and pretzels into his mouth and chewed, grinning at Olivia the whole time.

Olivia sighed in exasperation and went to fetch a waiter.

A grateful Rawlings placed an order for braised short ribs with horseradish mashed potatoes and sautéed greens. After selecting the lemon-and-herb roasted chicken with polenta and mixed vegetables and telling the waiter to set places for them at the bar, Olivia sat back in her chair and waited for Rawlings to speak.

"Mr. Vonn talked himself into a hole," Rawlings began. "During his initial interview, he claimed to have met Ms. Balena only *after* Gordon Bruce had been dating Vonn's sister for nearly a year. By this time, it was clear that Gordon and Vonn's sister—her name is Julia—were the real deal. In fact, Mr. Bruce had already purchased an engagement ring from Vonn's New Bern shop, so Arnold knew that Mr. Bruce was planning to propose before his sister did."

"Did he approve of the match?" Olivia asked.

Rawlings nodded. "Vonn claims to have liked Gordon Bruce from the start. Mr. Bruce was very forthright with Julia about his past. He told her about his battle with alcoholism, his previous marriage, and how nothing in his life was more important than his two children. He didn't conceal his arrest for assault or that his first wife was many years his junior and, because of her self-centered personality, tended to inject unwanted drama into his existence."

"And she accepted him after all that?" Olivia reached for her drink. "Gordon must have had lots of other redeeming qualities."

"According to Mrs. Bruce, he most certainly did," said Rawlings sadly. "When I spoke with her, she painted a picture of a down-to-earth family man. A guy who was happiest playing board games with his kids or cooking dinner along-side his wife."

Olivia stared at the ice cubes in her tumbler. "I wish Julia could have held on to that rosy vision of her husband. Instead, she has to learn of his online gambling addiction and . . ." She trailed off. "Is it bad? Their financial situation? And what about Gordon's children? Julia isn't the only person who will suffer. Those kids lost their parents within days of each other. Worse than that, both mother and father died violently." She shook her head. "I was so concerned about the kind of Christmas the Hobbs twins would have that I completely neglected to consider what this holiday will be like for the Bruce children. Can we do something for the three of them?"

"Let me finish telling you what happened and then we'll bat around some ideas." Rawlings gave Olivia a warm smile. "So Mr. Vonn's claim that he hadn't met Ms. Balena until Mr. Bruce was in a serious relationship with Julia Vonn was a lie. Thanks to your investigative work at Vonn's shop, we were able to pry a completely different story from him. In the updated version, Vonn stated that he'd first met Ms. Balena when she came to his store to demand more cash for the diamond engagement ring she'd sold to one of Mr. Vonn's associates the previous day."

"That would be Kat."

The waiter returned with a basket of warm French bread and a bowl of softened herb butter. "Would you care to move to the bar, ma'am?" he asked Olivia.

"Not yet. We're so cozy here that we'll wait for our entrées, thanks."

The young man bustled back into the dining room and Olivia held out the bread basket for Rawlings. There was still only one patron at the bar, but Olivia deemed it best to keep their conversation as private as possible.

"We kept Kat's name out of the inquiry," Rawlings continued. "For all Mr. Vonn knows, a friend of Ms. Balena's came forward with the pertinent information. The bottom line is that we got results. Vonn admitted to being intrigued by Ms. Balena from the moment they met. When she came into his office to complain, he took the opportunity to get to know her better, and as soon as it became clear that she was unattached, he asked her out on a date."

Olivia nearly dropped the heel of bread she'd been buttering. "What?"

"Mr. Vonn and Ms. Balena were lovers for half a year," Rawlings said, somewhat amused by the stunned look on Olivia's face. "When we asked for proof, Mr. Vonn was able to supply us with several notes and more than one video."

Because her mouth was full, Olivia could only raise her hands in protest, silently entreating Rawlings to spare her the details.

"I have no intention of spoiling our meal by describing what those two were into," he assured her. "Suffice it to say, these videos made a roomful of veteran cops grimace."

The latter comments didn't even register with Olivia. She was suddenly transported back to Millay's apartment, reading the exchange of Facebook messages between Steve and Stacy. All along, she'd assumed that the ex Stacy had been scared of was her former husband, Gordon Bruce.

As exes go, Arnold Vonn posed a far greater threat, Olivia thought. *If it turns out that he was the puppet master controlling the ring of jewelry thieves, then Stacy would have had to do things his way. She was too self-centered for that to have worked for long.*

Of course, Rawlings still didn't know that Olivia and

Millay had read those messages, so she couldn't voice these thoughts aloud. Instead, she said, "It's a wonder they made it six months. What caused the demise of this charming union?"

Rawlings chortled. "Here's where Mr. Vonn backed himself into a corner. When asked why he and Ms. Balena stopped dating, Mr. Vonn said he felt guilty about seeing Gordon's ex-wife behind his sister's back. Julia had no clue that he was dating anyone, let alone the mother of her boyfriend's children. Vonn doubted she would approve."

Olivia rolled her eyes. "Gee. I wonder why."

"Once it became apparent that Gordon and Julia were to be married, Mr. Vonn decided to call off his relationship with Ms. Balena. She took the news badly." Rawlings stretched out his hand to take a second piece of bread, reconsidered, and drank some beer instead. "Ms. Balena threatened Vonn with bodily harm and vowed to burn down his stores. She also threatened to tell his sister about their relationship. He claimed that she'd always been a little unhinged, but her unpredictability was strangely alluring until then. Vonn responded to these threats by pointing out that he was a wealthy, powerful man while Ms. Balena was a divorced mother of two barely scraping by. He told her that she'd better not start a war because she had neither the brains nor the resources to win one against him."

"That must have stung."

After casting another longing glance at the bread basket, Rawlings said, "If one believes Mr. Vonn's story, then yes, I imagine his retort would have taken the wind out of Ms. Balena's sails. However, Cook proposed an alternative theory: Ms. Balena was a genuine threat because she was aware of Mr. Vonn's involvement in antique jewelry thefts."

Olivia leaned a little closer, sensing that Rawlings was

nearing the denouement. "Why didn't he kill her back then? Why wait until now?" she wondered aloud.

"Mr. Vonn probably spent those six months training her to be his newest thief," Rawlings said. "Ms. Balena was an investment, and Mr. Vonn was ready to send her into the field. In reviewing Ms. Balena's employee history, we discovered that she was an RN at Carolina East Medical Center until around the time of her breakup with Mr. Vonn. Cook and I both found it hard to believe that she suddenly aspired to become a hospice nurse without Mr. Vonn's influence."

"Please tell me that you found evidence of the larceny ring in Vonn's house or stores," Olivia said. She was on the edge of her seat, her right hand closed around her empty glass in a white-knuckled grip, her left hand clamped around the arm of her chair.

Rawlings gently pried the glass from her hand and placed it on the table. "As expected, Mr. Vonn has lawyered up and refuses to cooperate. Working in conjunction with the New Bern Police Department, we obtained search warrants and discovered a notebook hidden in Mr. Vonn's home containing notations that match the descriptions of dozens of stolen pieces of jewelry."

Olivia exhaled in relief. "That's a promising start."

"It is," agreed Rawlings. "However, there's still so much ground to cover. Mr. Vonn's financial records have to be checked. Going back many years. Both personal and business accounts. Forensic teams need to examine three locations: Vonn's house, his shop in New Bern, and his shop in Bayboro. Most important, we need to identify the other members of this larceny ring. Which other hospice employees are stealing from patients? It's unlikely that Vonn recruited them all from Tidewater, as there are half a dozen companies in the region."

"With multiple people working for Vonn, why weren't there more reports of jewelry thefts? Why is this just coming to light now?"

Rawlings took a moment to organize his thoughts. "There isn't a simple answer to that question. For starters, the thefts have probably occurred in several counties. Also, many of the thefts weren't reported because, unlike Milton and Rachel Hobbs, many people pass away without first having created inventory lists of their valuables. Therefore, their relatives don't know what's missing. Lastly, it can be months after a loved one's passing before his or her possessions go through probate and all the rest of that legal red tape. By the time someone realizes a valuable is missing, my guess is that the descendants accuse each other of the theft."

"So it comes back to nailing Vonn. And he wouldn't have been dumb enough to use a regular phone or e-mail to contact his thieves," Olivia said. "Which means we have to hope a burner phone is uncovered or one of the employees at the jewelry shop is in the loop. No pun intended."

Though Rawlings rewarded her with a grin, it quickly faded. "With tomorrow being Christmas, most of this activity won't get under way until the twenty-sixth. In the meantime, Mr. Vonn will remain in custody."

To Olivia, it seemed as though the police were building a solid case against Vonn as a thief. But what of his role as murderer? It didn't sound as if they'd found any evidence to prove that he'd killed Stacy Balena, let alone Gordon Bruce. This worried Olivia, despite Rawlings's assurances that the investigation had only just begun and would take many days and a great deal of manpower to complete.

"Why do you think Vonn killed Stacy now?" Olivia asked. "They broke up years ago, and I doubt he cared that she was involved with another man. And yet the crime displayed such rage—it almost conveyed a message that Stacy deserved punishment." Seeing the waiter approach with a tray, Olivia hurried to finish her thought. "My guess would be that she had somehow become more of a liability than an asset to Vonn. As time passed, she either demanded a bigger piece of the pie or took too many risks. Whatever the reason, Vonn didn't want her to be part of his side business anymore. But you can't just fire a thief you no longer trust."

The waiter went straight to the bar and placed their entrées on the snowy napkins Gabe had laid out for them. Rawlings stood and offered Olivia his arm. "May I escort you to your table, milady?"

Olivia was too engrossed in Rawlings's story to deliberate over wine, so she settled for ice water. Rawlings ordered the same. He then insisted on taking a short hiatus from the current conversation in order to focus on their wonderful meals.

"I'm glad we didn't order more alcohol," Rawlings said several minutes later. "It's been so long since we've enjoyed a peaceful, leisurely supper together, or had a decent night's sleep, that Gabe and Michel would probably have to carry me to the car if I had another drink."

"In that case, you'd better start talking." Olivia gave Rawlings a playful nudge in the side. "Michel made a special chocolate cake to share with the staff and I thought we'd wash it down with a mug of Irish coffee."

Rawlings sighed in contentment. "Boy, did I know what I was doing when I asked you to marry me! What other man gets to eat like this on a routine basis? All right, where was I?" He paused to recollect where he'd left off. "Right. You were asking about Mr. Vonn's motive. Well, thanks to Harris, who was able to recover hundreds of deleted e-mails and documents from Ms. Balena's hard drive, we found a document written by Ms. Balena to Mr. Vonn in which she expresses her desire to become Vonn's wife and business partner. She makes it quite clear that she doesn't require a romantic relationship. What she'd like is to work fewer hours as a nurse, live in a nicer house, drive a more expensive car, and treat herself to designer clothes, jewelry, and regular beauty treatments. She goes on to say how unfair it is that Gordon gets to be happy and that she, Stacy, doesn't want to end up alone, with no one to take care of her. She—"

"What was wrong with that woman?" Olivia demanded incredulously. "She could take care of herself! She had a good job. And she was making money on the side stealing from helpless patients. That wasn't enough? She wanted to marry someone she didn't love and who didn't love her just to be on par with her ex-husband? I don't suppose she mentioned her children in this letter either."

Rawlings shook his head. "No, she didn't. In any event, Mr. Vonn refused her. We found a saved copy of his reply too. Thus rejected, Ms. Balena set her sights on other men. In between her relationships with Mr. Vonn and Steve Hobbs, she had two affairs. Both involved married men. These men were successful professionals who were at least ten to fifteen years her senior, and in each relationship, she pressured her partner to leave his wife, but neither man complied. Within six months of the commencement of each affair, it had ended. It would appear that these affairs remain secrets to this day."

Olivia made a noise of disgust. "Someone should send the wives an anonymous letter."

"I imagine every sordid detail will be printed in black and white once this case is finally put to bed," Rawlings said. "There'll be no place for those men to hide. And sadly, Laurel and her family will have to endure last week's horror all over again."

The thought sobered Olivia and she put down her fork. "It sounds like Stacy never got over Gordon. And when Arnold Vonn wouldn't have her, she searched for men who reminded her of her ex-husband. In the meantime, however, Gordon had changed. When he was married to Stacy, he'd been an alcoholic. He'd had anger issues. He was probably a lousy husband and father."

"That's just it. I believe Stacy wanted the better version of Gordon Bruce," Rawlings said. "The version Julia got. People always talk about how much better the second wives have it. I think Ms. Balena would have agreed with that sentiment. She saw herself as a victim—someone who'd gotten married too young to the wrong man. And when he became the right man—a good man—for another woman, Ms. Balena became so embittered over the new life her ex-husband built for himself that she would have sold her soul to have a similar-looking life."

"Stacy Balena *did* sell her soul," Olivia pointed out. "She tried to break up three marriages, she was too self-centered to invest in the raising of her own children, *and* she stole jewelry from terminally ill patients."

Rawlings dipped his head in somber acquiescence. "Yes. Pain, envy, bitterness, loss, and loneliness twisted that young woman's soul into something dark and ugly. I doubt any man or any amount of material possessions would have filled the empty hole inside. She was an unfortunate young woman who could never have peace because she refused to exorcise the demons from her past. She believed there was power in the ruination of others, and she was too blinded by this delusion to see that she was walking down a path that would inevitably lead to her own destruction."

"I'm still unclear as to Arnold Vonn's motive," Olivia said.

Rawlings nodded. "I did go off on a tangent. Sorry. Okay, consider two things. The first is the jewelry recovered from Ms. Balena's house. We matched those pieces to stolen and missing property reports, some of which were filed over a year ago."

Olivia understood the implication. "Stacy had no intention of handing them over to Vonn."

"It didn't look that way," Rawlings agreed. "She seemed to be holding out. For more cash from Vonn? Probably. After we reviewed her financial records, it was clear that she spent money as fast as she earned it. Clothes, concerts, dining out, facials and costly beauty products—she seemed incapable of saving a dime and she either didn't know or didn't care about investing her money."

"So she *wasn't* putting funds aside to sue for joint custody of her kids? That was just a lie she fed Steve?"

"Yes." The word was infused with sadness and Olivia knew that Rawlings was thinking of Stacy's children. "Many of Ms. Balena's messages and texts to Steve were fabrications. Amid the lies were kernels of truth, such as her fear of her ex. She never used the term 'ex-husband' or mentioned Gordon Bruce by name. Everyone reading those messages— Steve included—assumed she was referring to her former husband. And Steve never asked for clarification because he wasn't very interested. Learning details about Stacy's former lovers didn't jibe with his fantasy."

Olivia didn't think she would ever stop being angry with Laurel's philandering husband. "Do you think Stacy truly cared for Steve?"

"Not in the slightest," Rawlings said. "Nor did she care about Arnold Vonn or the other two married men. I do believe she loved Gordon Bruce and never recovered from the breakup of their marriage."

The waiter appeared to clear their plates. Olivia was deliberating over whether to linger over dessert and coffee or to call it a night and head home. Analyzing Stacy's character flaws had injected an atmosphere of gloom into their intimate conversation, but Olivia refused to allow the dead woman to spread any more negativity. Not in Olivia's restaurant. Not on Christmas Eve. Not when Arnold Vonn's arrest had instilled such hope into all of the Bayside Book Writers.

"Let's have our cake in the kitchen," Olivia suggested to Rawlings. "It'll be more festive to sit around the counter and drink coffee with the staff, and since we're closing early, there shouldn't be many people left in the dining room."

Gabe's other customer had left, so he grabbed two bottles of Baileys and followed Olivia and Rawlings into the kitchen. As they passed through the dining room, Olivia noticed that all the patrons were either on their dessert courses or settling their checks.

The kitchen was a cocoon of warm steam, delicious aromas, the hiss of running water, and jovial chatter.

Michel was in the midst of tucking his clean knives into a padded attaché case when they entered. After pushing the paring knife into its foam bed, he glanced at the threesome and beamed. "Excellent! Now the celebration can officially begin!"

"Will Shelley be joining us?" Olivia asked, taking a seat at the counter.

"She's on her way, and she's bringing treats for everyone!"

Hearing this, the sous-chefs and waitstaff already present in the kitchen gave a hearty cheer. They cheered again and added a round of applause when Michel ducked into Olivia's office and reemerged carrying the two-tiered chocolate cake he'd baked for his coworkers. Haviland, who'd been involuntarily shut in the office with the cake, trailed on Michel's heels.

After gingerly setting the cake down on the counter, Michel straightened, put his hands on his hips, and bellowed, "Voilà! My beautiful wife has been helping me perfect my art as a chocolatier. This truffle layer cake is the result of many failed attempts. It is a fudgy chocolate sponge divided by layers of dark and white chocolate ganache, all of which is covered in a most decadent chocolate frosting. The tree and snowflake decorations encircling and topping the cake arc cdiblc, of course, as they are piped white and dark chocolate."

Michel's audience made appreciative noises and a waitress came forward with a stack of dessert plates, forks, and napkins while a sous-chef handed Michel a long knife and a cake server. Gabe had just started taking coffee orders when Shelley entered through the rear doorway.

"Perfect timing, my love!" Michel cried, dropping the utensils and rushing to his wife's side. "I was just about to cut the cake. Here, let me help you with your coat."

Shelley gave him an affectionate shove. "Stop fussing over me, you big oaf. I can unbutton my own coat. Go serve your friends. I'm dying to see how your masterpiece turned out."

Michel raised a warning finger. "All right, but promise you won't sneak back outside to get the gifts."

"Yes, dear." Shelley gave him a pat on the cheek and then bent down to greet Haviland.

Everyone had fallen silent during the couple's exchange, and when Michel turned around to face Olivia, Rawlings, and his coworkers, they were all staring at him in amusement.

His cheeks flushed a bright pink. Shooting a plaintive glance at Shelley, Michel mouthed something at her and she smiled and nodded in reply.

Beaming, Michel reached into his apron pocket and pulled out a pair of tiny knit bootees. "*Mes amies*, I am the happiest man in the world! Tonight, I am pleased to share with you the news I have been bursting to share. My sweet Shelley and I are going to be parents! These little shoes will be worn by a baby chef."

Amid the congratulations, backslaps, and hugs that followed this joyful announcement, Olivia made her way over to Shelley and asked when the baby was due.

"My doctor said that he or she should be born around the first day of spring, but babies have their own sense of timing. I expect this kid to show up when we're least prepared." Shelley smiled. "And you might as well know right now that we've set our sights on you and Sawyer as this kid's godparents, so I hope you're ready to change some diapers."

"Can't I just write checks instead?" Olivia asked fearfully, and she and Shelley broke out into peals of laughter.

All traces of the heaviness Olivia had felt when she and Rawlings were discussing Stacy in the bar vanished like fog burned away by the summer sun. Standing in the warm kitchen, Olivia took in the glowing faces and sounds of happiness surrounding her. Michel, having delivered his big announcement, set about cutting the cake while Shelley assisted by serving the slices. Haviland moved from person to person, receiving pets and scratches. He wasn't allowed in the kitchen, so this was a rare treat, but since it would be closed for the next day and was scheduled for a deep clean the day after, Olivia decided it wouldn't hurt to give her poodle a pass just this once.

Haviland gave Gabe's ankle an inquisitive sniff as the bartender distributed the last of the Irish coffees. As soon as he was done, Olivia sidled up to him and whispered something in his ear.

"You got it," Gabe replied in an equally soft murmur.

"But have your cake first," Olivia said. Turning to Rawlings, she spotted a smear of chocolate on his upper lip and wiped it off with the tip of her index finger. "How is it?"

Rawlings rolled his eyes in appreciation. "I'm not much of a dessert guy, but this must be how the food in heaven tastes."

Having overheard his comment, Shelley shushed Rawlings. "Do not repeat that to Michel," she warned. "His head will get so inflated that his chef's hat won't fit anymore. Besides, I've had such a good time playing teacher to his student that I'm not ready to give that up."

"Are you saying that you want me to criticize the man wielding a large knife?" Rawlings asked, pretending to be nervous.

"You wouldn't refuse an expectant mother." Shelley flashed him a wry grin. "And since I only plan on having one child, I'm going to play the pregnancy card as much as I can."

Rawlings chuckled. "Thanks for warning us. Ah, I believe Gabe has something for you and Michel."

Gabe and two other waiters had quietly vanished and reappeared carrying bottles of champagne and sparkling cider. Multiple corks popped, people cried out in surprise, and Haviland barked in alarm, causing a ripple of laughter. Champagne flutes were lined up on the massive butcher block and Gabe expertly poured a splash of bubbly into each glass. Olivia took advantage of the prep time to search on her phone for the perfect toast for an expectant couple. She'd never been close to anyone starting a family before and she wanted to make this a bright and shining memory for Shelley and Michel. However, the quotes she came across were either too sarcastic or too sappy.

In the end, Olivia raised her flute, faced the couple, and

said, "To quote the wise and wonderful Winnie the Pooh, 'A grand adventure is about to begin.' Congratulations! Thank you for sharing your gift of happiness with us tonight."

Rims were clinked, more hugs were exchanged, and the room grew warmer and noisier. Eventually, Michel darted out to Shelley's car and returned with stockings stuffed with handmade candies for each of the staff members.

"I made special gingerbread houses for Laurel's boys," Shelley told Olivia. "If we put the houses directly in your car, can you get them to the twins tomorrow? I hate to impose because I wouldn't feel right stopping by their place on a holiday, but I really want them to have these treats."

Olivia smiled. "I'd be glad to do it. I'll take Haviland. He can act as Santa Paws."

Shelley squatted down and asked for Haviland's paw. "Thank you, Santa. I had a feeling you'd be involved, so I made something for you too."

Not only did Haviland give Shelley his paw to shake, but he leaned in and licked her cheek as well. Shelley laughed and glanced up at the ceiling. "Hey! I don't see the mistletoe. Where is it?"

Rawlings slipped his arm around Olivia's waist and pulled her to him. "That's an excellent question."

Olivia planted a featherlight kiss on his neck. With her lips hovering near his ear, she whispered, "I think I saw a particularly large bunch hanging over our bed."

"I'll get our coats," Rawlings said, suddenly moving with the alacrity of a man who hadn't had one of the most exhausting, stressful, and nerve-racking weeks of his life.

It was too much for Olivia to see him wildly weave through a knot of waiters and sous-chefs in an effort to reach the swinging doors leading to the dining room, and she began to laugh.

She was still laughing when he returned with their coats draped over one arm.

"This woman is clearly inebriated," Rawlings declared to the room at large. "I'm taking her home before she becomes a menace to society. Merry Christmas, everyone!"

Cries of "Merry Christmas!" followed Rawlings and Olivia into the star-filled night.

Chapter 15

Better a diamond with a flaw than a
pebble without one.

—CHINESE PROVERB

"I've spoken with Michel about seeking donations for the Bruce family at the Shakespeare Supper," Olivia informed the Bayside Book Writers in what seemed like their first meeting in months.

It was a Thursday evening during that strange, somnolent time between Christmas and New Year's when most people walked around looking dazed. It was as though the weeks of shopping, excess food, visiting relatives, parties, and exchanging gifts followed by a mailbox stuffed with credit card bills had put everyone into a trance. There was a sense of lethargy and inertia throughout town, and Olivia couldn't remember the last time she'd seen the streets so empty.

As for the Bayside Book Writers, they were eager for time to march on. December had been a horrible month and maybe, with both the police and the media viewing Arnold Vonn as the prime suspect in the investigation of Stacy

Balena's murder, January would have them all feeling that the worst was over.

Tonight, the five friends had gathered in the lighthouse keeper's cottage for a meal and a brief critique session of the query letter Harris had crafted to send out to a select number of literary agents. Olivia had ordered a variety of pies from Pizza Bay and stocked the fridge with her friends' favorite beverages. Rawlings had a fire going in the living room, and the cottage felt warm and snug.

Laurel was ensconced on the sofa, holding a glass of Chardonnay in her hand. There was an untouched slice of pepperoni pizza on the coffee table in front of her. "Donations?" she asked Olivia, sounding confused, and Olivia realized that she'd never told Laurel about Gordon's gambling issues. Laurel had no idea that Julia and the Bruce children were in need of financial assistance.

"If you want to cheer up the kids, order some custom treats from Decadence. My boys are still talking about their Christmas surprise from Shelley," Laurel suggested as she refilled her glass for the second time.

Harris opened the pizza box containing the ham and pineapple pie and helped himself to another slice. "What surprise?"

"Shelley made them gingerbread houses the likes of which I've never seen," Laurel said, her eyes shining at the memory. "One was actually a castle. On the outside, it had icing pennants, a saltwater taffy moat, and chocolate-dipped ice-cream-cone turrets. There were gumdrop and peppermint candy decorations too. And on the inside, there was a veritable army of gingerbread cookies. Knights, squires, ladies. Even a king and queen."

"What? No dragon?" Millay quipped. She propped her

black-studded boots on the coffee table and glanced over at Rawlings, who was digging around in the refrigerator. "Hey, can you grab me a cold one while you're in there, Chief?"

Rawlings called back that he'd be glad to be of service. He returned to the living room carrying two beer bottles in one hand and a plate with a generous slice of sausage and mushroom pizza in the other.

Laurel waited for him to settle down in his favorite chair before continuing. "The second house wasn't exactly a house either. It was a stadium. Like the castle, the outside was decorated with pennants and banners—all done in the colors of the boys' YMCA soccer team. The gingerbread cookie players inside wore the team colors as well. Dozens and dozens of different kinds of hard candies represented the heads of the fans. It was so incredible that the boys were almost reluctant to break off a piece. *Almost.*"

"It's a good thing their dad is a dentist," Olivia joked.

Everyone shot nervous looks at Laurel, silently wondering how she'd respond to this remark. Would she say something negative about Steve, or would she act normal because that was what she needed to do to move forward?

Reaching for her slice of pizza, which was undoubtedly cold and rubbery by now, Laurel fixed her gaze on her food. "Yeah. Aren't they lucky?" she replied blandly, and took a bite.

Olivia made a mental note never to mention Steve again unless Laurel made it clear that she wanted to discuss him. "Asking Shelley to be involved is a great idea," she said, hoping to redirect the conversation to a safer topic. "Though she'll probably want to work with a medium besides gingerbread. What confection reminds people of a new year?"

"Champagne truffles?" Millay suggested.

Rawlings laughed. "That might not be the best choice for children."

"No, but Julia Bruce might like the double dose of comfort provided by the chocolate and booze," Millay said. "I'm not sure if any amount of sweets will make Gordon's kids feel better, no matter how beautiful or delicious. They just lost two parents. And those parents died violently."

Laurel pulled a face. "You're right. It was insensitive of me to think that candy would cheer them up. I need to forget who their mother was and remember that her little girl and little boy are victims too." She swept her arm around the room. "What these kids will need is people. People to get them out of the house—to take them to movies and to restaurants, to invite them over for supper and for sleepovers. Julia will do what she can to help. I'm not saying she isn't every bit their mom just because she didn't give birth to them, but she's grieving too, and it'll be a challenge for her to be strong for them twenty-four-seven."

Harris looked at Olivia. "You're a master when it comes to getting the blue bloods of Oyster Bay's community to write checks for worthy causes, but how does someone fund-raise a support system for this family?"

"We'll post a sign-up sheet at the Shakespeare Supper," Olivia said. "That will get us the monetary donations and the support system. I just need to figure out who we know in New Bern. Who can help us with this?" She fell quiet and was considering the issue, when Laurel suddenly snapped her fingers.

"You could ask Lynne Chester for advice. She's been so sweet with Milton. I can hardly believe she's the same woman I met at Tidewater Hospice." Laurel shook her head in disbelief. "I have totally misjudged her. What I took for abrupt and pushy was really just efficiency and a no-nonsense attitude. Anyway, didn't you say that Gordon and Julia attended church in New Bern, Chief?"

Rawlings nodded. "Yes, and judging by the number of people who came to pay their respects at Mr. Bruce's funeral, you already have a significant support network through that church community."

"Lynne could probably tell you how to tap into that network," Laurel said. "I was thinking of giving Lynne two tickets to the Shakespeare Supper as a thank-you for going above and beyond the call of duty after Rachel passed away. I know she and Rachel were close toward the end, but Lynne proved to be invaluable to Milton, seeing as Steve and I didn't end up being of much use."

Millay studied Laurel. "Are you positive her heart has suddenly turned to gold? Or is it more a case of—" She shot a glance at Olivia. "What did Fred call it? Gold fill? Maybe Ms. Lynne is a gold *digger*. She stands to catch herself a pretty rich fish if she can get the hook in deep enough."

Laurel stared at Millay in confusion. "Lynne and Milton? No." She dismissed the idea with a shake of her head. "I honestly think Lynne's excited to be getting high-quality stuff for the church thrift shop. Maybe she's allowed first pick? And who cares if she is? In my mind, she's earned whatever perks she gets. It's not like I want any of Rachel's stuff, which is good, since she didn't leave me a thing."

"What about her jewelry?" Olivia asked. "I know she left the costume pieces to the church, but what of her fine jewelry? It was worth close to one hundred thousand. I saw the appraisals done for your in-laws' insurance company."

Olivia's revelation gave Laurel pause, but she didn't seem interested in asking her friend how she'd come to see these documents. "Rachel bequeathed the majority of her estate to Milton, including every piece of fine jewelry and art," she explained. "That's a fairly common practice—to leave most of your assets to your spouse. She also gave Steve a nice chunk of change and set up a trust account for each twin. They'll inherit the money when they turn thirty. Her clothes, costume jewelry, and an assortment of books and knickknacks were given to the church to be sold in the thrift shop. There was a short list of sentimental items for close friends as well. I believe Rachel left Lynne some art book that Lynne had always admired. As for me, my name wasn't mentioned in the will at all."

"That's so mean!" Harris exclaimed.

"I wasn't surprised," Laurel said without a trace of bitterness. "After the reading, Steve repeatedly apologized for the snub, but I'd been prepared for it, so he was far more upset than I was. I didn't want anything of Rachel's anyway, but Steve became super defensive on my behalf—a side of him I'd never seen before. I told him it was a *little* late for him to stand up for me against his mother. That brought on another round of apologies."

Olivia watched Laurel drop her unfinished pizza slice onto her plate. Clearly disinterested in food, she drained the rest of the wine from her glass instead.

"Are they sincere?" Olivia asked before Laurel could refill her glass for a third time. "The apologies?"

"I have no doubt that Steve is genuinely sorry for what he's done." Laurel sat back in her chair. "But I don't know if I have it in me to work on our marriage anymore. It would take so much effort to forgive him—to even be friends again, let alone trusting partners. I can take care of the boys and myself. I've already been doing that for years, but I don't know if I can handle propping Steve up as he examines his issues. I'm through with being his cheerleader. I'm tired of my ideas and dreams always being less important than his. It's time for me to focus on my needs for a change."

Millay picked up Laurel's plate, walked into the kitchen,

and tossed it in the trash bin. She returned with a fresh slice of pizza and a glass of ice water. "I don't know where your marriage is headed, but it sounds like you just described the final third of your novel to us. Maybe, just maybe, you should write the rest of the book as a vehicle of releasing your feelings. Even if you never use what you write, that kind of raw emotion shouldn't be wasted. This might sound a bit crazy, but I think your character would want you to pour all of this into her. Just dump everything into her and see what she does with it."

Laurel's gaze turned distant as she considered Millay's suggestion. For a long moment, during which the rest of the group remained silent, she stared out the window overlooking the ocean. It was too dark to see much. The water was a shadowy smudge beneath a gravel-colored sky, but something began to shift in Laurel's eyes. It was a subtle movement—an errant breeze rippling the surface of a stagnant wading pool—followed by a glint of light. A wink of sunshine on metal. A flash of inspiration, electric and nearly palpable, had struck Laurel and illuminated her from within.

"I like that idea," she said to Millay. And then she grabbed her pizza and started to eat.

By the time Harris had passed out the copies of the query letter for his friends to critique, Laurel had finished her first slice of pizza and was on her way to the kitchen for a second.

"I could kiss you," Olivia whispered to Millay. "That was brilliant."

Trying to hide her pleasure at the praise, Millay mumbled, "It's not me. We solve problems when we're here. Together. Why did we have to nearly fall apart before we figured that out?"

"I don't know, but at least we came around before it was too late," Harris said. "That would be an apt description for me and Emily too. We've had a bunch of super-honest, super-exhausting conversations over the last few days, and I feel like we're on track again. She's coming up for New Year's, and I can't stop smiling."

Laurel came back into the room and slid an arm around Harris's waist. "I hope you start the year on a high note."

Harris smiled down at her. "We could all use high notes and a fresh start. So let's remember what Millay said and go after them together."

The five friends clinked glasses and beer bottle rims in a wordless pledge and then got down to work.

Olivia had never been to Fred Yoder's house. Since their friendship included their dogs, they met at the community park when the weather cooperated and at Fred's shop when it didn't, usually during Fred's lunch break.

Now, as Olivia stood at Fred's door holding a wicker basket filled with goodies, she realized that her entire plan hinged on Fred inviting her in. Glancing down at Haviland, she said, "I'm hoping you can get me through the door, Captain. You need to give Fred that look. The 'I haven't eaten for three days and I'm going to die' look you give me every morning before I've even had the chance to pour a cup of coffee. The one that works *every* time."

Haviland wagged his tail and grinned.

"By that response, I'll assume you're willing to comply." Olivia rang the doorbell, setting off an immediate cacophony of barking from somewhere deep within the house. "Guess they're home," Olivia said to her poodle. Haviland sniffed the air and shifted on his feet in anticipation of seeing his terrier friend.

When Fred opened the door, he studied his visitors for

a moment before smiling. "Well, you've got the basket and the red coat. Can't tell if it has a hood or not. Am I supposed to be Grandmother because I live in the woods?"

"What mighty big ears you have," Olivia teased. Instantly turning contrite, she said, "Actually, Fred, I'm the wolf. The trickster. The liar. And I'm very sorry. I don't want to lose your friendship." Proffering the basket, she added, "I was hoping we could have a cup of tea and talk."

Duncan suddenly appeared in the space between Fred's legs and the doorframe. His black nose quivered and Haviland surged forward to rub noses with his friend. Fred looked down at the dogs, smiled, and opened the door wide.

"Come in," he said, ushering Olivia into the front hall. After shutting the door, he pointed at the basket. "This feels like more than tea."

Following Fred into his kitchen, Olivia could see why he preferred the kitchen at Circa. That room had a row of rear-facing windows that caught the morning sun and seemed to hold on to the light throughout the day. This room felt dim and close, despite Fred's attempts to brighten it with a display of Fiestaware and colorful place mats.

"I might have packed a few tea treats for you," Olivia said, watching Fred peer into the basket. "There are finger sandwiches. Salmon and crème fraîche and ham with Dijon. To satisfy your sweet tooth, you'll find cinnamon scones with clotted cream and blackberry preserves as well as fresh gingerbread and a Victorian sponge cake."

Fred rubbed his belly. "If I eat all that, Duncan won't be the only one in the house taking insulin."

"Let's have a scone for now," Olivia said. "Tell me where everything is and I'll set the table."

"Sit." Fred waved at a chair. "You're my guest. And my friend." He waited for Olivia to take a seat before continuing.

"You're also forgiven. It wasn't about me. You did what you did to protect Laurel, and you would have done the same for me, had I been the one in danger of going to jail for a crime I didn't commit. Both Laurel and I are lucky to have you in our lives."

Olivia leaned over the table and threw her arms around her friend. "Thank you."

Alarmed by the suddenness of her movement, Duncan started a bout of agitated barking.

Fred and Olivia both laughed and their congenial friendship was officially restored. "Calm down, Duncan," Fred chided. "I know beautiful women don't hug me often, but give a guy a break." To Olivia, he said, "Let me put the kettle on and you can fill me in on the investigation over tea."

While Fred filled the kettle with water, Olivia laid out two Fiestaware plates and a pair of forks from the drying rack next to the sink. Once Fred had the kettle on the cooktop and the burner's flame had been turned to high, he faced Olivia. "After I read about Arnold Vonn's arrest, I almost called you. I wanted to talk to you about it, but I was still too upset about Gordon. I did my talking at AA meetings instead. That's where I share the hard things." Fred placed mugs, spoons, and napkins on the table. "If I *had* called, I would have told you that I wasn't surprised that Vonn had been arrested. I always thought Vonn was shady. But a murderer?"

"That part surprised you?"

Fred shrugged. "Why would he kill two people? For money? I don't see a guy like Vonn caring about much else."

"Money is the most likely motive, but there's so much material for the authorities to sift through, and even with two police departments working together, they're making slow progress." Olivia echoed what Rawlings had told the Bayside Book Writers the night before.

"Sounds like a politician's answer," Fred said, giving Olivia a disappointed look.

Behind him, the kettle began to whistle. Duncan and Haviland whined in response to the high-pitched keening until Fred removed it from the heat. He then placated the agitated canines with dog biscuits.

"I think you two were exaggerating in order to wangle a treat out of me," he scolded.

Olivia waited before speaking again until the tea was poured and Fred had served himself a scone and scooped a dollop of clotted cream onto his plate.

"To be honest, I'm not sure if the police know what they're looking for," Olivia said. "This puzzle is still missing some pretty big pieces. For example, no one's been able to decode Vonn's notebook yet. Other than figuring out which piece of antique jewelry was referred to on each page, the notebook hasn't revealed the identities of the thieves, or what Vonn did with the stolen pieces once he received them. It's a good thing he's suspected of larceny *and* murder, because if he were just a murder suspect, Cook would probably have had to cut him loose by now. As it stands, the clock is ticking. They need to place Vonn at the scene of Gordon's murder."

"Hmm" was all Fred could manage with his mouth full. However, Olivia could practically hear the gears spinning as he turned the problem over in his mind.

"I keep coming back to what Millay mentioned at Grumpy's before Christmas," she went on as he chewed. "She noticed that all the stolen jewelry contained diamonds."

Fred swallowed and chased the bite of scone with a sip of tea. "Pieces small enough to pocket. Extremely valuable. Unique. Diamonds set in mostly gold." He seemed to be talking to himself, and Olivia didn't interrupt his stream of staccato phrases. "Gold can be melted. Sold by the gram. And the diamonds? Sold as loose stones?"

Olivia ate several bites of her scone while Fred ruminated. It was moist, buttery, and incredibly light. She skipped the clotted cream, preferring the blackberry preserves because the taste reminded her of summer.

"If Vonn's interest was diamonds, then he would have had the stones removed prior to selling the gold to a refinery. He'd be losing a pile of money doing this. Melting Cartier earrings is like scribbling all over an Hermès Birkin handbag with a permanent marker. Cartier earrings are worth what they're worth because they're made by Cartier. It's the designer name that matters. On the other hand, you can train people who aren't familiar with antiques to learn a few choice designers. Tiffany. Cartier. Et cetera. There's less risk of their stealing junk if they stick to pieces with recognizable hallmarks."

"Only to rip them apart and sell them as scrap?" Olivia couldn't conceal her doubt. "Why go through all the trouble? There couldn't be enough money in the gold."

"No," Fred agreed. "This must be about the diamonds, but since I haven't had a lightbulb moment just yet, let's talk about other things. If anything brilliant comes to me, I'll let you know. No one other than Julia Bruce wants to find out what happened to Gordon more than me."

Since Fred had brought up Julia's name, Olivia shared her plan to turn the Shakespeare Supper into a partial fundraiser for the Bruce family. "You're going to attend, aren't you?" she asked Fred. "When I looked over the RSVP list and saw that your name wasn't on it, I got worried."

"New Year's Eve parties are for couples," Fred said. "And they usually involve lots of alcohol. I'm a bachelor teetotaler. It's not the best fit."

Olivia pointed at the scone plate. "This party is all about

food. Food and the Bard. The poetry of flavors. The imagery of spice. The meter of texture. These aren't my words, mind you, but Michel's. This isn't a celebration for partners either. People are attending in groups, as singles, as couples—you name it. There's no assigned seating, so no one will notice if you come stag. And while cocktails will be available and there will be a champagne toast at midnight, nonalcoholic drinks will also be served."

Fred smirked. "You made quick work of my excuses. Do I have to break out my tux?"

"I could ask Michel if any of the men in his supper club have an extra pair of britches and hose you could borrow." Olivia grinned.

"For your information, I have *very* shapely calves. That's what comes from standing behind a shop counter for hours in a row," Fred said. "All right, I'll brush the dust off my penguin suit and polish my dress shoes, which I practically have to pry off my feet after—" He stopped abruptly.

Olivia watched him stare into the middle distance. "Fred?"

"The diamonds." Fred's eyes regained focus. "What if Arnold was swapping diamonds? Someone brings in a diamond ring to be resized. Vonn swaps the stone for an inferior one. He puts the better stone in an engagement ring setting and sells it in one of his stores. As long as the replacement stone *looked* the same, the duped customer would never know. As for the customer purchasing the engagement ring, Vonn can afford to give him or her a discount, because he's paid nothing for the diamond, only the setting."

Olivia whistled. "Maybe that's how he gained his reputation for fairness and quality. He does advertise his business as the place to shop for bridal jewelry, which is mostly diamonds." She tapped on her wedding band. "You know, if I picked up a ring after having it repaired, I wouldn't have a clue if someone switched the diamonds. As long as the stones were the same cut and size, I wouldn't be the wiser."

"Same cut, size, and color," Fred added. "You'd notice if your stones were yellow. But you'd need a jeweler's loupe to spot clarity issues—to be aware of tiny chips, wisps, cloudiness, or other flaws. And who goes around examining their jewelry with a loupe? No one. Besides, I'm sure Vonn didn't do this with every customer. He'd be discerning. He'd know exactly which customers trusted him and wouldn't consider having their pieces examined or appraised by another jeweler."

To Olivia, Fred's theory sounded quite plausible. "Even if a customer noticed a flaw at a later date, it would be nearly impossible to prove that Vonn's Jewelry was responsible."

"That's right. Because customers would have to report the crime the day they picked up their piece from Vonn's, and they'd have to back up the claim with evidence," Fred said. "Including documents and photographs from the original sale versus documents and photographs taken after the piece was repaired. What are the chances that would happen?"

"Slim to none."

Fred raised his teacup in a mock salute. "Those were odds Vonn could take all the way to the bank." He set down his cup, reached into his pants pocket, and pulled out something small and shiny. Olivia recognized his anniversary token from AA.

Fred rubbed it between his fingers. "The night Gordon fell off the wagon—the night I wasn't there for him—is haunting me, Olivia. I knew that he'd invested in Arnold's third store, but I also knew that he was facing financial problems, though he didn't go into specifics with me. At some point Gordon did mention Stacy. He said that he wouldn't be writing her any more checks after he was done speaking with her."

Olivia had gone very still. "Did he talk to her the night she was murdered?"

"I don't know," Fred said, and Olivia believed him. "But in hindsight, I think Gordon must have discovered that Stacy was stealing from her patients. I think he was going to refuse to pay her child support because he knew she had an extra income. An illegal income."

"If so, both Stacy and Gordon became threats to Arnold's diamond-swapping business." Olivia sighed. "However, how do *we* prove any of this? The cops have questioned Vonn's employees, and none of them admit to being involved with or being aware of underhanded dealings at either location. This includes the jewelers in charge of repairs."

Fred grew pensive again. In the silence, Olivia could hear the soft moans of the dogs. They'd both fallen asleep on the kitchen floor, their backs slightly curved and their front paws tucked into their tummies. They looked like a set of quotation marks.

As though sensing he was being watched, Duncan slowly rolled onto his back and sighed. Fred glanced at his dog, smiled, and then pushed back his chair, collected the empty teacups, and carried them to the sink.

Turning back to the table, he looked at Olivia. "One of the employees is lying. Vonn couldn't do this work alone. I'm not a jewelry expert, but I've heard enough talk at shows and auctions to know that it's no easy task to remove gemstones. Vonn doesn't have the acumen. The cops need to find the employee who does and make him talk."

Olivia felt a surge of energy. "Yes! And once Vonn sees that he's going down for the thefts, he might confess to all his crimes in hopes of a more lenient sentence." She took hold of Fred's hand. "You're not letting Gordon down now. And you and I are going to see that his family is taken care of. That's what would matter most to him, right?"

Fred nodded.

"When I see you on New Year's Eve, you and I will have the same goal. We can put our energy into helping two wounded women—Laurel and Julia—so they can look to the future."

"I'll drink to that," Fred said. "Just give me seltzer with a spritz of lime and I'll be good to go."

"Oh, I think we can do better than that." Olivia smiled. "This is a Shakespearean event. Everything you eat and drink will be named after the Bard's characters. Each dish will be artistically presented and stimulating to the palate."

Fred finished clearing the tea things from the table. "I just hope no one takes Will's plots too literally. The man penned his fair share of tragedies. Lots of bloodshed and poisonings." He picked up one of the leftover scones and studied it. Then he shook his head as though dismissing a thought and transferred the scone to a cookie tin. "Still, it's a good thing Arnold Vonn is behind bars. It'd be hard for most people to enjoy a party with a murderer at large."

Chapter 16

The object of a New Year is not that we
should have a new year. It is that we
should have a new soul.

—G. K. CHESTERTON

Following Olivia's conversation with Fred Yoder, Cook and Rawlings reviewed the Vonn's Fine Jewelry employee files and discovered that one man had been hired a year before Stacy and Arnold Vonn became lovers. This fit with the date Vonn had founded his larceny ring, according to the cops. They based their theory on a subtle spike in stolen and missing jewelry reports throughout multiple counties.

The employee of interest, a pallid, wiry man named Derek Johnston, had been the picture of confidence during his first interview. Now, however, as Olivia watched him being escorted toward the room where Cook and Rawlings waited, his eyes betrayed his fear.

For the last few days, Vonn's shops had been filled with people. Not with customers in search of post-Christmas sales, but with law enforcement personnel from New Bern and Oyster Bay. The two departments were working overtime to collect forensic evidence, inventory the jewelry, review financial records, and interview employees and select customers.

Using Fred as a consultant, Cook and Rawlings arranged some of Derek's equipment in the interview room. They then procured a diamond ring from a repeat customer of Vonn's—an extremely wealthy New Bern woman named Mrs. Troy. Fred believed that Mrs. Troy's three-carat stunner, despite its contemporary setting, was a stolen antique.

"The most popular diamond cut is round," Fred had explained to Rawlings, Cook, and Olivia as the four of them sat together in the chief's office earlier that morning. "Some of the other cuts are more modern. The oval came into being in the sixties. The princess cut in the nineties. The stone in Mrs. Troy's ring is an old European-cut marquise diamond." Fred handed each of them a printout showing a diagram of the cut. "People in the business sometimes refer to this cut as a 'moval,' and it could be seen in pieces from the Edwardian era. I found a similar stone set in an Edwardian Tiffany engagement ring that was purchased from an online auction site for around eighty thousand dollars."

"And this shape matches the ring on the stolen item report filed four years ago by Elizabeth Newcomb, now deceased," Rawlings had said.

Cook, who had a copy of the report in front of him, picked up the narrative. "Yes. The report states that Mrs. Newcomb's daughter didn't realize the ring was gone for several months. She assumed it was in the bank with the rest of her mother's valuables, but wasn't able to search for it because she fell ill herself. Cancer. It was only after she was up and about again that she realized that the ring had gone missing. By then, dozens of people had been in her mother's house and she had no idea who to finger for the crime."

Olivia had grunted. "We do. Was her mother receiving hospice care?"

"Not exactly," Rawlings had said. "Mrs. Newcomb received regular home health-care visits from a nurse, but she was never a hospice patient. She was only hospitalized during the final days of her life."

"This just gets more and more complicated," Cook had grumbled. "Hospice nurses. Traveling nurses. How are we going to track down these thieves?"

Now Olivia sat in the corridor of the police station and stared at Derek Johnston's back. She knew that everything depended on his interview. If Cook and Rawlings could get him to bend, then the larceny ring would fold. After that, Vonn would surely confess all his crimes—even murder. That was what Olivia, and everyone she cared about, was counting on.

"There he goes," Harris said when Derek entered the interview room and the door closed behind him.

"Do you think he'll talk?" Olivia asked.

Harris nodded. "I've learned lots of stuff about that man in the last twenty-four hours. His background is in chemistry. He uses nitric acid and hydrochloric acid heated on a hot plate to separate diamonds from gold. It's a great process. Doesn't damage the stones, and the pieces of metal are put aside and sold for scrap. One of the forensic guys from the New Bern PD found a receipt from the refinery where Johnston's shipping the gold. It's a year old and I'd bet you my desktop that Johnston was supposed to have shredded the thing the moment he got it, but there was a love note from a coworker written on the back and Johnston didn't want to throw it out. So he kept it folded inside his tool chest."

Olivia began to smile. "Let me guess. There's no record of where that gold was acquired. Vonn didn't purchase it from his customers, because Kat told me they stopped buying jewelry for cash."

Harris matched Olivia's smile. "Yeah. He's going to have a difficult time coming up with an explanation for that receipt and hundreds more like it. Once the cops had the name of the refinery, they were able to procure copies of all the receipts for Vonn's Jewelry. Cook has a whole folder of them in the interview room right now. That's why I'm feeling pretty good about how this is going to go." He checked his watch. "I'm just hoping we can get out of here by lunch. All of these late nights are killing me. I need a bacon cheeseburger before they start in on Vonn."

Luckily for Harris, Cook and Rawlings made quick work of Derek Johnston. As Rawlings explained to Olivia and Harris over a quick meal at the Bayside Crab House, the jeweler began to fidget the moment he was shown the receipts.

"He stuck to the line that it wasn't his business to ask where the jewelry came from," Rawlings said while loading his spoon with piping-hot clam chowder. "He just did what he was told and asked no questions. That was what he told us during his first interview too."

"But this time, you were able to use the name of his coworker crush to get him to talk, weren't you?" Harris asked in between bites of onion straws.

Rawlings nodded. "We led him to believe that she was in the next room and, as soon as we were done speaking with him, we were going to accuse her of being involved in the thefts based on the note she'd written on the receipt found in his tool chest. After all, if she wrote on it, she must have known about the selling of the stolen items to the refinery."

Olivia arched her eyebrows. "She didn't know?"

"No," Rawlings said. "The lady in question never turned it over. She simply saw a piece of paper sitting on Mr.

Johnston's workbench and used it to pen a note. She was in a rush because Mr. Johnston was returning from break. I believe her story. Cook does too."

Olivia sighed. "Is this another case of a good woman falling for a bad guy?"

"It's not that black and white." Rawlings sipped more soup and then put down his spoon. "Mr. Johnston was looking to get himself out of debt quickly. Unlike Mr. Bruce's, these were honorable debts. Student loans, a car loan, a mortgage, and a loan taken out to pay for a knee surgery during a time when Mr. Johnston didn't have health insurance. Basically, he got involved with Mr. Vonn because he saw it as his only way to get out from under these debts while he was still young enough to enjoy life." Rawlings switched his empty soup bowl for his shrimp salad plate. "His words. Not mine."

Harris made a thoughtful noise. "I know lots of guys like Derek. Guys in their mid-thirties who want to get married and start a family but can't imagine settling down until they've gotten some of the bigger monkeys off their backs. It must have been so tempting to do what Derek did. He must have thought that he'd only stay in the game for a few years— just until he was in the black again—and then he'd quit."

"He might have done it too," Rawlings said. "Because he wanted to be a man worthy of the woman he loved. That's why he told us everything he knew. And Derek Johnston knew plenty, including the names of the other thieves."

"Really?" Olivia asked, her voice rising in excitement.

Harris actually stopped eating. "All of them?"

"Every one. We have officers en route to their addresses right now." Rawlings took a few seconds to enjoy his salad. Olivia could see that he was also relishing the effect his narrative was having on his dining companions. "In addition to

Stacy, there were six thieves in Vonn's ring," he continued. "And they weren't all female nurses. The majority were, but there was also a male dietitian and a male nurse's aide."

"So what's next?" Harris wanted to know.

Rawlings glanced at his watch. "Cook was too pumped up to leave the station. He was going to grab lunch at his desk and make some calls. We're hoping Vonn's attorney will convince him to cooperate and we can put the robberies and the murder investigations to bed before tonight's party."

"Wouldn't *that* be nice?" Olivia shook her head. "Though it sounds unrealistic."

"The paperwork won't be wrapped up for weeks, especially since we're working with the New Bern PD, but if we could just get that confession—" Rawlings's phone, which rested on the table next to his knife, suddenly vibrated. It skittered sideways on the polished wood surface as though it were a living thing until Rawlings scooped it up and studied the screen.

Olivia didn't like the pinched expression on his face. "What is it?"

"Vonn will confess to running the larceny ring, but he refuses to admit to having anything to do with the murders. He also refuses to give up the name of the individual he believes to be guilty of the crimes." Standing up, he pushed his phone into his pocket. "Sorry to run out on our lunch."

"I'm coming with you," Harris said, wiping his mouth with his napkin. "Emily's flight lands in two hours and I want to help until the second I need to leave for the airport."

Olivia made a shooing motion. "Go! Both of you! Do whatever it takes to put the squeeze on Vonn. We want tonight to be a fresh start, remember? When those champagne corks pop, I hope to God we have a reason to celebrate."

* * *

Olivia spent the remainder of the afternoon at the Boot Top Bistro, assisting the supper club members with the decorations and trying not to read anything into the lack of calls or texts from Rawlings or Harris.

By the time she finally called it a day and headed home, darkness was falling. After feeding Haviland, Olivia decided to relax and read by the fire until either she heard from Rawlings or he showed up at the house.

At last, the sound of his tires crunching on the gravel made Haviland bark out a greeting, and a few minutes later Rawlings had joined Olivia on the sofa.

"That bad?" Olivia asked quietly, taking his hand.

"Mr. Vonn wasted the afternoon making ridiculous demands," Rawlings said wearily. "He'll never get the deal he wants, which is to walk. Even his lawyer realizes that his client has gone off the deep end, so we've given him until tomorrow morning to talk sense into Vonn. After that, any reasonable deal is off the table."

Olivia laid her head on Rawlings's shoulder. "I really wanted to tell Laurel that she no longer had to worry about the investigation. I wanted to see the look on her face and press a glass of champagne in her hand so we could all toast her freedom."

"We're so close," Rawlings said. "Hours away from an answer." He turned and tilted Olivia's chin so that her lips lined up with his. "Until then, we should seize as much happiness as possible. I've missed spending time with you. I've missed our nights on this sofa. Talking before going to sleep. Coffee and the newspaper before work. This case has been hardest on Laurel, but it's taken a toll on us all. So why not respond, now that we're almost at the end of it, by laughing louder and clinging even tighter?"

He didn't give Olivia a chance to reply. His mouth found hers and he plunged his fingers into her hair. His kisses grew hungrier and Olivia responded with equal hunger. Their hands moved urgently as they removed each other's clothes and carelessly tossed them on the rug. Olivia's sweater landed on Haviland, and the poodle headed upstairs in search of a more tranquil dozing spot. Neither Olivia nor Rawlings noticed his departure. They were completely focused on the dancing flames in the hearth and the merging shadows of their bodies.

The supper club members had turned the Boot Top Bistro into a holiday scene straight out of Elizabethan England using dozens and dozens of large candles and greenery. Garlands made of bay, holly, laurel, and ivy leaves hung from the ceiling, and additional laurel leaves had been dipped in gold paint and sprinkled over the surface of every table like confetti.

In addition to Michel's spectacular buffet, there were hors d'oeuvre stations throughout the bar, where attendees could load plates with treats like Othello's Olive Loaf, Desdemona's Stuffed Dates, Iago's Herb Pies, Ophelia's Oysters, or Cleopatra's Cheese Cakes, which were not the modern dessert but a savory cheese tart that Harris couldn't seem to get his fill of.

"I've loved everything so far," Harris said, wrapping his arm around Emily's slim waist. "Except the oysters. I'll pass on those."

Emily, who had a pixielike figure, seemed to be relishing every bite of her food. She possessed boundless energy, a positive outlook, and a ready smile. She wore her blond hair short and spiky, had matching dragonfly tattoos on the insides of her wrists, and came from a large, loud Texan family. All of Harris's friends liked her, and Olivia, who felt she was somewhat of a big sister to Harris, was delighted to see how thrilled Harris and Emily were to be reunited.

"I'm going to try everything!" Emily declared. "Even Petruchio's Pigeon. I've never had pigeon before."

"They're basically rats with wings," Millay said, sidling up to Emily with her date in tow. She'd introduced him as Quinn and seemed atypically shy around him. According to Harris, who'd managed to wheedle a few details out of her about the handsome, dark-haired, bespectacled young man she'd brought along to tonight's event, Quinn was also a novelist. He and Millay had met earlier that fall at a book signing their publisher had organized in Raleigh and had kept in touch. Seeing them together, Olivia could tell that a spark existed between them. She liked Quinn from the first, just as she'd liked Emily, and she hoped Millay gave their burgeoning friendship a chance to develop into something deeper.

The most surprising couple in attendance turned out to be Milton Hobbs and Lynne Chester. Olivia knew that Laurel had given Lynne a pair of tickets to tonight's supper, but she hadn't expected her to arrive on Milton's arm. Nor for her to look so comfortable holding it. Now, watching Lynne chat with Laurel and Steve, Olivia detected several instances of possessive behavior from Lynne. She repeatedly touched Milton in familiar ways. They were the touches one might see between two people who'd known each other a long time, such as a man and wife.

What are you up to? Olivia wondered.

"Heart of gold, my foot," Millay muttered close to Olivia's

ear. "That woman has an agenda. What is it with women and the Hobbs men anyway?"

Olivia didn't have time to give this question the consideration it deserved, for at that moment the swinging doors leading to the kitchen were held open and Michel and one of the sous-chefs appeared. They held a silver platter bearing an entire roast pig.

The men carried their burden to an empty table in the center of the room. After setting it down, Michel announced, "I present to you King Henry the Hog!"

After a round of applause, Michel revealed the other dishes on the buffet line, including Macbeth Meat Pies, Rosalind Rosemary Carrots, Laertes Leeks, Duke of Vienna Venison, Calpurnia Chickpeas, and Cleopatra Chicken with Grapes. The diners took their time with the food, sampling small portions in order to taste more dishes, and everyone was stunned by the complexity of the flavors.

"I thought Elizabethan food would be bland," Harris said, returning to the table he shared with Fred Yoder and the Bayside Book Writers. "But this stuff is awesome! Man, I can't wait to try the desserts!"

"Where are you going to find room for them?" Emily teased.

Harris rubbed his flat belly. "This is a bottomless well."

"It won't stay that way forever," Rawlings warned.

Harris grinned. "That's why I'm going to gather my rosebuds—and my Hamlet Honey Cakes—while I can."

"Why don't you gather me up instead?" Emily suggested. "I like this song."

"Me too," Steve said. Turning to Laurel, he reached for her hand. "May I have this dance?"

After tossing back the rest of her cocktail, Laurel said, "Okay. I can't remember the last time we danced."

Olivia and Rawlings joined their friends on the temporary dance floor that occupied half of the bar area, and when the song was over, they changed partners. Olivia and Fred danced while Rawlings took Shelley for a turn, seeing as Michel was putting out the last of the desserts.

The night wore on and the candles burned lower and lower. Harris sampled Hamlet Honey Cake, Falstaff Fig Tart, Antony Baked Apples, Prospero Pansy Shortbread Cookies, and more.

Finally, as midnight approached, Olivia asked the DJ for a microphone. After making a brief but heartfelt appeal for donations for the Bruce family, she introduced the minister from the Bruces' church. Olivia had called him several days ago, and was delighted when he and his wife had agreed not only to attend the party, but to coordinate all the donations and community efforts on behalf of Julia and the children as well. Though Olivia couldn't say why she hadn't taken Laurel's advice and asked for Lynne Chester's help, she was glad that she hadn't.

There's something predatory about that woman, Olivia thought. *She does an excellent job disguising it, but every so often I catch a glint in her eyes, like the flash of fish scales just below the surface of the water.*

When the pastor was done speaking, Michel took the microphone in preparation to conduct the official countdown to the new year.

Rawlings, who'd been helping the waiters distribute glasses of champagne, pressed one into Olivia's left hand and then folded her right into his. "Hello, lovely lady. Are you ready to spend another exciting and wonderful three hundred and sixty-five days together?"

"I am," Olivia said. After flashing him a tender smile,

she gave his hand a squeeze and glanced around the room. It was magical in the flickering candlelight, and she liked how all the faces gathered around the dance floor looked like small golden moons.

Michel and several members of his supper club had a bunch of noisemakers at the ready on a nearby table, and even more waiters were poised to pop more champagne corks. Olivia sensed a disturbance in the air to her left and pivoted slightly to find Laurel sidling up next to her. Steve was nowhere to be seen.

"This is hard," she whispered, her eyes filling with tears. "I feel incredible pressure to pretend that when this countdown is over, we can start afresh—that everything will be okay. But it still hurts."

"Of course it does," Olivia said. "Did you tell Steve how you're feeling?"

Laurel nodded. "He said that he was sorry and that he loved me. But I don't know what to do. The future is so unclear now."

Olivia saw the pain in her friend's eyes and wished she could take it away. "You don't have to decide tonight. Maybe you could focus on something simpler. Something smaller. Like dancing. How did that feel?"

Laurel smiled. "It felt good."

And suddenly, Steve was there, proffering a champagne flute just as Rawlings had done. "Thank you for taking care of my wife," he said to Olivia. "Especially when I didn't."

Not knowing how else to respond, Olivia raised her glass in acknowledgment before turning back to face Michel.

Michel, ruddy-faced with happiness and alcohol, had the microphone in one hand and an arm around Shelley's waist as he began the countdown. He glanced at his watch and shouted, "Ten!" and everyone began counting backward with him. At five, he abruptly interrupted the countdown and cried, "This will be the best year of my life!"

"Keep counting, you crazy man!" Shelley laughed, giving Michel a loving punch on the shoulder.

"Three . . . two . . . one . . . Happy New Year!" he shouted before tossing the mic on the table and giving Shelley a kiss.

Olivia had never been a fan of overt public displays of affection, so she and Rawlings exchanged a more demure kiss than some couples and therefore, they both saw how Laurel reacted to the sudden assault of loud noises in the dimly lit room. Champagne corks exploded from bottles, noisemakers rattled, and the celebrants—many of whom had overindulged on Shakespearean-themed cocktails—hooted and cheered. Worse, when it seemed as though the cacophony had reached its fever pitch, the DJ reclaimed the microphone, something went awry, and the speaker directly behind Laurel produced the earsplitting nails-down-the-chalkboard keening of feedback.

Everyone in the vicinity winced. Everyone but Laurel. Her eyes went wide with horror. And what Olivia knew was recognition.

Following Laurel's gaze, she saw that her friend was staring at another woman on the far side of the dance floor.

She was staring at Lynne Chester.

"Rawlings!" Though Olivia raised her voice to be heard over the noise, she needn't have bothered. Rawlings was already pulling Laurel behind the bar. Olivia followed a step behind, and by the time she caught up, the feedback sound had stopped and a song had taken its place. Olivia paid no attention to the music. For her, the world had shrunk and only three people existed—herself, Laurel, and Rawlings.

"I remember everything!" Laurel declared wildly. "The

night Stacy died—I saw Lynne! I saw her in the parking lot. It was right after I shouted at Stacy, and she got out of her car. I saw Lynne, and seeing her made me realize how insane I was being." Laurel was talking so fast that her words were almost tripping over one another. "She doesn't know that I saw her—I'm pretty sure of that—because I already had the door to my van open, and I saw her through the back window. Those windows have a special tint on them. You can look out but you can't look in. I guess it protects kids from strangers and the sun, you know. Anyway, Lynne got in Stacy's car. *In the backseat!*"

Olivia and Rawlings exchanged shocked looks. "You're doing great, Laurel. Go on."

Laurel started to cry. "Lord, I know why I blacked this out. Because I had totally screwed up threatening her. I came up looking like a drunken loser, and I was more filled with hate than ever. I shouted, 'I hope you die!' at Stacy. And then I drove away."

Taking hold of Laurel's hand and rubbing the smooth skin of her palm to help calm her, Olivia said, "Millay made a snide comment earlier tonight in which she wondered why women found the Hobbs men so attractive. First Stacy. Now Lynne. I don't think either woman was interested in a relationship."

"Neither do I," Rawlings agreed. "Mrs. Chester volunteers for Tidewater Hospice. She also serves as a deacon and assists with church funerals and thrift store acquisitions. On the surface, she sounds like a saint."

"A saint with horns under her hair," Laurel muttered. "Was this about Rachel's jewelry all along? Stacy seduced my husband to get to that jewelry?"

Rawlings made a noncommittal noise. "It's possible. It's certainly worth more than anything she'd previously netted."

"But Lynne's name never appeared in Mr. Vonn's notebook, so . . ." Olivia trailed off.

"Yes," Rawlings said. "Hers is the name Arnold Vonn refused to give up today. Lynne Chester is the murderer."

Olivia closed her eyes, wishing the three of them could have a moment of quiet. She felt simultaneously relieved and burdened. At last, they knew the killer's identity. But Lynne wasn't in custody. She was across the dance floor, sipping champagne and laughing it up with Milton Hobbs. The hundreds of silver sequins on her tentlike dress winked in the candlelight, and Olivia was reminded of the glint of light on steel. Lynne Chester. A cleaver of a woman. Ready to cut down anyone who came between her and her desires. A woman as cold as frozen metal.

"I have a plan," Rawlings was saying to Laurel. "You and Steve need to leave. Don't say good-bye. Don't let anyone know that your memory has come back. We have the element of surprise on our side right now. Later, when Milton is alone, I'll talk to him about laying a trap for Mrs. Chester. She's obviously after Rachel's jewelry, as I suspect Ms. Balena was as well—so we'll ask Milton to have a New Year's epiphany. He's going to give you the jewelry, Laurel. He'll get it from the bank when it reopens and invite you over for a chat. Mrs. Chester won't be able to resist the opportunity to make a grab for it. But we'll be waiting."

"What about tonight?" Laurel asked fearfully. "Isn't he in danger?"

Rawlings put an arm under Laurel's elbow. "I'll make sure an unmarked car follows him home and watches his house. Olivia, take Laurel back through the kitchen while I find Steve. He can collect your coats." He paused. "You're not driving, are you?"

This elicited a humorless laugh from Laurel. "Lord, no. Steve's only had the champagne toast. He's driving."

Olivia looped her arm through Laurel's. Together, the two friends headed out of the bar area, around the buffet tables in the dining room, and through the swinging doors into the kitchen.

The glare of the overhead lights caught Olivia off guard and she blinked dumbly several times before her eyes became accustomed to the brightness.

"I had the same reaction when I first walked in," Shelley said with a smile in her voice. Her tone quickly changed when she looked at Laurel. "Are you okay?"

Laurel nodded, averting her gaze. "I'm just ready to go home. The chief is getting Steve."

Rawlings must have had no difficulty locating Steve, because Laurel's husband entered the kitchen, paused for a second to adjust to the light, and then immediately rushed to his wife's side. "Can I help?" he whispered solicitously.

"We just need to go," she answered, reaching for her coat. "I'll explain in the car."

"Okay." Steve held out her coat, and once she had it on, the couple made their way to the rear exit.

Laurel had her hand on the door when she glanced back at Olivia. Her eyes were so large and haunted that Olivia began moving toward her friend. She'd closed half the distance when the *whoosh* of one of the swinging doors signaled the arrival of another person and the expression on Laurel's face abruptly changed.

Seeing the terror registered there, Olivia stopped her forward progress and swung around. She saw Lynne Chester standing just inside the doors, gripping a subcompact pistol in both hands.

Olivia noticed two things at once. First, Lynne wasn't holding the gun properly, which indicated that she might not have had experience with the weapon. But even if she had poor aim, she still had too many chances to hit someone.

"Well, well. So this is where the real party's at," she said. Her eyes met Laurel's. "I saw you staring at me. I could tell that you remembered something from the night I killed Stacy, the world's stupidest nurse, so I couldn't let you leave. I can't let any of you leave."

"Why stupid? Because she failed to steal Rachel's jewelry?" Rawlings asked. "Is that why you killed her?"

Lynne pointed the gun at him. "I'm not interested in answering your questions, Chief. But since you're about to die, I'll satisfy your curiosity on one count. Yes, Stacy was supposed to get close to Steve to get the jewelry. One morning, when she was taking care of Rachel, she was snooping and found an inventory of the jewelry, so we knew what the collection was worth. We also knew it was tucked away in the bank. Our best bet was to use Steve to get it out. He was easy prey. An overweight, going-to-gray man with a busy, successful wife and a high-stress, overscheduled life. He was primed for a midlife crisis and an affair with a younger woman—a cliché waiting to happen." She shot Steve a wicked grin. "I read you like a book."

"Not quite," Olivia argued. "Because when push came to shove, Steve didn't want to leave his family. You only wanted the jewelry, but Stacy wanted more. She wanted to trade her scrubs for tennis whites, and when she sensed that Steve was going to reject her, just as Arnold Vonn and her previous two lovers had rejected her, she became unstable, didn't she? She demanded a bigger cut, and you weren't about to give it to her. *You.* Arnold Vonn didn't direct the thieves. You did. You're the ringleader. You recruited them and he trained them and collected the jewelry."

"It was a smooth, profitable operation until Stacy came along and screwed it all up," Lynne said in what sounded like a snarl. "I enjoyed burning her. And I knew the cops would blame the scorned wife." She shifted her cold gaze to Laurel. "Stacy told me what you said to her the day you found her hubby in bed with her. She told me how you wanted to see her burn. That dumb cow thought we were such good friends. And you, Blondie, you gave me the idea. Burning Stacy seemed like a good way to get rid of evidence and pin the murder on you all at once. I figured a good citizen like you would confess what you said that night in Stacy's house as soon as they put you in handcuffs. Guess I misjudged you. Guess we all keep secrets, don't we?"

Rawlings made a dismissive sound that was somewhere between a grunt and a snort. "Laurel didn't give you the idea to smack Gordon Bruce over the head with a cleat."

Lynne's hands were trembling and Olivia suspected that the metal pistol was growing cumbersome.

"No, but I was smart enough to scout out that spot ahead of time. I'm no MMA fighter, but I knew if I clocked Bruce with a cleat, he'd topple off the dock. After that, the cold and the water would do the rest." Lynne pointed the gun at Shelley, who gave a squeak. "Open the door to the walk-in."

Once Shelley had the door to the huge refrigerator open, Lynne barked out her next command. "All right. Everybody in."

"If you fire that weapon, dozens of people will rush in here," Rawlings pointed out calmly. "You will be captured."

"Are you sure they'll hear the shot over the music?" Lynne asked, a smug smile on her plump face. "Are you sure you want to take that risk with your wife's life? With your friend's life? How about a pregnant woman? What do you say, Chief?"

Laurel, Steve, and Olivia entered the walk-in. Rawlings gestured for Shelley to enter, but Shelley seemed frozen in fear.

"Get her in there, Chief!" Lynne shouted, her eyes gleaming with nervous rage.

Rawlings prodded Shelley toward the chilled cavity where the rest of them stood huddled close together, but Shelley panicked and lunged in the opposite direction.

There was a scream and the shocking report of gunfire.

The door to the walk-in closed, but Olivia rushed forward and pushed on the knob, her heart beating so fast that it threatened to break through her rib cage like a freed bird.

"He saved me!" Shelley wailed when she saw Olivia emerge from the cold space. "I'm so sorry, Olivia! I'm *so* sorry!"

Shelley was pressing a folded apron against Rawlings's forehead. As Olivia watched in horror, the snowy-white cotton turned red.

There was no sign of Lynne Chester.

Chapter 17

For last year's words belong to last
  year's language
And next year's words await another
  voice.
And to make an end is to make a
  beginning.

—T. S. ELIOT

It felt like an eternity before other people entered the kitchen, but after they did, time sped up until the minutes blurred together like wet ink. Before Olivia knew what was happening, Rawlings was being taken to New Bern on a Flight for Life medical helicopter and Millay was bundling her into the passenger seat of her car.

"Cook got Lynne Chester," someone had said. Olivia didn't know if she'd heard this five seconds or fifteen minutes ago. Certain words and phrases were just permeating the fog in her brain. "Cook chased Lynne down and tackled her in the middle of the street. She shot at him, but that didn't even slow him. Seeing the chief lying on the floor like that—he wasn't going to let her get away, and he didn't."

Olivia hadn't responded to this remark or to any others. Her dress was sticky with Rawlings's blood. Someone—Laurel, maybe—had led her to the prep sink in the kitchen and helped her wash her hands. It had been someone with a gentle mother's touch and a patient mother's whisper. Olivia had tried to stay focused, because she knew that Rawlings needed her, but the image of his vacant stare and the way the sink water had turned pink as the soap cleaned the blood from her skin was too much. She'd retreated to a far corner of her mind.

She couldn't remember the drive to the hospital. At some point, she was given a pair of blue scrubs to wear and Millay and Laurel led her into a restroom to change. When she reemerged, Charles Wade was standing in the waiting room. His presence, so incongruent with the rest of the night's events, finally snapped her out of her state of shock.

"Dad?" She hadn't meant to say the word. After all, she was angry with him. At any other time, she would have called him Charles or pretended he didn't exist. But he was here. Tall and debonair. Wide of shoulder and quietly authoritative. And when he moved toward her, his arms opening as he walked, she rushed to meet his embrace.

"Oh, honey," he murmured into her hair. "I'm sorry I ran off. But I'm here now, and I'll never leave you again. Not ever."

Olivia let him guide her deeper into the large waiting room designated for families and friends of patients undergoing surgery. It had been filling up as the hours passed. Rawlings's sister, Jeannie, and her family arrived, along with Dixie and Grumpy. Many people who'd attended the New Year's Eve party had gone home, changed clothes, caught a few hours' sleep, and now sat or stood in clusters, holding take-out coffee cups in lieu of champagne flutes. By the time the morning of the New Year fully broke as a pewter-hued, somnolent January day, word had spread through Oyster Bay that Chief Rawlings was fighting for his life.

Michel and Shelley arrived just ahead of a group of cops.

It was clear that Shelley had been crying. When she knelt in front of Olivia, fresh tears spilled from her eyes.

"This is all my fault! I don't know what came over me. I just felt this inexplicable panic. I don't know if it's because I'm pregnant or what, but I thought that if I went inside the walk-in, that would be the end for all of us. The chief . . . he jumped in front of me. He pushed me out of the way and saved my life." She touched her belly. "Both of our lives."

"That's who Rawlings is. It's what he does," Olivia said calmly. "None of this is your fault. It's Lynne Chester's fault." Unlike Shelley, Jeannie, Laurel, or Dixie, Olivia hadn't shed a tear. In her mind, to cry was to admit that Rawlings might lose his fight, and she refused to concede this possibility, despite what the surgeon had told her. She'd heard the damning phrases. She knew that "extreme blood loss" and "severe damage to the tissue of the frontal lobe" were grave. She was also aware that having to undergo emergency procedures to "relieve the pressure on the brain" and "avoid organ failure" were less than hopeful, but she would not give up on her husband.

Of all the people who streamed into the waiting room, the last person Olivia expected to see was Officer Cook. Everyone stepped aside to allow him unhindered passage to Olivia's side. Laurel, who'd been sitting next to Olivia, instantly gave up her chair.

Cook dropped into it, looking years older than he had seemed the last time Olivia laid eyes on him.

"What's the latest update?" he asked Olivia.

She shook her head. "It's touch-and-go. That's all they'll say. They're pumping him full of everything they've got. I know that. They're doing their best. I know that too. I saw the X-ray." She paused, took a breath, and continued. "How can such a small piece of metal do so much damage?"

Cook grabbed her hand. Thinking of how far she and Cook had come from the days when they'd shared a mutual dislike, Olivia rewarded him with a smile. "What's your news?"

"When Vonn learned that we had Lynne Chester in custody, he was clawing at the cell bars to get our attention. Guess he realized that his hopes for a deal had just gone down the toilet."

"I can't seem to feel any sympathy for the man," Olivia said in a dry voice.

Cook shook his head. "No one does. He sang like a nightingale anyway. I guess he's hoping it'll make him look remorseful when it comes time for sentencing. And once he gave his confession, it didn't take long for us to get Lynne's. The woman is arrogant, Olivia. She was eager to brag about how she successfully orchestrated this larceny ring for years. And the murders? Same thing. Arrogance kept her talking and talking. Stacy was greedy and emotionally weak, so she had to be killed. Gordon's murder wasn't as personal, but he found out that Stacy was a thief and so he had to go too."

Millay, who'd been listening in from a chair across the aisle, leaned closer to Cook. "How did Lynne lure Gordon to that fishing dock? I can't believe he would have been dumb enough to meet anyone there—let alone someone he didn't know."

"He thought he was meeting Arnold Vonn. And he agreed to the meeting because he wanted to protect his marriage," Cook said. "People will do desperate things when they have a secret to keep."

"The online sports betting?" Harris guessed.

Cook nodded. "Lynne e-mailed Gordon at his work address using Vonn's home computer. She knew where Vonn kept a spare key to his house. She also knew that his security system was mostly for show—he rarely turned it on. After she sent the e-mail to Gordon, she warned him not to reply and erased all signs of her activity."

"Pretty tech-savvy for a woman her age."

"She's probably fifty-five. That's hardly old," Millay said irritably. "And she might be a nasty egomaniac, but she isn't stupid." She returned her attention to Cook. "Was it a blackmail message?"

Cook paused to consider his reply. "It was presented more as an offer to trade services. A 'you scratch my back and I'll scratch yours' type of thing. Except for the tone of urgency and the repeated warnings to keep both the message and the meeting a secret, it could have been an invitation to a Christmas cookie exchange."

"Having seen Vonn's TV commercials too many times to count, I'm having trouble picturing him rolling out cookie dough over a flour-dusted countertop." Millay smirked. "The guy liked to get his hands dirty, but only if that filled his pockets with another type of dough."

Ignoring Millay's interruption, Cook continued his narrative. "Mr. Vonn said that he'd heard of Gordon's financial issues from the loan officer at the bank. Seeing as Gordon was an investor in Vonn's third store, this was quite possible. Of course, it was Stacy who learned of Gordon's gambling debts. Gordon was still using an old e-mail address from when they were still married, and Stacy had a habit of logging on to it and reading his e-mail."

"That woman was a serious piece of work," Olivia said, feeling a fresh wave of disgust. "One usually hears redeeming qualities about a person after she's passed away, but I've yet to discover a single positive character trait pertaining to Stacy Balena."

Cook threw out his hands as though to say that he was

unable to supply anything either. "Believe it or not, Stacy planned to blackmail her ex-husband into spending time with her. She probably intended to sabotage his marriage and—"

Laurel uttered an expletive that made Cook falter.

"Sorry," she said, coloring.

"Lynne knew this would end in disaster," Cook continued. "Between Stacy's failure to secure Rachel's jewelry, her obsession with her ex, and her desire to quit work and step into another woman's shoes as the wife of a successful professional, she was a liability. However, it wasn't until Lynne was in the back of Stacy's car and had injected her with a syringe loaded with morphine that Stacy told her she was too late—Gordon already knew about the thefts."

"Wait, wait!" Laurel interjected. "So Stacy *tried* to blackmail Gordon, but he not only refused but turned around and told her he knew what bad stuff *she* was up to?"

"Exactly," Cook said. "The New Bern PD finished combing through Mr. Bruce's digital correspondence and they found a series of deleted cell phone texts from the night Gordon fell off the wagon. That was the same night Stacy contacted him."

Olivia frowned. "But how did Gordon find out about the stolen jewelry?"

"This is the craziest part of the whole story," Cook said. "Their kids found out. Stacy and Gordon's. They were in Stacy's bedroom while Stacy was at the store. She'd been gone for ages and the kids were bored. They started digging around for things to try on and they found a shoe box of beautiful jewelry. Gordon had given the eldest kid a smartphone in case she ever needed to call him, and she used it to take a photo of the jewelry. Gordon saw the photo, considered Stacy's profession, and put two and two together. Not right away, of course."

Laurel gaped at Cook. "If he'd gone to the authorities, his kids would still have a father. What was he thinking?"

Olivia answered before Cook could. "Like Cook said, people will go to great lengths to keep a secret."

"I can understand that kind of crazy. What I can't comprehend is why Lynne didn't leave last night's party." Harris waved his empty coffee cup in the air. "Why not just walk out the front door and drive away? Why the dramatic scene in the kitchen?"

A protective arm curled around Olivia's shoulder and she looked to find Charles staring at her in concern. However, she'd been asking herself the same question. In fact, it had been torturing her. Almost as much as the waiting.

She faced Cook again, knowing that he wouldn't speak again unless she indicated that he should. She gave him a small nod of encouragement.

"Lynne Chester had totally snapped by the time she grabbed her handbag, headed to the kitchen, and pulled out that Smith and Wesson subcompact," Cook said. "She'd never even fired that gun. A nurse's aide had recently stolen it from an elderly man's home—a man with no family. The gentleman didn't have a permit for the pistol, so it was the perfect weapon for Lynne to pocket." He shot a glance at Laurel. "With Vonn in custody, Lynne knew she was running out of time. Her plan was to use the gun to threaten Milton into surrendering the key to his safe-deposit box to her."

Laurel gasped. "Would she have killed him after he surrendered the key?"

"I believe so." The gravity of Cook's words and the different scenarios that could have played out hung over their small group like a thundercloud. "Lynne assumed Milton had followed the rest of you into the kitchen. She didn't see him because he and Steve were having a heart-to-heart in the men's restroom." Cook's eyes simmered with anger and he balled his hands into tight fists. "We should have pressed Vonn harder. We shouldn't have given him until this morning. If we'd put the screws to him, we'd have had Lynne in custody and the chief wouldn't be in there." He jabbed his white-knuckled fist toward the operating room doors.

Olivia laid a hand over Cook's. "We can't do that to ourselves. Those what-if scenarios. They'll drive us insane. And we're not the ones who came unglued. Lynne is. What was her motive, though? What drove her to become this person?"

"I'm no shrink, but I'd have to say it was power. She thrived on having control over others she viewed as weaker than herself," Cook said. "When I asked about her life as a working-woman, she turned bitter like that." He snapped his fingers to demonstrate. "Claims she had a series of chauvinistic bosses who treated her very unfairly."

"They exist," Millay said. "Believe me, I have friends who work for guys like that now."

"And women still don't receive equal pay for equal work," Laurel added. "I can understand a measure of bitterness." Her eyes cut to Olivia. "I'm not defending Lynne's actions, believe me."

Cook shifted uncomfortably. He wasn't interested in engaging in a feminist debate. "As for preying on the elderly, I'd have to guess that Lynne was holding on to old anger. She was a late-in-life baby. Her parents were forty and forty-two when she was born. They hadn't planned on having children, and she says they weren't exactly warm and loving. Also, they both had medical issues and Lynne got saddled with taking care of them. She never got to take time to do things for herself. There was never money for her dreams. She didn't get to make her own choices until her folks were gone. Lots of resentment there."

"Wow," Charles said, speaking for the first time since Cook's arrival. "The damage we can inflict on our families—on our spouses and children—is unfathomable. If only someone really strong shook us by the shoulders every so often and yelled, 'Treat the ones who love you right! Nothing matters as much as they do!'"

"That would be a good service," Laurel said. "Maybe Harris could design a smartphone app to replicate that. It could include music, photos of your family and friends in a slide show format, and maybe a haptic buzz."

Millay rolled her eyes. "It'll take more than a haptic vibration for some people to get a clue."

"Like me," Charles said. "I needed a Taser."

Olivia glanced at him. "How did you get here so fast anyway?"

"I was at a hotel in Raleigh when Laurel called to tell me what happened." Charles paused to flash a grateful smile at Laurel before focusing on Olivia again. "I wanted to spend the upcoming year, and all the rest of my years, in Oyster Bay. I bought a house not too far from you on the Point. I also spent the last few days on the phone, working things out with Emmett so that we can divvy up responsibilities at the bookstore and he can finally take a vacation." He gazed at Olivia with the same deep ocean water blue eyes as hers. "I thought it would be best if I didn't just show up at your door. I wanted to let you get used to my being back."

"I know why you left," Olivia said. "But you should have stuck around. You underestimated the people of Oyster Bay. They'd have taken you in. You were one of us. They didn't blame you because bad things happened. They blamed those responsible for the crimes. Just as now. Lynne and Arnold and Stacy and the bad people here. No one else."

Charles glanced down at Olivia's hand, which was enfolded

in his. "I couldn't believe that, you see. Because I *felt* responsible. I felt like a bad man. I had to get away to realize that I was running from the best place—and people—I'd ever found."

"People do really stupid things when they think they've let down the most important people in their lives," said a new voice. Everyone turned to find Steve Hobbs standing in the aisle between two rows of chairs. He held a shopping bag stuffed with presliced bagels in one hand and a bulk cardboard coffee box with a dispenser in the other. "I knew I wasn't doing a good job as a husband and father," he said, addressing Laurel. "I felt like a failure. I felt like I couldn't face you and the kids, so I did bad things to try to hide from myself. I'm truly sorry, Laurel. And I'm sorry to everyone here too, because you had to step in time and time again to support my wife after I'd let her down. But that won't happen anymore. I'm going to prove that I'm worthy of her. I'm going to work really hard to be a man she deserves."

Laurel looked both pleased and embarrassed by Steve's speech. She stood, smiled, and murmured something to him. He then handed her the bag of bagels and the two of them began moving through the waiting room, passing out food and coffee.

"That couldn't have been easy," Millay said. "I hope he means it."

"Me too," Harris said. "I want them to make it. I'd like to know that there are people who survive the 'for worse' part of the marriage vow."

In the silence that followed, Olivia wondered if the rest of them were thinking what she was thinking. Would she and Rawlings survive the "in sickness" part of that vow? She'd known from the start that falling for an officer of the law carried a high level of risk, but she couldn't help her feelings. Her heart had found its home in Sawyer Rawlings. Besides, all true forms of love came with risk. Perhaps the only risk worth taking. Life had taught Olivia Limoges that much.

Her silent musings were abruptly interrupted by an automated hiss, indicating that the wood doors leading to the operating rooms were opening.

The surgeon's gaze scanned the waiting room in search of Olivia. His mask was pulled down beneath his chin and he looked haggard. The fatigue etched into his face proved that he'd been working ceaselessly for hours, doing everything in his power to give Rawlings a fighting chance. But had his efforts paid off?

Olivia slowly got to her feet, making it easier for the doctor to pick her out in the crowd. She knew he'd have no trouble spotting her. Not many women were nearly six feet tall with a shock of moon pale hair.

And when the surgeon's eyes met hers across the room, the world suddenly went very still. For when Olivia saw the shadows pass over his gray irises like wind shifting a winter sea, she knew that her husband was gone.

Six months after the funeral, Olivia had yet to write a single word.

She would take out her notebook from time to time, but the words wouldn't come.

She hadn't abandoned her other routines. They were what kept her afloat. Her restaurants. Her partnership in Through the Wardrobe. Lunches with friends. Suppers with her father. Walks on the beach with Haviland. She did these things because they gave her life a semblance of meaning, but she couldn't remember the last time she'd laughed with genuine abandon or looked to the future with a thrill of anticipation.

Olivia Limoges wasn't one to give in to despair because she'd been dealt an unfair hand. She was made of sterner stuff. But when she didn't feel like getting out of bed, she thought of her ancestors on the Wade side—the men and women who rose when it was still dark, shrugging into clothes that smelled of salt spray and sweat, preparing for another long day of hard labor. The men would do battle with the sea, hoping to return home with full nets, while the women cooked, laundered, mended, cleaned, worked in the garden, looked after children, and performed dozens of other tasks. These people—grandfathers and grandmothers to Willie and Charles Wade—didn't quit when a storm blew in. They lowered their heads, buttoned their coats, and stepped out into the wind and driving rain.

Olivia looked in the mirror each morning, acknowledged that she was now a widow, and knew she must also walk through a storm. And though the wind and rain resided within her, she fought against it with every dawn.

But on a dazzlingly sun-filled July day, she felt a slight easing of her grief. For Michel called her landline from the hospital—the same hospital where Rawlings had died—to tell her that Shelley had just delivered their baby boy. He was a big boy too. Almost ten pounds.

"It's all the protein Shelley ate!" Michel cried, unable to contain his joy. "Olivia, he is so beautiful! I've never seen anything in this world more beautiful! And he has this *smell*! *Mon Dieu!* It is the perfume of the angels clinging to the crown of his little golden head. I can't stop sniffing him. Or looking at him. His tiny fingers. His fat legs. His skin is like a seashell."

"This child isn't going to be spoiled. Not at all," Olivia said, a smile playing at the corners of her mouth. She was already picturing Michel buying his son a pint-size kitchen complete with pots and pans and a chef's outfit, and all this before the boy had learned to crawl.

Michel giggled with glee. "Without a doubt! Where are you? Is your cell phone nearby?"

"I'm on the back deck. Haviland and I were just about to go for a walk before it gets too hot."

"Get your cell. I sent you a picture of my son. The *first* picture, seeing as you're his godmother."

Olivia's smile grew larger. "All right, I admit to being curious. Don't expect me to squeal, though. You know I don't lose my mind over babies the way some women do."

"That's going to change, *ma cherie*," Michel declared firmly. "You are about to fall in love."

Now Olivia was freely laughing. She laughed until she went inside, picked up her phone, and saw the face of the baby staring out of her screen. Michel hadn't been exaggerating. The child was beautiful. Olivia was so entranced by his eyes, which seemed to reflect all the hues of the sea at once—from its bright tidal pools, to the darker water where the schools of big fish swam, to the shadowed trenches where only ghost light reached.

"His name is Sawyer," Michel said softly. "Sawyer Michel. I had to be included somehow. My ego wouldn't accept anything else. But the moment we saw him, we knew. Those eyes. They are so much like the chief's, no?"

Olivia had to swallow the lump in her throat before she could reply. "He would be so pleased."

"So buy a new dress!" Michel continued giddily. "We are going to have a huge christening in six weeks! You'll have to help Shelley deal with my family, Lord help you both. And come to the hospital this afternoon. Sawyer wants to meet his godmother. By the way, you are now *Fée* Olivia. The French word for godmother is much more charming than the English one, don't you think?" Without giving Olivia a chance to reply, Michel barreled on. "I must find coffee. I refuse to drink coffee that comes out of a *vending* machine. Talk to you soon, *Fée* Olivia."

Olivia did go to the hospital, though part of her resisted the idea. She experienced a fresh wave of pain when she passed through the first set of automated doors, but as soon as Michel placed the baby in her arms, she forgot about her grief. It was impossible not to smile at such a beautiful child. And Michel was right. He smelled of something inordinately sweet. An aroma that couldn't be identified or defined. Something otherworldly.

Olivia didn't suddenly become a baby person then and there. The child didn't cure her grief or gain more of her affection than her niece and nephew already claimed, but gain her affection he did.

By the time of his christening, she and the child had formed an unbreakable bond. Baby Sawyer's face lit up whenever his *fée* Olivia came into his range of view, and when she gazed into his fathomless blue eyes, she was inspired to rock him late into the night and whisper to him of the people of Oyster Bay.

Olivia wanted to put aside all thoughts of people like Stacy Balena, Arnold Vonn, and Lynne Chester. She wanted, she realized, to write about a roller-skating dwarf named Dixie. About an antique store proprietor and his beloved Westie. About a computer geek who moonlighted for the cops and had finally won over the girl of his dreams. About a bestselling novelist with exotic looks who'd released her second novel to record sales and talk of a movie deal. About a mother, wife, and successful journalist who was one of the strongest and truest people in the whole town. About a police chief who created wonderful art in his garage, loved chocolate milk, classic rock, Hawaiian shirts, and tales of pirates.

But Olivia would write about herself first. Not her current self. Her childhood self. She wanted to write simple stories about a girl who lived in a lighthouse keeper's cottage. She would make these happy stories, she decided. Fictional stories. The girl would have a dog. A black poodle. He would be her best friend. Her companion through thick and thin. Together, they would hunt for treasure on the beach. They would share many adventures and encounter a multitude of wonderful and memorable characters. Sea captains and barmaids, librarians and fruit stall vendors, bakers and boat builders. Olivia could practically hear the words singing in her veins.

"Let's take a walk. When we get back, I'll start," she told Haviland one early September morning, and slung the metal detector over her right shoulder.

Following the poodle over the dunes, she passed through the shadow of the lighthouse and headed for the finger of sand stretching out into the water. As was her custom, she didn't lower the Bounty Hunter until this point. She now began sweeping the head of the detector over the sand in a wide left-to-right motion, listening to the chirps and bleeps coming through her headphones.

Haviland had sandpipers to occupy his interest, but when Olivia paused to dig in the sand, he obediently stopped chasing the birds to assist her. She unfolded the trench shovel, scooped sand into the sieve, and shook the sieve until the sand rained through its holes.

"Nothing," she informed her poodle.

Using his front paws, Haviland dug beside her while she repeated her sifting process. On the third scoop of sand, something rattled around the bottom of the sieve.

"What do we have here?" she asked, pinching a coin between her thumb and forefinger.

Normally, Olivia would pocket her find and soak it in a vinegar bath once she was back home. She'd then store the cleaned and dried item in a jumbo pickle jar labeled with the year. Today, however, the sea breeze was so refreshing and the water had such a starry sparkle that she kicked off her shoes and waded into the surf to scrape the crust of grime and dried sand from the coin with the edge of a clam-shell.

After a minute of concentrated labor, she straightened with a laugh. "It's a penny! All that work for a penny."

She would keep it, of course. It would go into the jar with the rest of her treasures. And for the moment, she would simply stand and relish the feel of sunlight on her shoulders and the way the damp sand squelched between her toes.

The penny winked in her palm as though demanding her attention. She glanced down at the coin. Raising it closer to her eyes, she squinted at the embossed date. It had been minted the year Rawlings was born.

Olivia Limoges stood in the shallows, the water gently bobbing around her calves, and closed her hand around the coin. Fixing her gaze on the lighthouse beacon—the brilliant, dependable, and never-faltering light that had been with her since childhood—she smiled.

To see how it all began, turn the page
for an excerpt from the first book in the series,

A Killer Plot

Available now from Berkley Prime Crime.

Chapter 1

Writers should be read,
but neither seen nor heard.

—DAPHNE DU MAURIER

Two of Oyster Bay's lifelong citizens were in line at the Stop 'n' Shop, gossiping over carts stuffed with frozen entrées, potato chips, boxes of Krispy Kremes, and liters of soda when Olivia Limoges breezed through the market's automatic doors.

"Here she comes, Darlene. The grouchiest woman on the entire North Carolina coast," the first woman remarked, jerking her head toward the produce department.

"And the richest." Darlene watched as Olivia examined a pyramid of peaches, turning the fruit around and caressing the flushed velvet skin of each golden orb before placing it in her cart. "She's good-lookin' enough. Doesn't have the curves most men wanna hold on to at night, but with all that money, you'd think she could net at least one fish."

"She might have more money than Oprah, but she ain't *exactly* a ray of sunshine," her companion pointed out. "Half the town's scared of her."

"That's because half the town works for her, Sue Ellen." Darlene pulled a sour face as her friend dumped a family-size Stouffer's lasagna on the moving belt.

"She ever smile at you, Mandy?" the woman named Sue Ellen questioned the cashier.

Mandy cracked her gum and shrugged. "Ms. Olivia is nice enough, I reckon."

"Maybe she likes *younger* men. You know, one of those male models or somethin'. Or maybe she wants 'em to be rich and speak three languages and be as high and mighty as she is. She's too fussy if you ask me. That's why she doesn't have a man," Sue Ellen whispered, clearly impressed with her own insight as the cashier ran her friend's check through the register. "Who knows what's goin' on in that big ole house of hers?"

Darlene's dull brown eyes turned misty. "If *I* had all that money, I'd go on one of those cruises with them chocolate buffets. You ever heard of such an amazin' thing? Whole fountains of chocolate! You can dunk strawberries or cookies or little bits of cake right in 'em. Lordy! I'd eat chocolate until I couldn't move."

Sue Ellen unloaded two jumbo-size bags of potato chips and a bouquet of scentless carnations onto the belt. "She oughta *give back* to the community. After all, she grew up in Oyster Bay. Lots of folks kept an eye on her when her daddy was off on one of his trips."

"Which trips?" Darlene snorted cruelly. "The fishin' trips or the ones where he drifted along the coast with a net in the water and a case of whiskey by his side?"

"Either one. With her mama passin' on when she was still at such a tender age, that girl needed folks to look in on her. I recall *my* mama bringin' her a tuna casserole more than once. And how about that lighthouse cottage?" Sue Ellen was becoming flushed in righteous indignation. "The way she's lettin' it fall to pieces—it's a disgrace! She should fix it up and let the town use it. It's not *our* fault her daddy left her all alone out on that boat in the middle of a storm for—"

Bam! The woman's words stuck in her throat as a twenty-pound bag of Iams Premium dog food was slapped onto the belt, instantly flattening the potato chips and the tight cluster of carnations.

"Good morning, Mandy." The tall woman with white blond hair greeted the cashier as though the other customers did not exist. "Just the peaches and the dog food, please. And whatever you've already scanned from my neighbor's cart. You can charge me for the chips and flowers twice, seeing as they'll both have to be replaced."

Mandy nodded, biting back a smile. She rang up Olivia's fruit and kibble as well as the other woman's frozen dinners, rump roast, potato chips, flowers, cookie dough ice cream, and maxi pads. Olivia swiped a credit card through the reader, shouldered the dog food bag as though it was filled with helium, grabbed her peaches, and wished Mandy a pleasant day.

She walked out of the store, squinting as the sun bore down on her. She slid glasses over eyes that had been fiery with anger a moment ago but had now returned to a placid lake water blue.

Inside her Range Rover, Captain Haviland, her black-furred standard poodle, barked out a hello.

"You may find that a portion of your kibble's been pulverized into crumbs, Captain. I'm afraid my temper got the better of me." Olivia gunned the engine, drove seven blocks north, and swung into an available handicapped parking space. Haviland barked again and added an accusatory sniff.

"It's tourist season. There's no place else to park and if I *do* get ticketed, that'll just add more funds to the community treasure chest. Apparently, I don't give back enough," Olivia snidely informed her dog, and together they marched into Grumpy's Diner. Olivia established herself at the counter, ordered coffee, and perused the headlines of *The Washington Post*. However, her concentration was repeatedly broken by a group of people seated at the diner's largest booth. They were tossing out words like "dialogue," "point of view," and "setting," and since Olivia had been trying to write a book on and off for the past five years, her curiosity was aroused.

She kept the paper raised, as though an article on escalating interest rates was inordinately captivating, while she listened intently as a woman read aloud from what sounded like a work of romantic fiction.

"Maureen put her eye to the keyhole and gasped. There was her mistress, the duchess, in the arms of a strange man. His fingers were unlacing her gown, slowly, letting each piece of delicate silk slide over his powerful fingers."

"What drivel," Olivia Limoges muttered to Haviland as the reader paused for breath. The poodle sneezed. Feeling that her canine companion hadn't been in clear agreement with her assessment, Olivia leaned to the right in order to eavesdrop further.

"He then turned her around, roughly, and pushed her frock to the floor. I could hear her gasp as he caressed the ribbons on her petticoat, his dark eyes never leaving the duchess's amber ones."

Olivia snorted. "Cats have amber eyes. *People* do not." She cast a glance at the author who had abruptly ceased speaking, seemingly reluctant to continue. She was a pretty woman—small-framed and smooth-skinned, with hair the color of sunlit wheat—but her face was discolored and puffy, indicating a consistent lack of sleep.

"Go on, Laurel, my dear. I sense we're nearing the *juicy* part," a middle-aged man with carefully gelled hair, a peach silk shirt, and finely manicured hands urged.

"Maureen knew she should back away from the door, but the stranger's movements were hypnotizing. His hand, which resembled the callused palm of a man engaged in trade, not the smooth, pampered hands belonging to a gentleman, eased apart my lady's bodice. His eyes lingered on the heaving swell of her breasts—"

Olivia couldn't contain herself. "Not heaving breasts!" she exclaimed with a wry laugh. "Anything but those!"

The woman named Laurel blushed furiously and dropped her paper onto the table in front of her.

"If you'd like to share your opinion, it'd be a mite easier if you joined their group instead of hollerin' across the counter. It's this kind of behavior that makes folks think you're an odd duck," a high-pitched voice emanating from Olivia's left scolded. "Good morning, Captain," the woman greeted the poodle warmly. "Your usual, sir?"

Haviland issued a polite bark and parted his mouth in order to smile at the familiar speaker.

"Good morning, Dixie." Olivia folded her paper in half and smoothed out the wrinkles. "And for your information, people think I'm odd because I'm rich and single and perfectly content. All three of those factors are a rarity here in Oyster Bay." Olivia lowered her empty coffee cup from the counter so the vertically challenged diner proprietor could fill it with her famously strong brew.

At a total height of four feet seven inches tall, including the two inches provided by a pair of roller skates and an inch of comb-teased, sun-streaked brown hair, Dixie Weaver had the body of a kindergartener. She was not as young or as well proportioned as a five-year-old however, being that she was a dwarf.

"Dwarf" was the term Dixie preferred, and the residents of their coastal town had learned long ago never to refer to her as a "little person."

"I'm of short stature," she had told Olivia soon after Olivia had moved back to town and had struck up an immediate friendship with the feisty, roller-skating diner owner. "I'm not *little*. 'Little' implies young or innocent. Like a cute puppy or a baby bird. I'm a middle-aged waitress with a litter of children and a permanent tan. I smoke and do shots of tequila and I'm *not* cute. 'Sides, I haven't been *innocent* since the eighth grade. And do you have any idea how much I hate havin' to wear clothes from Walmart's kids' department? I can't *exactly* pull off sexy wearin' Strawberry Shortcake, now, can I?"

Today, Dixie was garbed in denim overalls, a green-and-white-striped T-shirt, and rainbow leg warmers. Her hair was meticulously feathered as though she were a diminutive version of Farrah Fawcett and her large ale brown eyes were amplified by a layer of frosty baby blue shadow that spanned the entire area of skin from upper lid to brow.

"Someone's in my booth," Olivia complained to Dixie, gesturing at the table in the corner of the room. Most of the Oyster Bay residents knew better than to plant their buttocks on the red vinyl cushions of that booth between eight and eight thirty a.m. That was when Olivia frequently showed up at Grumpy's to claim a booth. She'd then spend the better part of the morning there, eating, sipping coffee, and writing.

It was the only booth not surrounded by Andrew Lloyd Webber paraphernalia, as it butted against the diner's front window. Dixie, who practically worshipped the king of musicals, had filled her establishment with posters, masks, and themed-decorations celebrating the composer's work. It was an adoration Olivia did not share with her closest friend, and she preferred the street view to being seated beneath a pair of Dixie's used roller skates and a poster of *Starlight Express* illuminated by strings of pink Christmas lights.

"You sound like one of the three bears." Dixie lowered her voice to a squeaky growl. "Somebody's been eatin' in my booth and they're still *there*!"

The current occupants were not locals. They hadn't been seated for long either, as they had only been served beverages. Olivia was surprised to see four college-age boys awake, dressed, and functioning so early in the day. Normally, they'd have been slumbering with their mouths open on the floor of a six-bedroom vacation home surrounded by empty beer bottles, brimming ashtrays, and overturned bongs.

"You can eat here at the counter for once. It would do you good to rub elbows with your neighbors. Livin' out there on the Point, all alone with your ghosts, with only a dog to keep you company." She quickly stroked Haviland between the ears. "No offense to you, sweet darlin'." Dixie cocked a steaming coffee carafe aloft. "It ain't good for you to be all work and no play. Why don't you take your highfalutin ass over to the *Song and Dance* booth and join that writer's club? They call themselves the Bayside Book Writers, and since you're tryin' to write, it seems to me like you all were destined to meet."

Olivia grunted. "What do you mean by 'trying'?" Still, she cast a quick glance at the document on her laptop screen and sighed. "I never realized it would be so hard to write a book. Do you know how many times I've started this novel? I've never consistently failed in achieving a personal goal before."

Before Dixie could reply, an elderly couple entered the diner and immediately looked befuddled. Dixie skated over, handed them menus, and pointed at the empty *Evita* booth.

She then disappeared into the kitchen for several minutes, which Olivia suspected were spent smoking Parliaments out the fire door. When Dixie reemerged, she was carrying Olivia's breakfast on a decoupage tray. Pivoting onto the toes of her skates, she pushed the heavy china platter onto the counter.

"One spinach and feta omelet with half a grapefruit." She slid another plate in front of Haviland. "And scrambled eggs and sausage for you, my pet."

The poodle held out his paw. Dixie accepted it and then leaned against the empty stool next to Olivia. "So the book's not exactly writin' itself then?"

Olivia pushed her laptop aside in order to eat her breakfast. "I've reworked the first five chapters a dozen times. For some reason, I can't seem to move on to chapter six."

Dixie pretended not to notice a customer signaling for the check. "What's goin' on at the end of chapter five?"

"Kamila, my main character, has just been selected to join the harem of Ramses the Second. It's a huge honor, but she's determined to become his wife, not just a woman he couples with a few times a year. Once she separates from her family, however, and is inside the palace, she's terrified and insecure, despite her exceptional beauty. After all, she's only fourteen."

Dixie whistled. "That ain't too early to be a conniving slut. You walked into a high school lately?" Turning to nod at her impatient *Phantom* customer, Dixie said, "It seems to me that you'd describe the palace at this point in your story. How did folks treat this girl? Where is she sleepin'? Did she get a bunch of fancy clothes and jewelry when she moved in? Does everybody hate her 'cause she's the new girl? Are the other girls from foreign places? What does she eat? Folks love to read about food, ya know."

Olivia cut off a corner of her omelet. "I wish you'd read what I've written so far. I think you've got an editorial ear."

"No chance in hell, 'Livia. You're one of the few people I call friend. I am not gonna mess with what we've got by pullin' apart your novel." Dixie turned away. "If you want to get someone's opinion, get off your rump and go talk to that writers' group. I'm tellin' you, *they* are what you need."

Haviland opened his eyes wide and made a sneezing noise—a signal to Olivia that his canine ears had picked up a solid recommendation.

"I don't know, Captain." Olivia concentrated on her omelet, trying to imagine reading page after page of grammatically incorrect, verbose claptrap, or florid romances such as the woman Laurel was penning. "I wonder what the rest of them are writing?" she asked her dining companion and stole a glance at the writers' group.

In addition to Laurel, there was a stunning young woman with glossy black hair tarnished by stripes of electric purple. She had large sable brown eyes and tea-hued skin, which she had pierced in multiple locations as though she'd deliberately set out to mar her exotic beauty. She wore a tight tank top embroidered with a pirate's flag, and her exposed arms were muscular and sinewy. Olivia had no difficulty picturing the girl creeping out at night in the form of a sleek black panther.

Sitting across from her was a young man in his mid- to late twenties with a dramatic case of rosacea. His unfortunate skin condition precluded one from seeing that he was handsome, in a boyish way. With his elfin eyes, brilliant smile, and waves of reddish, unkempt hair, he reminded Olivia of Peter Pan.

The well-groomed middle-aged man in the expensive peach silk shirt completed the assemblage of writers.

As Olivia blatantly stared at them, the man in peach caught her looking. He murmured something to his group and they quickly dispersed, their laughter trailing them out the door. He then settled onto the stool next to Olivia's and began to study her as she renewed her pretense of being fascinated by the day's news.

"I come in peace," the man said, and held up his hands in a gesture of surrender. "*In fact*, Dixie advised me to speak to you, but to use extreme caution." He smiled, showing off a row of chemically whitened and perfectly straight teeth. "She spoke as though I'd be approaching a coiled cobra instead of the *vision* of feminine power and beauty that sits beside me."

Haviland whined and the man laughed. "Oh, you're right, friend. I'm laying it on too thick. But seriously." He focused on Olivia again. "Dixie says you might be able to solve our problem." He looked pained. "Our little critique group is looking for a new place to meet. I simply cannot concentrate within *miles* of that *Jesus Christ Superstar* poster."

Amused, Olivia struggled to keep her expression neutral as she openly assessed her neighbor. "What do you write?"

"I pen a celebrity gossip column. Under a female pseudonym, of course. Ever heard of Milano Cruise? That's me. But don't go shouting that from the rooftops or I'll be out of a job." He wiggled a pair of neatly curved brows. "Most of my stories find their way onto the Internet. Milano's My-Space page is one of the most popular in the world."

"You hardly need a critique group for that kind of work," Olivia said with a dismissive wave of her fork.

"No, indeed," the man agreed with a laugh. "I must confess that I'm *quite* good at my craft. However, I'm spending the summer in Oyster Bay in order to work on a top secret story. You see, it's my intention to create a fictionalized biography of sorts. Names and dates changed—that sort of thing." He lowered his voice. "Everyone would know who I was writing about, but I can't get sued this way, you see?" He cleared his throat and puffed his chest out. "There are just piles of money waiting to be made on my idea."

Olivia found herself warming toward the man. Firstly, Haviland seemed comfortable in his presence, and Olivia found him refreshingly candid. Most importantly, he was well mannered and clearly intelligent. "I have a banquet room in my restaurant, but it would be rather costly. How often do you meet, Mr. . . . ?"

"Camden Ford, at your service." He bowed his head in exaggerated gallantry. "We've only had two meetings, but we'd like to gather once a week. And 'costly' isn't *really* the adjective to which I was aspiring."

"What about the library?"

"Those spectacled harpies won't let us partake of any alcohol." He smirked. "How can we be proper writers without booze? Coffee and eggs are not acceptable substitutes for old Scotch or a fine Cabernet. Also, two of my fellow writers have scheduling conflicts with morning meetings. One has to care for a pair of imps in diapers while the other sleeps until noon so she can work the night away sliding beer bottles across a dirty, sweating bar to equally dirty, sweaty men."

A laugh escaped Olivia's throat. She felt inclined to introduce herself and Haviland to the entertaining newcomer.

"Limoges?" he asked in interest. "As in the fine porcelain?"

Pleased, Olivia nodded. "My family name comes from the French city where the porcelain was produced."

"'Tis also the birthplace of my favorite comic hero, Astérix, *mais non*?" Camden stirred sugar into his coffee. "So are you a fabulously wealthy porcelain heiress?"

"Oak barrel heiress, actually." Olivia passed him the cream. "The kind specially produced for storing fine cognac."

Camden looked dutifully impressed. He then made a sweeping gesture with his arms. "Oyster Bay's not the type of town where I'd expect to meet someone like you. Unless you're hiding from a sordid past? An abusive lover? The IRS . . . ?"

Olivia disregarded his speculations. "We're hardly Beverly Hills gossip material either. There's neither a renowned plastic surgery center here nor an exclusive detox facility, so whose trail are you following?"

After taking a dainty sip of coffee, Camden winked. "Wouldn't *you* like to know?"

Indeed, she would. Olivia liked to be informed about the goings-on in her town, no matter how insignificant. "*Do* tell." She came close to pleading and then decided to come off as unconvinced. "There can hardly be any celebrity news to be gleaned in Oyster Bay."

"That is where you're mistaken, dear lady." He rose. "Come, let's move to a booth where I can gaze into your Adriatic blue eyes."

Olivia took her coffee and laptop and relocated to the vacated window booth. As soon as they were settled, Haviland ducked under the table, stretched out his front legs, and put his head on Camden's shoe. Olivia was surprised. It normally took the poodle quite a while before he felt comfortable with a stranger. The gossip writer seemed content to provide a pillow for the groggy canine. "Do you know the Talbot family?" he asked.

"Certainly. The Talbots are real estate developers."

"Not developers. Tycoons. Think big. As in Donald Trump big." Camden lowered his voice to a conspiratorial whisper. "*That's* just the parents. There are three kiddies too. The daughter designs haute couture and sleeps with NFL quarterbacks. The older son likes snorting coke and fondling beautiful young men, and the baby boy is the lead singer of a hot punk band. He's nailed half the starlets on E!'s up-and-coming list, and *I* know for a fact that he's brought his latest paramour here, to the Talbot beach house. Oh, and did I mention that the gorgeous creature he's wooing is barely legal? *And* she's appearing in two big-budget films this summer after wrapping a third season as the star of a hit television show?" He crossed his arms smugly. "Milano Cruise will dine off this story for years, thank you very much."

"Are the Talbots the family you plan to write about in your novel?"

Camden put a finger to his lips. "*Absolument*. I wrote the first three chapters on the plane from LA to DC, but I require help choosing which of the so very, very juicy, dark, and scandalous events I should focus my poison pen upon." He stroked Haviland's soft ears, and both man and poodle sighed contentedly. "Madame Limoges, we need an alcoholic haven in which our creativity can flow. Dixie mentioned an unused cottage on your property. An isolated lighthouse keeper's house with the ambience sure to encourage even the most reluctant of muses. Would you open it up to us for an hour or two each week?"

Olivia signaled Dixie angrily with her eyes. "That place has been uninhabited for years. It's falling apart—utterly unsuitable for your purpose at this point in time."

"At *this* point in time," Camden repeated. "Dixie also

relayed that your work in progress is historical fiction and that you've reached an impasse." He looked at Olivia warmly. "We need one another, my dear. Join the dark side. Sweep the dust out of that cottage, share your manuscript, and let's hit the bestseller list together." He reached over and gave her forearm a playful swat. "Don't pout, *ma cherie*. It'll be fun. I'll handle all the insipid organizational stuff."

Olivia was silent for a long time. It was impossible to remain unaffected by Camden's charm. "I'll think about both offers," she promised sincerely.

"I have long since learned to take all I can get. Do call me if you're willing to take a chance, my dazzling, halo-haired Duchess of Oyster Bay." Camden placed a business card next to her water glass and then gently slid his foot out from beneath Haviland's snout. "Excuse me, my fine sir."

Olivia watched him walk away, strangely conflicted by the encounter. Camden was quite charismatic and she would have enjoyed spending more time in his company. But to commit to his group required some adjustments on her part. For one, such a change meant she'd have to walk into the home of her childhood. A structure haunted by loneliness and loss.

"Is Dixie right? Am I living with ghosts?" she murmured to the snoozing poodle. "Perhaps I am, or near enough anyway. Perhaps the time has come for an exorcism."

Olivia examined herself in the reflection of the mirror lining the back wall. She didn't see the handsome, confident woman her neighbors saw, but a skinny, frightened, and friendless child with white blond hair and eyes that spoke of the sea's secret depths.

Blinking, Olivia passed her hand across her face, as though she were wiping it away in the mirror. She nodded to her reflection and Haviland stirred as his mistress squared her shoulders and came to a decision.

Her purposeful feet might not have carried her so lightly through the door, had she known that one of the diners she'd seen at Grumpy's that morning would soon be dead.

And it would be a death the likes of which the residents of Oyster Bay could never have imagined.